PLACE OF REFUGE

BASKIN FAMILY FOSTER JOURNAL SERIES
BOOK 1

DANIEL BISHOP

Place of Refuge
By
Daniel Bishop

Previously published as Ralley Point: Place of Refuge
Second Print Edition

Published by Foster Fiction Books
ISBN: 978-1-7344540-1-7

This is a work of fiction. Some events in the book are loosely based on real
events but have been altered to fit the convenience of the book. Some of the
characters are loosely based on real life characters. Some of the organizations
mentioned in the book are real organizations but are used fictitiously.

ACKNOWLEDGMENTS

I would like to thank my wife Joelle for her ideas, suggestions, and her tireless efforts improving the manuscript. My daughter Amberly Bishop for her support, as well as my brother Mike Bishop, his wife Christine, and their children. They have been the ultimate beta readers and supplied great feedback.

Special thanks to Ginger McBrayer Washington for ensuring the accuracy of the DCS procedures.

Last but not least, I thank my editor Melanie Saxton for her belief in the importance of a fostering and adoption tale, and her efforts in working through the chronology.

Author Photo by Lynette Eason. https://lynetteeasonpho tographyllc.pixieset.com

Cover design by Hannah Linder Designs. https://hannahlinderdesigns.com

This book is dedicated to children in the foster care system and the foster parents who nurture them, as well as families who invest their love and devotion in the adoption process.

Proverbs 14:26
*In the fear of the Lord there is strong confidence, and His children will have a **place of refuge**. (NKJV)*

CONTENTS

PROLOGUE
KNOXVILLE, TENNESSEE

June 2054

"Dad?"

"Yes, Ralley."

"What's up with these binders?" I asked, plunking the box on his countertop. He smiled and put his hand to his chin. He always does that when he's thinking. My dad, Leif Baskin, is an eighty-four-year-old widower. My mom, Dyanna Jo, passed away a few years ago. Dad lives alone in a rancher with attic storage above the garage. A few months ago, I came over to visit, and he asked me to get something out of a box in the attic. Easier said than done! It took me almost an hour due to the clutter, so I decided to come back later and organize the attic chaos.

Today is that day. I've been toiling mightily and have the sweat to prove it. About three-fourths of the way through, I found a box simply marked BOOKS. I assumed it was a jumble of old books he'd read and didn't want to toss, so he shoved them in the attic.

Boy, was I wrong! Imagine my surprise when I explored the

contents and found a collection of three-ring binders. The contents flooded my heart with memories. I lugged the box down the ladder, happy to leave the hot attic.

"Oh. Those are the books I wrote several years ago."

"They don't look like books."

"Actually, they're our journals. They need to be edited and turned into books. I just never got around to it. It would be nice if they were published, but I don't really want to mess with it now."

"This is about our family, right? The fostering and adoptions?"

"Yep. Remember, I asked you to write a few of the chapters."

"Oh yeah! I completely forgot about that."

"Mom wrote some of the chapters, too," he commented.

"Now, I remember. Remember how she would always mix up her words? She would be talking, and suddenly she would replace a word with another that completely changed the meaning of what she was trying to say." I smiled at the memory.

"We got a good laugh out of that, didn't we?" he chuckled. "It would drive her crazy."

"What you and Mom did was important, Dad. It mattered a lot," I said, feeling a sudden swell of emotion.

"I think so. It was important to us, that's for sure," he agreed.

"Hey, do you mind if I take them home with me so I can read them again?" I asked.

"That's why I wrote them," he answered.

"I would love to work on getting them edited and published," I added. "It would be a shame not too after all the research and work you put into them."

"I think I would like that," he agreed. "I definitely did a lot of research, but I wasn't able to find out everything. I pieced what I could together and wrote what I thought might have happened. Some of it is my speculation on how things went."

"When Haley and River were older, didn't we find their birth parents?"

"Yes, they both asked us to find their biological parents. They said they had a message for them."

"I remember that. Did you write about that?"

"Yes, that's in the third journal. In fact, I called that journal *The Message*. Haley and River's birth parents shared their stories with us. They wanted their stories told as well."

"I see the first journal is called Place of Refuge," I commented as I dug through the box. "The second one is Family Tree."

"Isn't that the one where you corresponded with that retired History Professor?"

"Yes, her name is Sylvia Wilson. I found her because I discovered our families had a connection in the past. She had discovered that as well and was glad I contacted her."

THE THREE-RING BINDERS chronicled our time as a foster family — a time capsule written from our various points of view. Dad started working on them in 2016. It took him several years to write them because he had a thing called a full-time job. On the weekdays, he would get up an hour early to work on them. He didn't work on them at night or on the weekends. He wanted to make sure he reserved that time for us. He combined the chapters Mom and I wrote with his own, most of it about our early lives together and how we added my sister and brother to the fold. My siblings were foster children, and Mom and Dad eventually adopted them. I'm now fifty-seven, Haley is forty-six, and River is forty-five. My sister and brother have been such a blessing to us all. They have different birth parents, and their stories are potent sagas of refuge, redemption, and restoration.

It wasn't always comfortable being a foster family, though. It was uplifting yet shocking at times. Most of our foster children had lived in deplorable conditions. Some had been abused. I'm thankful Mom and Dad opened their home to all the kids who came through our house. The whole process meant a lot to all of us.

"Dad, I'm going to go home to take a shower. Then I'm going to start reading these binders. Do you need me to do anything before I go?"

"No, I think you've done quite enough," he said, trying to sound upset. "You've messed up my carefully organized attic, and now I'll never be able to find anything. You've also accused me of being mischievous. You just run along now. I've had about enough of your help and accusations for one afternoon."

I walked over to him and kissed him on the cheek. His eyes had a mischievous twinkle.

"I love you, Dad."

"I love you too, and thank you for all your help."

I patted him on the shoulder, and then I headed home. After showering, I told my husband, Chandler, that he was on his own for dinner. I headed to my home office and curled up in my favorite chair. Then I picked up the first binder and began reliving how we became a Place of Refuge.

1

PLUSES AND MINUSES

I'm Leif Baskin, and Ralley is my daughter from my first marriage. Our journey has a lot of pluses and minuses, so to speak. We've had times of mourning, periods of adjustment, and plenty of celebrations, trusting God through it all.

Janet, my wife, died of breast cancer when Ralley was five years old. The treatments didn't help, and both Ralley and I were devastated, for Janet was an exceptional mother and wife. On that fateful day, October 17, 2001, I became a widower and never thought I'd meet someone who could be a mom to Ralley and a wife to me. Then Dyanna Jo came into our lives. We married on February 27, 2004. That is a story unto itself.

I'm widowed again after losing Dyanna Jo. We spent many adventuresome decades together, but our roots as foster parents were planted when she miscarried. It's bittersweet as I look back and remember how the process unfolded.

❡

Leif's Journal, **May 2007**
 "Dad?"

"Yes, Ralley."

"I hope everything's okay with the ultrasound."

Ralley, who was ten at the time, was my blue-eyed, blond-haired daughter with a cute row of freckles going from under one eye, across her nose, to under the other eye.

"I do, too," I agreed.

My wife, Dyanna Jo, was pregnant, and we were going to our second ultrasound in six weeks. Dyanna Jo was a petite woman—five feet three inches tall—but a ball of fire. Her hair was dyed red, but when I first met her, it was dyed blond. Her hair color changed just about every time she went to the salon. Her eyes were a smoky blue, and she had a cute little nose.

She wanted kids. I was okay with just having Ralley, but I didn't think it was right to keep Dyanna Jo from experiencing pregnancy and birth. So, we started trying right away but weren't successful. It was very disheartening to work for so long and not have any results.

After three years of trying and failing to get pregnant, we decided to be more scientific in our efforts... which was funny because Dyanna Jo was far from a model student in high school. She barely graduated. The thought of her doing anything scientific was comical until I recalled how talented, tenacious, and intelligent Dyanna Jo was as long as the end goal was something she wanted. Once she set her mind on it, she was an unstoppable force of nature and proved it by timing her ovulation, taking her temperature, and getting all kinds of charts and graphs. It was remarkable, and I half expected to see her with a boiling pot, making some kind of pregnancy potion.

On March 31, she called me at work.

"I, um, did something today," she confessed after I answered the phone.

Oh, boy. "What did you do this time?" I asked, knowing she either embarrassed herself or made an idiot of herself or both.

"Why do you say, 'this time'? You make it seem like I do stuff regularly."

"Probably because you do. So, did you embarrass yourself or make an idiot of yourself?"

"I would have to say I did both," she laughed. "But I was excited, and you're going to be excited too."

"Why were you excited?" I played along.

"You have to promise me you won't be mad," she said in a syrupy sweet voice.

"I promise."

"Two days ago, I thought I was pregnant. I got a pregnancy test to see if I was. Do you know how they work?"

"Yes, you pee on them, and then you wait for the results."

"Yes, I got one that shows a plus sign if you're pregnant and a minus sign if you're not. After I waited the amount of time, I checked it. It looked like it was a plus, but it was so faint I couldn't tell for sure. I decided to call Dr. Swanson to have her do a test. I went there today. Mom is with Ralley."

"Are you pregnant?" I asked, hopefully.

"Let me finish my story of how I idiotically embarrassed myself."

"Okay."

"I brought the test with me. When I got there, I showed it to the receptionist. I was just so excited. I put it up close to her so she could see how faint the plus was. She didn't look too thrilled and scooted her chair back a little. 'I get it,' she huffed. I then sat in the waiting room, and there were five women there as well. I proceeded to show them."

"Did you shove it in their faces too?" I asked, already knowing the answer and shaking my head.

"Well, I had too," she emphasized. "The sign was so faint."

"Yeah, that makes perfect sense," I said sarcastically. "I bet they were nonplussed about it." My pun sailed right past her.

"I sat there for about ten minutes. When the nurse called

me, I showed it to her, and she looked at me funny. As we walked down the hall to the room, I showed it to everyone I came across. They all looked at me like I was crazy!"

"Imagine that."

"Oh, shoot! I missed my turn."

"Are you driving?" I blurted.

"Yes. I missed my turn, and I don't know where I am. I've been so distracted by talking to you that I don't know where I am."

"How about you pull into a parking lot and finish talking to me. Then figure out where you are."

Is she going to be this crazy the whole pregnancy? I asked myself. I was quiet for a minute.

"Okay, I'm parked now, and I think I know where I am."

"Well, as long as you think you know. That's probably the best we can hope for."

"Where was I?" she asked.

"You were about to tell me if you're pregnant," I sighed.

"I am definitely pregnant."

"Yes!" I exclaimed.

"Are you okay?" she asked, sounding concerned.

"Yes, why do you ask?"

"You don't usually show that much excitement."

"It's not every day your wife tells you she's pregnant."

"That's true. Dr. Swanson scheduled an ultrasound for two weeks from now. I made the appointment so you can go when you get off work. I want you with me."

"Good. I want to be there too."

"Well, I should go. I've kept you on the phone long enough."

"That's okay. I enjoy talking to my idiot wife."

"Haha, I don't embarrass you too much, do I?"

"I'm used to it."

"You're not mad at me for not telling you until today?"

"No, you wanted to make sure before you told me. I'm fine with that."

"Good. I'll talk to you when you get home."

We hung up. *This is going to be an amusing nine-months,* I thought.

THAT NIGHT, we took Ralley out to dinner and put a stuffed baby giraffe on the table in front of her. After Dyanna Jo got off the phone with me, she finally figured out where she was and where she was going. She went to the baby store and bought the stuffed giraffe.

"What's this for?" Ralley asked.

"You're going to be a big sister!" Dyanna Jo gushed.

"You're pregnant?" Ralley asked, stunned.

"Yes, she is," I beamed. "And, in two weeks, she's having an ultrasound, and you and I are going too."

Ralley was excited about that. I was too.

"I got a baby giraffe for you and one for me. At night, when we go to bed, we can snuggle with our giraffes and pray for this sweet baby who will soon be joining our family," Dyanna Jo explained.

Two weeks later, we went to Dr. Swanson's for the ultrasound. The ultrasound room had a monitor on the wall, so Ralley and I could see the ultrasound as it was happening. I liked that. After the ultrasound, Dr. Swanson talked to us in her office.

"It looks like you're about seven weeks along, but the heartbeat isn't as fast as it should be. It's ninety-four, and it should be around one-twenty. I would like for you to come back in two weeks to do another ultrasound."

"Do you think the baby is in trouble?" Dyanna Jo asked nervously.

"I don't think so. Sometimes, the heartbeat is slow at first, but by the next ultrasound, it's fine. However, I want to be cautious because of how long it took you to get pregnant. I will be doing a couple more ultrasounds than I usually do."

We were a little concerned after the appointment but decided not to let our imaginations run away with us.

"Dad," Ralley said as I was driving us to the doctor's office for the second ultrasound.

"Yes, Ralley."

"Are you hoping for a boy?"

"No. I'm hoping for a healthy baby, and I don't care if it's a boy or a girl."

"Well—" That's my wife speaking up. She can't go too long without throwing her two cents in— "I think its a boy. If it's a girl, I will be just as happy, and yes, the main thing is for the baby to be healthy. But I think it will be a boy."

"And what makes you think it will be a boy?" I asked.

"I don't know. I just do."

"Ah. Women's intuition. This should be interesting to see if you're right."

We got to the doctor's office, checked in, and then proceeded to wait. Our appointment was at 10 a.m. We got there a few minutes before ten. The ultrasound tech, Lisa, came and got us about fifteen minutes later. She was the same one who did the ultrasound the other time.

We got back to the room and were all happy and jovial. Dyanna Jo wasn't too keen because it was a transvaginal ultrasound. She didn't care much for that, but the doctor wanted it done because it gave a better view of the uterus.

Lisa had everything ready. She started the procedure once Dyanna Jo was on the table. She did a few things on her control panel. I noticed that the baby looked smaller than the previous time. I figured it was because I didn't know how to read the ultrasound and was lucky just to be able to make out the baby.

Lisa did a few more things on her panel, put markers on either end of the baby, and made some measurements. She had gotten noticeably quieter. Dyanna Jo picked up on it and asked what was wrong.

Talk about a startling change in the atmosphere. One minute there was laughter and happiness because we were seeing the baby again, and the next, there was this deep feeling of dread.

"What's wrong?" Dyanna Jo asked again, feebly.

"I'm just finishing up," Lisa replied gently with a tentative smile. "the doctor will go over everything with you." She did a few more things on her keyboard and then told Dyanna Jo she could get dressed.

After Dyanna Jo got dressed, Lisa walked us to the doctor's office. We had been in her office before, however, I hadn't noticed the pictures of her two kids on her desk. They looked like they were about five to seven years old.

"I've looked at the ultrasound," Dr. Swanson began. "I'm sorry to say that we were unable to detect a heartbeat."

All we could do was stare and nod. Dyanna Jo reached for a tissue but took the whole box.

"What?" Dyanna Jo asked quietly.

"You've had a miscarriage," Dr. Swanson confirmed. She paused for a couple of minutes and continued by saying, "Before I had these two," she pointed to her kid's picture, "I had two miscarriages. I want to say you did nothing to cause this. You might be thinking there's something you did that brought on the miscarriage, but that's not the case. These things happen, and you don't need to feel guilty."

"Well, what caused it then?" Dyanna Jo mumbled between

sniffs. "I had a couple of drinks before I found out I was pregnant. Could that be it?"

"No, it's just one of those things. The chromosomes were probably too damaged, and once it reached a certain point, it couldn't keep developing."

"I thought that," I admitted. "Dyanna Jo having a beer or two before she found out she was pregnant, couldn't have caused this. That happens to lots of women, so I'm sure that wouldn't have caused a miscarriage."

"No, it wouldn't. Repeatedly drinking alcoholic beverages during the entire pregnancy would cause major problems for the baby, but not a drink or two so early in the pregnancy."

"So, what do we do now?" Dyanna Jo whispered.

"I would recommend seeing a fertility specialist. Since you've had a hard time getting pregnant, had a miscarriage, and your current age is thirty-nine, I think it would be good to see one."

"Do you have someone in mind?" I asked.

"Yes, Dr. James Kennedy. I'll send him a referral, and his office will call you to set up an appointment."

"Okay."

"Do you have any more questions?"

"No," I answered.

Dyanna Jo just shook her head.

We left the office and walked to the car. None of us felt like talking. We got in the car and drove home, still not talking. I wondered what Ralley must be thinking. She didn't seem to be as upset as us and seemed a little confused.

We got home, parked the car in the garage, and we all went inside the house. Dyanna Jo went straight to our room. Ralley went to her bedroom, and I followed her.

"Do you know what has happened?" I asked her.

"Mom lost the baby," she replied.

"I asked because you looked confused, and I just wanted to make sure you knew why your mom and I are upset."

"I am confused. I mean, I guess not confused, but disoriented. I'm trying to change how I've been thinking."

"What do you mean?"

"I've been thinking of all the things I planned on doing with my brother, and now I won't have a brother, and it's just all unsettling and topsy turvy."

"I can understand that. It is unsettling and topsy turvy. Did you think it was going to be a boy?"

"Yes."

"Why?"

"I don't know. I just thought it would be, and I named him River."

"Dyanna Jo thought it would be a boy also. She hadn't thought of a name, though. River is a good one. I'll have to tell her."

She laid down in her bed, and I made sure she was as okay as she could be, considering the circumstances. Then I went to our bedroom and laid down. Dyanna Jo was lying there, holding her baby giraffe. One last thing Dyanna Jo was going to have to do was go back in three days for a D&C. Dr. Swanson said she needed to get the placenta and any fetal matter out because it could cause an infection if not removed from the uterus. Dyanna Jo wasn't thrilled to have to go through that.

RALLEY'S JOURNAL

One minute, Mom and Dad were joking around, and the next, they were intense and wearing pained expressions. Talk about a drastic change in the mood. It was like all the air got sucked out of the room. It took me a while to understand I wasn't going to be a big sister. My mood changed. I don't think I felt as bad as Mom and Dad. I mean, I wasn't crying like they were, but I was on the verge of it.

As we sat in Dr. Swanson's office, I thought about all the things I had planned on doing with my brother. I just knew it was a brother. I could help with changing diapers, feeding him, giving baths, making faces, and hearing him laugh. Tickling him and hearing him squeal. Dr. Swanson told us about the heartbeat as soon as she sat down at her desk. I was glad she didn't beat around the bush and prolong things. Just get it over and tell us.

While the adults talked, I thought about what I would have liked for his name to be. I thought he should be called River. Why River? No reason, it just sounded cool.

They said something about fertility and a specialist, and I lost track of what they were saying. So, I daydreamed—random thoughts that made sense to a ten-year-old. Like if mom visited a fertility doctor, would he or she give her fertilizer to make her more likely to get pregnant? Or, would she get pregnant, and then the fertilizer would make the baby grow? I was silly. I didn't exactly know what a fertility doctor did, but I knew it didn't involve fertilizer. I was just trying to be funny with myself to lighten the mood a little, at least for me.

After they talked for a few more minutes, we drove home. We were all so sad and didn't speak. Mom kept dabbing at her eyes with a tissue. Dad looked like, well, Dad. He never showed much emotion. I spotted a few tears in the doctor's office, and that constituted a significant cry for him.

When we got home, mom went up to her room. Dad explained to me what happened. I guess he figured I didn't understand because I hadn't cried or shown much emotion. I knew what happened but was more worried about them. I had never seen them like this before and wasn't sure how to act.

Dad made sure I was okay about everything, and then he headed to his room. I laid down in my bed and thought some more about River. I cried and prayed. I asked God to help Mom and Dad feel better and to be able to have another child. I fell asleep and dreamed about River. He was a Pillsbury dough-boy. Chunky, fat rolls on the legs, wispy blonde hair, and bright blue eyes. I was going to miss that guy.

2

———

LOOKING BACK

After our kids grew up and flew the coop, I recall how much Dyanna Jo and I enjoyed it when they came back home for visits. They would bring their children with them. Wow! Grandkids are genuinely the best thing since sliced bread. After Dyanna Jo passed away, Ralley stepped up as the glue that held us together. She's so driven lately to chronicle our family history. Yes, once Ralley hit her late fifties, she became full of questions, especially since finding my box of "books" in the attic. She's experienced our joys and sorrows as a foster and adoptive family. She feels that our story should be shared, and I agree. Maybe it will encourage other families to foster and adopt, but also give them a real eye-opener about the process.

By the way, it feels odd to have a child who has lived more than half a century. That makes me old, Eighties old. But keeping up with Ralley, Haley, River, and the grandkids is an anti-aging recipe, and keeping up with our old journals has jumpstarted my brain. Reliving our early years is bittersweet but worth the trip down memory lane. And what glorious recollections we have, some funny, some downright heart-breaking, but most of all full of love as we stitched our family together, piece by piece.

"Dad," Ralley called to me a few weeks after the miscarriage.

"Yes, Ralley."

"Could you tell me again how you and Mom met?"

"I would be happy to tell you how your mom threw herself at me."

"Oh boy, here we go," the mom in question chimed in. "More lies." I was glad to see that her mood was improving. The last two weeks had been rough for her.

"Well, I can't help it if you saw me talking to those two women and decided to act a fool."

"You weren't talking to any women when I came over to talk to you."

"I was earlier, and you saw me. Later in the evening, you got desperate and barged right in on the conversation I was having with those guys at the table."

"Yes, you're just a regular casserole. You have women watching your every move."

I wasn't sure what she was trying to say. "I'm a casserole? Is that what you said?"

"Oh, you know, that guy who always had women around him and swept them off their feet."

"Casanova is who you're thinking of, and he doesn't hold a candle to me."

She turned to Ralley and said, "I'm leaving before I throw up, and remember to take what he says with a grain of salt. He tends to embellish things."

Ralley seemed amused by the whole exchange. I'm sure

calling me a casserole added to it. I waited for Dyanna Jo to traipse into the kitchen to prepare dinner. Then I got started on relaying to Ralley the correct and complete version of when I met Dyanna Jo.

I MET Dyanna Jo at church about nine months after Janet died. Time had helped Ralley and me to move on, although I was concerned about Ralley for a few months. She was unusually quiet and mellow. She was never a hyper or rambunctious child, but she was active and always had a smile. But those few months she didn't smile much and looked sad. We talked, and I was encouraged by what she told me.

"I just need some time, Dad," she explained.

I had to keep telling myself she's five. She's always been an old soul. I've had people tell me when they talk to her; it's easy to forget her age. After a few months, she started acting like her usual self.

"What about you, Dad?" she asked me.

"I need some time, too," I admitted. "I know we'll both move on, but for now, we should just take our time." So, that's what we did. My parents and my sister, Dana, helped watch Ralley while I was at work. I didn't know when I'd be ready to start another relationship. I would just have to let God decide that, and I wasn't in any particular hurry.

I asked Ralley how she felt about me getting married again. She said it would have to be the right person.

"What's your definition of the right person?" I asked.

"The right person," she intoned, "would be someone who lets me do whatever I want and does whatever I ask them to do."

"Where do you suppose I could find such a creature?"

"I don't know, Dad," she answered like she was exasperated. "Ask God."

"Why, yes. I don't know why I didn't think of that. I will petition the Almighty and breathlessly wait for His answer." She nodded like it was a done deal, and then she laughed. I knew she was okay with it.

When Janet was still alive, we went to a married couple's small group at our church. I continued attending after she died but started to feel a little out of place. I decided to start going to a single adult group. I wasn't interested in meeting a woman. I just wanted to go and have some fun.

My first time at the singles group was at a Fourth of July party. I left Ralley with Mom and Dad to spend the night since I would probably be out late.

A married couple in our church had five acres out in the country, and that's where I met Dyanna Jo, at six o'clock to be precise. Our hosts fired up the grill shortly after we arrived and grilled hamburgers and hot dogs to celebrate Independence Day. Before the food was ready, two women come up to me separately. I knew who they were but had never talked to them. There had never been any reason to since I had been married. But now that I was single and eligible, that all changed.

I got me a hamburger and some potato chips and sat down to eat with a few people I knew. I hadn't been eating long when this Lunatic came over (yes, Lunatic with a capital L) and practically shoved a guy out of the way to sit beside me. She was aggressive and practically asked me to marry her right there and then.

I didn't know how to take her. I'm exaggerating a little bit, but she did make it clear she was interested in me. After I got over the initial shock of her arrival, we settled into a conversation.

"I'm Leif," I introduced myself.

"I'm Dyanna Jo."

"So, Dyanna Jo, I like your name. Does anyone ever call you D.J.?"

"No, no one calls me that. My name is spelled D Y A N N A J O with a space between Dyanna and Jo. My birth name is Dyanna, but as time went on, I developed the nickname Dyanna Jo, and it stuck."

I liked her but wasn't thinking of asking her out. After we finished eating, we parted company and talked to other people. I played corn hole, horseshoes, and some other games and just hung out and talked until it got dark. Then came the fireworks. I enjoyed my time and the people I met.

The Fourth of July was on Thursday that year, so the party was on Friday the fifth. I saw Dyanna Jo again on Sunday, and she met Ralley for the first time. I talked to her after church, and she mentioned going to West Town Mall to eat lunch and asked if we wanted to join her. I figured, *Why not?* We got there and dined in the food court. We found out Dyanna Jo was from San Diego. Her parents, Joe and Pat, were also from San Diego but moved to Knoxville in 1995 because their retirement funds could go a lot further here than there. Dyanna Jo followed them to Knoxville in 1996 after getting laid off from her job. She's two years older than me. She was thirty-four when I met her.

She had been married once before when she was twenty-three. Unfortunately, the guy kept cheating on her, and they divorced after a year. I realized then why she was so aggressive towards me. She had been single way too long and was on the hunt for a husband. Then I discovered something about her that was shocking at first. She was and is incredibly LOUD.

We finished eating and started walking around the mall. We went into the Disney Store and looked around. There weren't that many people in the store, so it was quiet. She saw something cute and was enthusiastically yelling at Ralley even though they were next to each other. I looked around to see if anyone was staring at us. Nobody was. I'm a quiet, reserved person, so her volume was startling.

I bought the thing she thought was cute, and then we walked around the mall some more. Of course, I had my coffee from the Starbucks in the mall. I always stopped there to get a mocha or a latte.

"Dad," Ralley said after we got in the car to leave the mall.

"Yes, Ralley."

"She's loud."

I laughed. "I was going to ask you what you thought of Dyanna Jo, and now I don't have to."

"I think she's nice, but ..." she paused and shrugged her shoulders.

"I know, Ralley, I know," I said dramatically. "I think she's nice, too, and she's pretty. But I don't think there's a person in the world who can talk over her or drown her out."

Janet was quiet and soft-spoken. Ralley and I were also. I liked Dyanna Jo but didn't know for sure if I was ready to date yet. I was just getting my feet wet and wasn't prepared to dive in.

Dyanna Jo's Journal

Now I get to correct all the malicious things Leif said about me in his journal entry. He so enjoys picking on me.

When I met him at the singles Fourth of July party, I didn't "throw myself" at him. Was I eyeing him? Yes, I was. The single men at church were slim pickins' and to see a new, good looking guy at the party was encouraging and rather exciting. Was he marriage material? I had no clue, but I was going to talk to him one way or another.

For about seven years after my divorce, I wasn't the least bit interested in getting married. When I turned thirty, I started thinking about it and knew I wanted to have kids.

When I decided it was time to start dating, I found I was always attracted to the wrong kind of men. I dated way too many frogs and was very discouraged. I wasn't getting any younger.

One day my mom told me to stop dating and make a list of all the things I wanted in a husband. Pray over the list and ask God to lead me to the man I should marry. I followed her advice. To say my list was long is an understatement. There was no way I was going to find one man who had all the qualifications on my list. I needed to pray and trust God.

Just because I made a list and asked God to lead me, I still got a little too excited and jumped when I saw the new guy at the party. I was eager to talk to him. I made a beeline for his table, and maybe my actions bordered on lunacy. It's who I am; I don't do anything calmly. Especially when I see something I want. Now that I've been married to him for years now, I can admit that it was definitely a moment of insanity.

Leif was busy talking to the guy beside him. The table was full, but I waited, not too patiently. When the spot opened on the other side of him, I didn't hesitate. I bolted! He turned briefly to see what idiot was flying into the seat next to him. Leif looked at me for a split second and quickly resumed his conversation with the guy on the other side. He kept ignoring me for at least thirty minutes. I acted like I was there to talk to the other people at the table. Finally, he turned and introduced himself.

After we talked for a few minutes, he said he thought he detected an accent and asked if I was from Knoxville. I told him I was originally from San Diego. That interested him and said he'd always wanted to go there. In the half-hour we talked, we got to know a little about each other —our roots, our families, jobs, and things like that. I found out he was a widower. It was apparent he wasn't thinking of marriage, it was too soon. I was going to have to do the one thing I wasn't good at — be patient.

Once my mind got set on something, I wanted it right then. In the meantime, I was going to make him see I was a catch.

In just a short time of talking, I could already tell he was so many things on my list. The problem? I was going to have to wait for Leif, a fact he likes to remind me of frequently.

3

REMEMBERING JANET

Ralley's Journal

Sometimes I think about my first Mom, although the older I get, the fuzzier my memories become. Dad told me that a few weeks after she gave birth to me, she started her cancer treatments. After about a year of treatments, her cancer was in remission. It had cost her left breast. Over the next few years, she had regular mammograms and other tests to see if the cancer was still in remission.

All of that is sort of a blur, but I'll never forget when she took me to the zoo. I was four. She was in remission from her cancer and so full of life.

It was the first time I'd been to a zoo, and I was looking forward to it. Mom had shown me pictures of animals I would see — elephants, giraffes, lions, tigers, hippos, monkeys, and my favorite, penguins. So, on that lovely spring day in May, we first went to Cracker Barrel for breakfast. I had country ham and scrambled eggs, and she had three pancakes. She loved pancakes. She ate them every Saturday morning. I didn't like them very much, but they were her favorite. When my food arrived, she got out some green food coloring and put a little on my eggs.

"Why did you make my eggs green, Mommy?" I asked.

"I knew you would want eggs," she began. "And since *Green Eggs and Ham* is one of your favorite books, I thought I would make your eggs green."

"You're silly, Mommy."

"I'm silly? You're the one with green eggs. Who eats green eggs but silly people?"

"You're the one who made them green, Mommy."

"What? Me?" she feigned innocence. "I didn't make your eggs green. You're silly and crazy."

"Mommy," I laughed.

We ate our breakfast and headed to the zoo. School had let out the day before, so we were celebrating the first day of summer vacation. I was homeschooled and had just finished Kindergarten. I was born in September 1996. Even though I was four, Mom went ahead and started me on a kindergarten curriculum in September 2000. I liked having school at home. People sometimes told Mom they didn't think homeschooling was right for kids because they didn't get much socialization. She would nicely tell them that I got plenty of socialization. I was in Children's Church and a home-schooling co-op. I went to the co-op two days a week and was in classes with other kids. So, I got plenty of socialization.

I remember the zoo being a prominent, exotic place. I loved the elephants and giraffes the most. At least, I did until I saw the penguins. I loved watching those little guys. I loved how they waddled around, and it looked like they were wearing a tuxedo. Of course, I was four and didn't know until I was older about tuxedos, but at the time, I thought their colors were neat.

We had lunch and spent the whole day there. When it was time to leave, we had to go through the gift shop to exit the zoo. Mom bought me a stuffed penguin along with a book about them. I still have both. I talked Mom into buying me some shirts and earrings with penguins on them. I had so much penguin stuff. I named the stuffed penguin, Waddles.

When we got home, Mom wrote in the penguin book she bought at the zoo. She wrote, *I am so proud of you and loved being your teacher. You were a great Kindergarten student. I look forward to many more years of trips to the zoo and green eggs and ham.* She signed it with a heart.

THE NEXT DAY, she had a follow-up doctor appointment. She had a mammogram the week before and was getting the results.

When she came home, she tried to put on a happy face for me, but I could see that something wasn't right. She wouldn't tell me what was wrong. She and Dad wouldn't talk about it while I was around, but I overheard them sometimes. I worried that the cancer would come back. After this last doctor visit, she found out that she had it in her right breast, and it had spread to other parts of her body. She would have a mastectomy and start cancer treatments in a few weeks.

Finally, Mom and Dad sat me down and talked to me about it. I think I understood it a little better, but my four-year-old understanding couldn't completely grasp it. The main thing I knew was that Mommy was sick.

She started the treatments and lost all her hair along with her energy. Dad and I shaved our heads to match hers. Dad asked me if I was sure I wanted to get rid of my hair, and I told him I was. So, he let me get it shaved. But everything happened so fast. The treatments didn't work, and just a few months after the diagnosis, she was in the hospital knocking on heaven's door.

A week before she died, I sat in her hospital room, holding Waddles.

"Ralley," she called. "could you get my lipstick out of my purse?" I rummaged through her purse and found her lipstick.

"I haven't felt like putting makeup on, but there's something I want to do." She held the lipstick, took off the cap, and twisted it until I could see a pretty bright pink lipstick. I watched her add a lot of the lipstick to her lips. "Now, hand me Waddles."

I passed it to her, and with a faint smile, she gave it a big kiss on the cheek. It left a big impression of her lips.

"Ralley, you know that soon mommy will be with Jesus." She paused, grabbed a tissue, and dabbed her eyes. I began to cry. "I wanted to put a kiss on Waddles, so you could always know my love is always here with you. I know you love Waddles, and now you'll always have my kiss."

She couldn't talk anymore, and I couldn't either. We didn't bawl. We just cried quietly. Mom never cried much, and when she did, it was quiet.

A week later, she passed away. Dad and I were with her every day and just about every minute up until she died. Most nights, we even slept at the hospital. I'm so glad we did. I will always remember that time with my mom. When she had the strength, she would read her bible and talk about being in the arms of God. Even through the pain, she always had joy when she told me about God.

I still have Waddles with the lipstick on its cheek. It always sat on the top of my bookshelf in my room. Right beside a picture of my mom. They are the only things on that shelf. I will always cherish that penguin and my mother's kiss.

Mom gave me a gift, and I will always remember the love she had for me. She knew she was going away and wanted me to have something to remember her by. The cross means the same thing to me. It always reminds me of God's love for me.

AT FIRST, I didn't know the part Dyanna Jo would play in our lives. I can say now that she was an awesome stepmom. She took great care of Waddles and Mom's picture. She dusted the shelf and the frame every week. She was always willing to listen when I talked about Mom, which wasn't very often. Dad and I had moved on, but we still reminisced about her sometimes, and Dyanna Jo didn't mind one bit. When we visited Mom's grave and left flowers, Dyanna Jo always brought some of her own. She would softly touch the tombstone and thank Mom for loving us so deeply.

Later, Dad told me that Mom—my biological mom—was a foster child. She was never adopted. She became a foster child when she was thirteen. Her parents died in a car wreck, and with no family, she was all alone. Her foster parents took good care of her but never attempted to adopt her. She liked living there but never thought much about being adopted. Her foster parents continued to foster other children over the years. When Mom was seventeen, her foster parents started the process of adopting two younger children who had been in their care for over a year. Mom asked them why they never adopted her. Because she was older and never talked about adoption, they assumed she didn't care or want to be adopted. By the time they finalized the adoption of the younger children, she would be close to her eighteenth birthday, so they didn't think it mattered to her.

Dad said that she told him it did matter to her. She wanted to know she belonged and feel like part of a family. Her foster parents apologized and petitioned for adoption. Unfortunately, the hearing was scheduled for after she turned eighteen. She couldn't be adopted after she turned eighteen. So, she was never legally adopted, but her foster family had adopted her in their hearts. Later she realized that it didn't matter if they legally adopted her. They treated her like their daughter, and that's all that mattered.

That's what made me think she would like us to be a foster family. I know she would approve. If she were here, she would be an awesome foster mom. Sometimes I think it's unfair that she died when I was so young, but then I see these foster kids, and I know it pales in comparison to how unfair life seems to be for them. After all, I know my mom loved me and took great care of me. None of these foster kids could say that.

Dad said he would always try to adopt any foster children available for adoption, no matter how old they were. Yes, Mom would like that. It also made me think about someday becoming a foster parent myself. I know I want to get married and have kids. I also know that there are so many children who need homes. I could share God's love with those kids and maybe with the parents, too, if it worked out.

I know it will be hard work. Being a parent to your kids is hard enough, and then trying to be a parent to kids who have been through some bad things is even harder. But as Dad tells me, it was also hard for Jesus to die on the cross for us. Looking back, I wasn't always comfortable being a foster sister, but I know it was good for me. It helps me see I have so much to be thankful for in my life.

4

A TENTATIVE START

Leif's Journal

After spending the afternoon at the mall with Dyanna Jo, I liked her. She seemed to adore Ralley, and I think the feeling was mutual despite how loud she was. We would have to get used to that.

Over the next few months, Dyanna Jo and I talked on the phone several times a week. We saw each other at church on Sundays and sometimes went out to eat. Ralley was always with us. When the singles group met, we sat with each other. Sometimes after the meetings, we went out with some of the other singles.

So, we never really went on a formal date for several months. Two other women at church had talked to me some, and I could tell they were interested. However, when they saw the Lunatic throwing herself at me, they stayed away.

Looking back on it, I can see that God was arranging things for the Lunatic and me to be together. It took me a few months to realize what had been in front of me the whole time. I knew Ralley liked her, and the Lunatic was good with Ralley. But I still plodded along and took my sweet time, much to the Lunatic's dismay.

DYANNA JO'S Journal

I should have known from the beginning that Leif would test my patience. Since he's calling me the Lunatic in his chapters, I'm calling him the Snail in mine. I specifically prayed, and I know that God heard my prayers, and He brought me that special man. They say you should never pray for patience. Since I don't have any, I prayed for a man with patience. God definitely answered that prayer. Leif has more patience than anyone I know. I thought I had learned patience when I was single all those years, but apparently not.

I liked Ralley from the moment I first saw her. She was so adorable with a cute row of freckles across her nose. I could tell from their interaction that the Snail cared deeply for Ralley, and she loved her dad. She wasn't very talkative with me, but she answered me when I asked her questions. I could see myself being her stepmom. I didn't want to replace her mom, but as she got older, it would be good for her to have a woman help her with the changes she would go through.

The Snail says my memory is mistaken, but his memory isn't anything to write home about. It took him seven months to ask me on a date, not "several" months. Seven months of me waiting. Seven months of wondering when God was going to let him know he needs to get serious about me. God may have been letting him know, but it was taking a while for it to sink into that Snail brain.

We talked quite a bit during that time and developed a good friendship. I also developed a good relationship with Ralley. Despite my impatience, it was probably good that he waited to ask me out. It pains me to admit that. So, we moved at the Snail's pace, and I just about pulled my hair out.

RALLEY'S JOURNAL

I remember not being too sure about Dyanna Jo when I first met her. She seemed nice. Nice and loud. She was fun to hang out with, but I wasn't sure if I wanted Dad to get serious about her. Of course, I was five by then, so I wasn't sure what serious meant. I just knew I didn't want whatever that was. I had heard adults talk about being serious with each other, and it sounded, well, serious. At first, I didn't want any part of that.

When we got home after the trip to the mall, I went to my room and looked at Mom's picture on top of my bookshelf. I still had a hard time thinking about her death. I held my stuffed penguin and wondered what she would think of Dyanna Jo. I knew she would like her, but she would probably get some earplugs, though.

"Dad," I said after I came downstairs and found him.

"Yes, Ralley."

"I've been thinking."

"Uh, oh."

"Are you serious about Dyanna Jo?"

He laughed and cocked his head to the side and briefly touched his chin with his hand. I noticed he did this when he was thinking before speaking. He didn't do it all the time, just sometimes when he was thinking of a serious reply.

"Why do you ask?"

I don't like it when they respond to my question with a question. They, being adults. Can't they answer the question and then ask me why I'm asking?

"Just wondering," I said. "Like I told you, I've been thinking, and that's what I came up with."

"No, I'm not serious about her. Today wasn't planned. She asked us on a whim, and I figured we weren't doing anything else, so we may as well have lunch with her."

By this time, we were sitting on the couch. We both sat for a few minutes. I could tell he was thinking. I was still holding the penguin and tracing Mom's lip print with my finger. She had such pretty lips.

"Are you worried she'll replace your mom?" he asked in a concerned tone.

"Maybe a little. That's why I wanted to know if you're serious about her."

He turned, even more, to look directly at me. His expression was solemn, and he touched his chin. "I'm not serious about her," he said and touched my hand. "We've just met, and all I see her being right now is a friend. She could never replace your mom. If you ever feel uncomfortable with her or any woman I may date, don't be afraid to tell me."

"I will."

I was glad he was taking my feelings into account. I didn't think I would have to worry about any woman he was friends with, but I also figured he would eventually get married again. It would be nice to have a stepmom to shop with. Mom always got my clothes, and Dad had no clue. He sent me to a Christian school in first grade, and when we had to go shopping for school clothes, let's just say it was a disaster!

I remember when we went to a kid store in the mall, just Dad and me. At first, he tried to pick out clothes and stuff, but none of them matched.

The lady who worked there asked, "Do you need any help?"

Dad replied, "Please." It sounded like he was begging.

The lady laughed. "You aren't the first dad who's come in here and gotten lost."

She helped me pick out several outfits and all the accessories. Dad just followed us around and grunted whenever we asked if an outfit was okay with him.

It took a couple of hours, but we finally got everything. The lady helped me get a few extra items I really didn't need, but we figured Dad wouldn't know if they were required or not. He didn't notice. It wasn't a lot or very expensive, but they were some things I wanted. The lady and I winked at each other like we were in cahoots. Dad was oblivious. On second thought, maybe I should have kept Dad all to myself.

"Do you think you got everything you needed?" he asked as we were driving home.

"Yes, I think so."

"That's good. I was worried maybe we didn't get enough." I noticed him glancing at me in the rear-view mirror. "I saw the lady wink at you and get you some extras you didn't need."

I was too stunned to speak. He was smiling.

"You both thought, dear old dad wouldn't notice, didn't you?"

I just nodded. What else could I do? I mean, seriously.

5

COURTSHIP AND MAYONNAISE

I wondered what God had in store for me when I actually asked Dyanna Jo out on a first real date. Just the two of us. We'd been friends for several months — make that seven months, according to her — I figured I'd kept her on the hook long enough. It was time to reel her in. I was starting to realize she was a good catch.

I had been praying for God to bring someone across my path to date and see if they were potential wife material. They had to be mother material, as well. Admittedly, I hadn't been thinking of the Lunatic in that regard. But in February 2003, I had an epiphany. *Why not ask the Lunatic out on a real date?*

Although it was February, I didn't envision a Valentine's Day date. I never liked that holiday. Janet and I never celebrated Valentine's day. We both agreed it was just a greeting card company's made-up holiday. I wasn't about to start celebrating now. I wouldn't bring it up and see if Dyanna Jo said something on our date. It had never come up in our conversations, but since this was February, I thought there was a big chance she would talk about the romantic holiday. If it was a big deal to her, then we would just stay friends. I couldn't celebrate a holiday I terribly disliked.

We went to see a movie. I don't remember which one because I was so enamored with the Lunatic, now that we were o-fficial. O-fficial first date, that is.

~

DYANNA JO'S Journal

What a load of bunk. Sounds good, but it's completely untrue. We weren't o-fficial. Leif was just testing the water, and I knew it. After the movie, we went to Panera Bread to get a light meal and coffee. It was nice; we were one of the only couples in the restaurant. It was a perfect place to sit and talk.

After about an hour, a cute couple walked into the restaurant. The girl was holding a beautiful bouquet of flowers. I had to laugh. It was the month of love. They seemed so young, and the guy seemed a little uncomfortable. Leif heard my laugh and turned to see where I was looking. When he turned back to me, he looked a bit awkward.

"Looks like a Valentine's date," he said after a very long pause. "How do you feel about Valentine's Day?"

"Is this a trick question?" I asked as I took a bite of my French fry. He watched me chew. He told me years later that it was like watching a cow chewing her cud. Of course, that was after we were married. Well, now, I choose to eat slowly. I was taught manners and to be proper at the table. Leif, however, is a speed eater. He always looks like he is afraid someone will take off with his food. This has been a topic of conversation for years and years. Thank God our eating habits weren't a deal-breaker.

Back to our dinner date and the Valentine's test.

"No, it's not a trick question. I just want to know how you feel about Valentine's Day," Leif continued.

I slowed down my chewing even more and swallowed. Then I took a long drink, all the while staring a hole through him. I'm not quite sure, but I think he squirmed a bit.

After seven months of friendship, I learned that Leif had a sense of humor and loved bantering back and forth.

"How do you feel about Valentine's Day?" I asked back.

I giggled inside because I could tell he was not expecting me to turn it back on him. Pins and needles. Playing with him, sure was fun.

"I don't like it. I think it's a stupid holiday," Leif replied. "If you think it is an important holiday and expect me to celebrate, then I think we should just end things now. I don't want to waste my time."

"Waste your time!" I replied indignantly. "I really don't care one way or the other about Valentine's Day! I think it has too much emphasis put on it. Poor guys get suckered into giving gifts on Valentine's Day when they should be showing love every other day of the year. People do things on that day because it's expected. Their heart isn't even in it. Your mighty smug aren't you? 'Waste my time!'" I continued with distaste on my face.

He just stared at me—no facial expression.

"You think I am so enameled with you, don't you?" I asked loudly.

Now it was my turn to watch Leif chew. I could tell my choice of words gave him pause. He took a long drink and stared at me. I stared back.

"Enameled?" he asked. "That's a curious choice of words."

For some reason, he was grinning.

"What?" I asked.

"You have a glob of mayo on your chin, and I think the word you're looking for is enamored."

Pause.........

"Oh," I said calmly and wiped my mouth with a napkin. I

am sure my face said it all. I could never hide my feelings. "You are totally picking on me aren't you? Man! I am going to get you back when you least expect it!"

He was funny and not romantic—two more things on my list.

We headed to the car and drove back to my house. The bantering continued in the car. I couldn't help but smile all the way home.

LEIF'S JOURNAL

She had a humorous look on her face. That glob of mayo she tried to wipe off her face had fallen onto her shirt. I pointed to it, and she looked down. She took her napkin and dipped it into her glass of water and dabbed at the blob. When she looked up, I was grinning. She threw her napkin at me—such maturity.

On the drive back to her house, I continued our conversation.

"So, you don't care one way or the other about Valentine's Day?" I asked smiling

"No."

"Well, then, try this on for size. If we wind up continuing this relationship and get married, I don't want to hear any bellyaching about me not doing anything for Valentine's Day, say, five years down the road. I'm letting you know now that I won't be doing anything for it, so don't start griping and complaining and nagging." I emphasized nagging.

"Oh, spare me the drama," she said with an emphasis on drama. "I won't nag you," she said, overemphasizing the word nag.

"I know you won't because you're enameled with me."

She laughed.

I enjoyed the bantering back and forth and playing with each other. It was the most comfortable first date ever. It was because we had taken the time to become friends and were comfortable teasing each other. It became our "thing"—the Lunatic and the Snail and our wordsmithing.

We both enjoyed ourselves, and I was glad I had finally asked her out for a real date. I knew she was beside herself with joy despite her tough girl act. She was utterly head over heels enameled with me.

~

RALLEY'S JOURNAL

Over the seven months, Dad procrastinated about being o-fficial, I had grown to like Dyanna Jo. Back when they weren't dating, I knew after a few months that he should get serious about her. It would take more effort on Dad's part. In the meantime, he let Dyanna Jo take me out from time to time. She took me to movies, out to eat, and for manicures and pedicures.

In September 2002, as her birthday present to me, she took me to the zoo. It was my sixth birthday. I didn't know how to respond. I just smiled and tried to look happy. It was the first time I'd been to the zoo since Mom died. I couldn't stop thinking about that time: the penguins, the news of her cancer returning, and her dying.

Everything we saw reminded me. I lost it when we got to the penguins. I cried softly, trying not to let Dyanna Jo see.

"What's wrong?" Dyanna Jo asked with concern in her voice.

"This is the first time," I mumbled through the tears, "I've been to the zoo since Mom died. That was the last thing we did together. She bought me a stuffed penguin. The next day she found out she had cancer again, and then she died."

"I'm so sorry," Dyanna Jo consoled me and put her arm

around my shoulder. "I didn't know. Do you want to leave?" We were about halfway through the zoo.

"No," I shook my head. "I'm fine."

She handed me a tissue she dug out of her purse. I wiped my eyes and got everything dried up. I was better for the rest of the day. I was still more subdued than a six-year-old should be at the zoo, but I did perk up some after the penguins. Dyanna Jo kept apologizing. I told her it was okay. I have good memories of my time with Mom. It was just, well, being at the zoo made me think more about her than I had in a while.

Even though our zoo day was melancholy, I did enjoy it. Looking back, I enjoyed being with Dyanna Jo. She was drastically different than my mom, and I liked her for her. Dad had told me it wasn't fair to compare her to Mom. They were completely different people, and Dyanna Jo would do things differently than Mom.

He hit the nail on the head with that statement. She was a lot of fun in a crazy, goofy, fly-by-the-seat-of-your-pants kind of way. Mom was fun, but she always organized her fun and scheduled it. She was organized at home too, and oddly enough, Dyanna Jo was the same way. At least when it came to our cupboards and closets. Later, when Dad and Dyanna Jo got married, I found out how meticulous Dyanna Jo really was when organizing. In the linen closet, she labeled melamine shelves for the hand towels, bath towels, and washcloths. All those things had to be folded a certain way and put precisely where the label was on the shelf. She had plastic bins for medical supplies and cleaning supplies. Those bins were labeled, and the spot where they went on the shelf was marked.

Every room was like that. Everything was assigned a place to go, and if it wasn't put in that place, it would bug her to no end. She wouldn't get mad, but I could tell she'd be agitated. Sometimes Dad misplaced things just to bug her, and that was funny.

So, while he procrastinated, Dyanna Jo and I goofed off and placed bets on when he would ask her out on a real date. If I won, she agreed to get her nails done in bright pink. She hated that color. If she won, I agreed to paint my nails lime green.

I bet it would be March, and she bet it would be January. I knew how slow dad was, just like a Snail. That was Dyanna Jo's nickname for Dad. She was impatient and hoped to prod him some. So, what did he do? He asked her out in February. Since neither of us could claim victory, we got manicures anyway in the colors we liked.

LEIF'S FAMILY

Dyanna Jo's Journal

I admit to being a bit anxious about meeting Leif's family. When he told me about his parents, Pam and Lee, he told me he was a lot more like his dad, and his mother was kind of like me. That piqued my curiosity.

"Care to collaborate?" I asked

"Collaborate? Sure, what would you like to collaborate on?" he replied with a Cheshire cat grin.

All I could do was groan under my breath and say, "Oh, you know what I mean!" I hate it when I do that. My brain seems to be constantly working on overdrive that when I talk, I mix up my words. Unfortunately, I do it often. Leif loves it and always gets a big laugh.

"Yes, I would be happy to elaborate," he said, emphasizing elaborate. "My mom has a type-A personality, just like you."

"Ok, I need you to elaborate a bit more." Yes, I emphasized elaborate.

"My mom has a dominant personality. She tends to be

bossy, controlling, set in her ways, and in her opinion, she is rarely wrong."

"Gotcha, sounds like she and I will get along just fine; or not."

The Snail continued to tell me all about his family tree. He had an older brother, Charles, who was married to Lisa. They had a son Charles the second, not Junior, who was nine months older than Ralley. Leif also had an older sister, Dana. She was single and lived with Pam and Lee. She paid them rent and worked at a hospital in medical records.

Leif is an identical twin. He talks about his twin all the time. I was most nervous about meeting him. Leif had shown me pictures of Anders and his wife Charlotte, along with their two children, Phillip and Katherine. Phillip was the same age as Ralley, and Katherine was a year and a half younger. It was extremely difficult to tell the twins apart.

I had never met someone who was an identical twin. Fraternal? Sure, but not twins who completely looked the same. Seeing the photos of Anders and his family, was like staring at Leif with a woman and children I had never seen before. When I finally meet Anders, will I be able to tell them apart? Most likely not, and I just knew there would be a lot of embarrassing moments in my future.

Charles and his family lived in Johnson City, a few hours away from Knoxville. Anders and his tribe lived in Stafford, Virginia. They were about eight to nine hours away, so I didn't know when I would actually get to meet them. His parents and sister lived just a few miles down the road.

Leif talked about his family a lot, but he wasn't in a hurry to have me meet them. Since I was so anxious, maybe that was a good thing. But in my crazy mind, I thought it meant that the Snail wasn't getting as serious as I had hoped. The Snail was never in a hurry.

The more time I spent with Leif, the more I saw he was the

man I had prayed God would bring to me. He was the man who's characteristics were on my list. I had never met a man like him, and I really believe that I didn't have enough faith to believe God would bring me such a perfect man.

I guess I just need to be patient and wait for Leif to move things along. Oh, how I hate to wait.

TIME SLOWLY PASSED. Finally, in June, four months after our first date, I met Leif's parents and siblings who lived within driving distance.

Leif's family was having a family luncheon one Sunday after church. Leif thought it would be a perfect time to meet them. We all met at his parent's house. Immediately, I could see exactly what Leif meant about his father. He was kind, slow mannered, and was welcoming in every way. A gentle teddy bear is the best way to describe Lee.

His mom, Pam, was a very in-your-face, blunt-type of woman. She was completely in charge. She definitely intimidated me. Dana, his sister, was like her dad. She was very friendly; I liked her. His older brother, Charles, seemed to be more like his mother. He was a bit louder, but not in a bad way. He laughed a lot. His kids were well mannered and polite.

It was a great luncheon, and they all made me feel welcomed.

FOURTH OF JULY 2003, was on a Friday. Leif was planning on hosting a family get together at his house to celebrate. Anders and his family were coming down to Knoxville.

Exactly one year ago, I met the Snail. Would I have been happier to be farther along by now? Yes, but again, Leif was in no hurry. Even though it had been a year, I still hadn't seen Leif's house. He was extremely conservative. When we would get together for a date, he never came into my house when he picked me up or dropped me off. He was a gentleman and would walk me to the door, but he always declined when I offered to have him come in. I never met a man like that. The men in California were not like the men in the South.

I was happy to be taking this next step; however, I was not excited to be meeting Anders for the first time. Especially in unfamiliar surroundings.

Anders and his crew drove down on Thursday the third and were staying with the Snail. Because Leif was hosting, I drove myself to his house. I walked to the porch, rang the doorbell, and anxiously paced as I waited for him to open the door.

Leif answered the door wearing a goofy grin. He didn't welcome me with a kiss. Not surprising, Leif never showed PDA (Pubic Display of Affection). Mr. Reserved.... I couldn't help but giggle. That helped me relax a little.

Most of his family was on the patio. Instead of showing me around his house, the Snail took me straight out to the patio. All eyes were on me. My anxiousness overwhelmed me. I gave everyone a sweet smile but didn't speak. Leif broke the ice and hollered for Anders to come out and meet me. I remained silent. Anders came out and introduced himself. Instead of taking my hand in a shake, he threw his arms around me. I was as stiff as a board. When he pulled away, he grabbed my face and planted a huge kiss right on the lips.

I was mortified! When Anders finally released me, my mouth flew open, but no words came out. All I could do was stand there with my mouth wide open and my eyes as big as saucers. The sound of laughter filled my ears and knocked me out of my shock. I looked around at all the faces on the porch. I stopped when I saw Ralley. She looked nervous and a little scared. I immediately turned to Leif, trying to understand why he didn't do something. He doesn't even show PDA. How was it okay that Anders did that. Leif was laughing along with everyone else. I looked back and forth between Leif and Anders. Back and forth, back and forth. Then I realized it was Leif who kissed me.

"Oh My Gosh! No, You Didn't! You are so mean!" I yelled as I started slowly laughing along with everyone else. I stood there laughing, looking from face to face, and when I reached Leif and Anders' faces, I realized they were both wearing the same clothes, everything the same from head to toe. No way! Their jokes were far from over. Ralley ran over and gave me a huge hug. Her little face was smiling. I think she was relieved that I was finally laughing.

I had always heard that twins play tricks on people. Leif was good at picking on me, but this was over the top. Anders finally stuck out his hand and said, "Hi, I am Anders." I took his hand and shook it authoritatively. I had to show him I could take it. The first chance I got, I slugged the Snail right in the arm. I did not hold back. It was nice to hear him say, "Ouch!"

The more time I spent with Leif and Anders, the more I noticed that this whole identical twin thing was eerie. They shared the same mannerisms—they walked, moved, talked, and generally did everything the same way. It was like they were carbon copies. It was going to take a lot of getting used to that. Fortunately, Anders didn't live close.

A while later, as I talked with Anders and his wife Charlotte, I heard the story of how they met and the road to their wedding. They told me the stories of how the twins played jokes on Charlotte. Charlotte seemed like a good sport. I liked her. I learned that Anders proposed to Charlotte six months after they met. That was blazing fast! I had to wait seven months for a first date. I guess the boys weren't as identical as I originally thought.

Throughout the day, I mixed and mingled with the whole

family. Everyone was great. I made sure to keep Leif in my line of sight for the rest of the day. There were a few small jokes, but nothing I couldn't handle now that I was expecting it.

I stayed clear of Pam. Not to be rude, but I was so intimidated by her. She wasn't shy about airing her opinion on just about every topic and let everyone in hearing distance know precisely how she felt about things. I had a feeling that we would be butting heads on more than one occasion if the Snail ever got around to marrying me. I later found out from Lisa and Charlotte that they had butted heads with her several times.

Overall, my first meeting with the whole family was a good one. They were just like every family. They had their peculiarities and characteristics. It definitely wasn't any worse than my family. We had our share of characters too, and some who might seem a bit crazier. I was glad that Anders was going back to Virginia. I liked him, but I needed to see him in small doses until I got used to this whole twin thing.

When the day ended, I said goodbye to Leif; I leaned in as if to tell him a secret. "You know, Anders only took six months to propose to Charlotte." I raised my eyebrows and tilted my head in a questioning way.

"Hmm, well, we wouldn't want to rush into anything, would we?"

"No, Snail, no we wouldn't." I smiled and walked out the door to my car.

7

———

DYANNA JO'S FAMILY

Leif's Journal

Well, Dyanna Jo did just fine with my family. I mean, she kissed my twin brother (ha-ha) and put my older brother in a bear hug. My dear old dad had to beat her off with a stick. A Lunatic, I tell ya.

I have come to realize that no matter what she is eating, she usually gets food on her shirt. That seemed to be her modus operandi whenever food was involved. She'd take a bite and a drop of mustard, mayonnaise, ketchup, relish — whatever condiment happened to be in play — plopped on her shirt. She hated it, but I found it comical.

Despite her embarrassing behavior, my family liked her. My mom thought she was a little too loud and outspoken, though. I had to laugh at that. Talk about the pot calling the kettle black. I think it's funny how people see something in others, but don't see the same thing in themselves. If you suggested to my mom, she was overbearing or outspoken, she'd think you were off your rocker and say so — loudly.

Now, it was my turn to meet Dyanna Jo's parents, Pat and

Joe. Joe was the Lunatic's step-father. She had one step-brother, Joe Jr. He lived in Florida with his wife, Sharon, and their daughter, Jean. They didn't come to Knoxville very often. Luckily, I only had to impress two people with my charm.

I hadn't thought much about meeting her parents since I'd been keeping Dyanna Jo at arm's length. Now that we were official and it had been several months since our first date, I suggested it to her. She didn't seem excited about the idea. When she described her parents, she said they were "unique". My interest was piqued. She said she needed to get her hooks into me a little more securely before she let me meet the parents. Now that she had met my family and they had survived her lunacy, I felt like it was time to meet hers. They couldn't be any more of a Lunatic than her.

In the meantime, we continued to date. She got food on more shirts, and we laughed a lot. Dyanna Jo was fun to be around. Ralley got more and more comfortable with her. Ralley had done some things with my sister over the years, and they always had a good time, so now I let her go out with Dyanna Jo. They seemed to enjoy themselves. I was glad Ralley had a woman to be there for her. Even if that woman was a Lunatic.

It was September when I finally got to meet Dyanna Jo's parents. She was the one moving at a snail's pace for a change. I resorted to bribery and told her it would speed things up if I met them. She quickly arranged a meeting.

We decided to go out for dinner at Olive Garden. My sister, Dana, watched Ralley. We got there before Dyanna Jo's parents arrived and put our name on the list. It was about a fifteen-minute wait. Pat and Joe showed up right as we were being seated. The first thing I noticed was that Dyanna Jo was almost a carbon copy of her mother.

Pat looked like she was about five feet five inches tall and about a hundred twenty pounds. She wore glasses and had completely white hair. Dyanna Jo told me she thought her mom was sixty-nine or seventy. She was actually sixty-four. Pat was born in 1939, and since it was 2003, she was definitely sixty-four. She wasn't too pleased when she found out Dyanna Jo said she was almost seventy. I've learned that Dyanna Jo isn't very good with dates or ages.

Joe was eight years older and a few inches shorter than Pat. His hair was just as white. He was bald on top with a comb-over. He wore glasses and a neatly trimmed beard.

When we got to the table, Dyanna Jo introduced us. Even though it was 5:30 p.m., Joe said, "Good morning." Without thinking, I said, "Good morning" back to him. He smiled. I learned he always had a smile on his face. We got seated and looked over the menus and ordered.

"We've heard a lot about you," Joe commented while we were waiting for our food.

"I've heard nothing about you two," I replied.

"Not a word?" Pat asked.

"Not a peep," I declared as I looked at the Lunatic. "I've asked several times for information about you two, but she won't tell me anything."

"Everything she's told us about you," Joe smiled, "has been good."

"It's hard to find anything bad to say about me," I grinned.

"She said you were humble," Joe laughed. "I can see she was right."

"I know you all moved here from California, but where are you from originally?"

"I'm from Chicago," Joe said.

"I'm from West Virginia," Pat said.

"How did you all meet?" I asked another hard-hitting question.

"We met in California," Joe began.

"We met at church," Pat interjected. "My first husband, Dyanna's biological father, was in the Navy, and we were stationed in California. He passed away shortly after Dyanna was born."

I noticed Pat didn't call Dyanna Jo by her nickname.

"I was a CPA and worked for an accounting firm," said Joe. "Pat worked at a church, and I kept their books. She was a good looking broad, and I noticed her immediately."

"Joe! Behave," Pat said, looking a little agitated.

"What? You were a good looking broad."

Their exchanges entertained me. "Pat had a good heart," Joe continued. "She ran the church's food bank. We saw each other from time to time, and one thing led to another, and I asked her out. She practically fell all over me."

"Now Joe," Pat scolded like she was patiently correcting a child. "Let's stick to the facts."

"But the embellishments are so much better," he protested.

The food arrived, and we let the waitress get everything settled. We all eagerly dug into our meals.

"Oh, shoot," Dyanna Jo and Pat both blurted at the same time after we had been eating for a few minutes. They both had dropped some food on their shirts. Joe gave me the side-eye, as if to say, *I tell ya, I can't take them anywhere.* They dipped their napkins in Dyanna Jo's water and gently dabbed at their shirts. They'd got most of it off. The apple sure doesn't fall far from the tree, or I should say, the food doesn't fall far from the mouth.

We continued to talk as we ate our meal. I learned that they lived in Southern California until 1995 and then moved to Knoxville, so their retirement money would go farther. California was eating up their savings. Dyanna Jo stayed in California for another year.

"Why, Knoxville?" I continued my probing, hard-hitting questions.

"We were retired and took trips every summer in our fifth-wheel camper. Over the years, we had traveled to all the states. We always liked East Tennessee," Joe explained. "We stopped in Knoxville for a few days because Pat got sick. While she was laid up, I went exploring and found a house I liked and bought it."

"I'm laid up in the camper with a stomach bug, and he's out gallivanting around East Tennessee and puts an offer on a house I've never seen," Pat relayed matter of factly. She didn't seem to have any residual bitterness about it. She just calmly told the story.

"How long were you sick, and what did you think when you got to see the house?" I asked.

"I was sick for a little over a week," Pat answered. "We had talked about moving to East Tennessee multiple times. We would often drive around looking at houses when we drove through on one of our trips. At first, I was really ticked at him, but when I saw the house, I liked it."

"So, what did you do with your place in California?" I asked.

"We sold it," Joe answered. "It sold in seven days."

"Do you still have the camper?"

"We do."

"Do you still take trips with it?"

"We take a few trips a year. We go to Pennsylvania to the Amish country a lot. That's Pat's favorite place to visit. We visit the Gulf Coast in Alabama and Mississippi. When we're there, we like to visit the old Antebellum Mansions."

"That sounds like it would be fascinating."

We talked a little while longer. I liked her parents. I didn't understand why it was such a big deal for Dyanna Jo. When it came time to pay, Joe jumped in and told the waitress to give him the check. I started to protest, but he was adamant that dinner was on him. I thanked him for his generosity.

The waitress came, took his card, and went to process the payment. She returned and gave him the receipt to sign. She quickly left again but came back a few minutes later with some to-go boxes. While she was gone, I noticed Joe took out a two-dollar bill and placed it under the receipt.

As we were leaving the restaurant, the greeter thanked us for coming. Joe replied, immediately saying, "thank you and Happy Ground Hog Day." The greeter looked a little puzzled. Pat and Dyanna Jo rolled their eyes and continued walking out the door.

In the parking lot, I reached into my pocket to get my car keys. As I was pulling them out, they dropped to the ground.

"Well, you don't have to get mad and throw it on the ground," Joe said, smiling.

I laughed. Again Pat and Dyanna Jo rolled their eyes and kept walking. This time, however, I thought I heard a couple of groans.

Dyanna Jo and I got in my car. I immediately commented on the things Joe said throughout the night. I thought he was funny. Dyanna Jo didn't seem amused.

"I have heard those phrases over and over my entire life, and they stopped being funny a long time ago," she informed me. "If you stick around, you'll see what I mean. He has a lot more of them." She emphasized "a lot".

"I think I'll stick around just to hear them all," I said, laughing.

"You won't' stick around for me?"

"I'll stick around for you just to see all the ways he gets on your nerves."

"So, my dad didn't run you off?"

"Nope. I don't see why you thought he would."

"I was just concerned because normally you're so quiet and

he's very talkative. He doesn't know a stranger. I thought maybe he'd talk your ear off, but you talked more tonight than I have heard all month."

"You're so loud and talkative that my hearing is gone anyway, so it didn't matter how much he talked."

"Ha-ha," she said intelligently.

"I'm also thirty-three, I've been in the Army, and I've had to put up with all kinds of people. Weird ones, mean ones, nice ones, the whole gamut. Your dad is mild compared to some of the people I've dealt with."

"Okay, Mr. Man of the World," she said sarcastically.

"No need for sarcasm. I've noticed when people revert to sarcasm, it's to hide their insecurity."

"I didn't pervert to sarcasm to hide insecurity."

I started laughing. She was worth hanging around just to see which word she'd mess up the next time. By now, she knew when I laughed after she said something, she'd messed up a word. She used to ask me why I was laughing, but she doesn't anymore. She just impatiently waits for me to stop laughing. Sometimes I even get a groan or two out of her.

We got to her house, and I walked her up to the front door. I held her hand and prayed; then I gave her a quick kiss on the cheek. I could tell she wanted me to kiss her more. I wanted to also, but I knew how attracted I was to her, and didn't want to allow my flesh to compromise.

WHEN I GOT HOME, Ralley was asleep. Dana told me about their night. They worked on some puzzles, and Dana painted her fingernails.

"Are you going to ask Dyanna Jo to marry you?" Dana asked.

"I'm thinking about it."

"Well, I like her and think she'd be good for you and Ralley."

"I think she would be too. I think in the next month or two, I'll ask her."

"When do you think she'll want the wedding?"

"I think it will be soon because she doesn't like to wait, and I have made her wait long enough."

"Is that okay with you?" she asked, unsure of my answer. Before I could answer, she immediately asked another question. "Are you going to have a big wedding or a small one?"

"A small one," I quickly replied before she could ask another question. "We've both been married before and already had big weddings. I think this time we'll have a small, simple wedding."

"You've already talked about it?"

"Actually, we haven't. She has mentioned it once or twice in passing, but I know she won't mind having a small one."

"A Valentine's Day wedding would be great."

I inwardly groaned when she said that. She liked Valentine's Day. I hadn't yet told her about my Valentine's dislike.

"It won't be on Valentine's Day. I want it to be separate from that."

"That makes sense. Have it be your own day."

DANA LEFT, and I checked on Ralley. She was sleeping peacefully. I turned the hall light on so there would be a little bit of light in her room. She had one hand outside her comforter, and I looked at her fingernails. They alternated pink and purple. *That figures,* I thought. My sister always was a little eccentric in her style. I gently laid my hand on Ralley's hand and prayed for her. I prayed for God to bless her and fill her with His peace.

I went to my room and got ready for bed. I laid in bed, thinking about when I would ask Dyanna Jo to marry me. Even though I knew she'd say yes, I was still nervous about asking her. *Was it the right time?* I asked myself. *Was she right for Ralley? Should I wait longer?* All kinds of thoughts and questions stirred in my brain. Deep down, I knew she was the right one, but I still had those thoughts sometimes. I just asked God for guidance on if and when I should ask her. I left it in His capable hands.

Having another woman in our lives was a big thing. It was part of moving on from Janet's death. She told me before she died that I should get married again. Ralley would need a mom in her life, and it was crazy to expect me to stay single because I didn't want to dishonor her memory.

"Grieve for a time, and then move on," she said. "You must move on."

So, I was going to marry a woman who was all the time telling me to get moving.

My family hadn't run her off, and hers hadn't run me off. It looked like we were stuck with each other.

DYANNA JO WORRIED every time I did something with her dad.

A few weeks after I met Dyanna Jo's parents, we went to visit them at their house in a subdivision called The Villas of Barrington. Their home was more like a townhouse. Most of the people who lived there were retired. In their garage, Joe had a bunch of woodworking tools. He took pride in his tools. A lot of the hand tools had been owned by his dad and were made in the early 1900's. Joe's dad had taught him woodworking and passed on his tools when he died. Joe gave me a tour of their house. The tour was mainly seeing everything he had built for Pat. Woodworking interested me.

We stayed for a while and visited. Pat served us cookies and Root Beer. Dyanna Jo must have mentioned that I love Root Beer. The conversations seemed very animated. The more time I spent with Joe and Pat, the more I realized that Dyanna Joe's whole family was loud. Even though I was usually the quiet one, I noticed that her family was able to bring me out of my shell. Joe joked a lot.

By the end of our visit, Joe and I decided we would build a bookshelf together to put in their sunroom. The villas had big garages with room for two cars and his woodworking tools. Pat had the house decorated in a country style. Lots of knick-knacks, flowers, twinkling lights, and everything had a place. The bookshelf would hold her books and possibly more knick-knacks. When I went into their sunroom, I was impressed with all of the Pats books. She had multiple Bibles, Bible studies, Christian fiction, and commentaries. She had a lot of books that needed storage.

A few days after we had been over to their house, Joe and I went to Lowes to get the wood for the project. The plan was to use oak plywood. We got to the wood section and looked at some plywood. A couple nearby discussed what kind of plywood they should use. They both seemed to be in their forties. The man had a beard. The guy told his wife he thought they should use birch plywood.

"Never trust a man with a beard," Joe barked and smiled.

The guy had his back to us and turned around with an unhappy look on his face. When he saw Joe and his beard and that smile, he laughed.

Joe quickly said, "Happy Ground Hog Day to ya," and they both laughed. "What project are you working on?"

"It's my first time doing a woodworking project, so I'm not sure what wood is good for it," he said. "We're building a box for our son to keep his sports stuff in."

The guy's name was Randy. He and Joe talked for about ten

minutes and were best buds after that. I had come to realize that Joe could make friends with anyone. After he visited with the couple, we picked up everything we needed and headed back to Joe's house.

We began to work on the bookshelf in Joe's garage. Joe was very thorough. He detailed every step, taught me how to use every tool, and told me the purpose of the items we purchased at Lowes.

It took about a week with me coming over after work. I thought it was fun doing the project with Joe. He cut the oak plywood pieces several times to sneak up on the correct length, and when it still needed to be cut again, he said he didn't understand because he cut it three times and it was still too short. I found that humorous. Sometimes we would do something that would accomplish two things at once, and he would say we killed two stones with one bird. Joe unleashed that expression often while we were gallivanting around.

We used some edge banding — a thin strip of oak that was a little over three-fourths of an inch wide — to cover up the edge so it wouldn't look like plywood. It had heat-activated glue on the back. We put it in place and then ran an iron over it, and it stuck to the plywood. We used a roller to smooth it out. Then we trimmed the little bit hanging over the edge.

When the project was finished, we showed Dyanna Jo; she was impressed. Joe looked very pleased; I was too. It was a lot of fun making that bookshelf, and It left me wanting to make more things.

"Dad really enjoyed himself," Dyanna Jo told me later. "Dad tried to do woodworking with my brother, Joe Jr., when he was younger, but he grew up, went to college, and got a great job in Florida. Joe Jr. really never showed an interest in woodworking. Dad's excited to be doing woodworking with someone again. Being able to teach and possibly have a son who will have a love for it just like he does."

The sentence, '*possibly have a son who will have a love for it just like he does,*' didn't escape me. I left her hanging by, not commenting. I knew that would drive her crazy.

"I liked it a lot. I'd be happy to learn more about it from him."

"Are you sure you can stand him? He teases a lot and will say the same thing over and over again."

"He doesn't bother me. I think he's funny."

"I guess it's because I've heard all of his sayings all my life. Over and over and over again. He's got a new audience, so it won't bother you now, but it might later."

I got used to him chatting up anyone within earshot and telling people Happy Ground Hog Day. I could see why he was a good businessman. He was good at making friends with people and fostering connections.

Joe and Pat approved of Dyanna Jo and me getting married. They were just as impatient for me to propose as she was. Dyanna Jo hadn't run me off yet, so they figured she needed to lasso me and hogtie me down before I came to my senses. I was shaking off my lethargy, especially if it meant I could do more woodworking projects. I could kill two stones with one bird. I could marry Dyanna Jo and do more woodworking. That just might spur me into action.

8

HE POPPED THE QUESTION

Dyanna Jo's Journal

I was utterly shocked when Leif and Dad hit it off so well. Leif really enjoyed working with my dad on the wood-working projects. God was definitely answering my prayers, and every day I could see little things appear that I had prayed for on my list. I knew beyond a shadow of a doubt that Leif was the man that God intended me to marry. It was a shame Leif hadn't figured it out yet.

Thanksgiving was upon us. Leif, Ralley, and I were going to Leif's parent's house for lunch. This family event, however, would include my parents. This would be the first time our families would all be together. I was nervous, but at the same time, excited.

Leif's twin, Anders, and his family weren't able to make the drive down to Knoxville. The rest of Leif's family would be there. I was relieved Anders wouldn't be there. I know that sounds bad. It was just so stressful with him around because I knew that the twins would have something up their sleeves. A joke on Thanksgiving with my parents meeting Leif's family didn't sound like a good time. I know Leif really wanted Anders there. The Snail and his twin were extremely close. I loved how close Leif's whole family was.

Leif and Ralley came to pick me up, and when I opened the door, Leif surprised me and barged right on in. I shut the door, hesitated, and went into the living room cautiously.

"Just come right on in," I said. He was fidgeting with a gift bag, and Ralley looked a little too nervous. All I could do was look at them suspiciously. The gift bag in Leif's hand was a little strange. This wasn't Christmas or my birthday. What was he up too?

"My dad has something he would like to give you," Ralley said. My heart thuddered. I headed to the couch and sat down. Ralley and Leif came and sat next to me. Ralley on the left and Leif on the right. Leif handed me the gift bag but said nothing. I took the bag and looked at them both once again. As I opened the bag, I noticed a folded piece of paper and a toy train. I looked up at Leif. His face was emotionless. I reached into the bag and pulled out the piece of paper. When I unfolded it, I saw it was a poem. I looked at Leif once again. Finally, I read the poem to myself. When I reached the very last line, it read, *will you be my wife and Ralley's mom?* This was a proposal. Instead of answering the question, I reached into the bag and pulled out a little wooden train. The train was a toy that could be taken apart and be put back together again. Similar to blocks. The train was painted red, blue, green and black. As I observed the features, I saw a beautiful ring sticking out of the hole where the conductor would be sitting. As I pulled the ring out of the hole, I could hear Leif say, "Well?"

I looked from the ring up into Leif's eyes. His blue eyes could melt a woman right in her tracks. I composed myself and quietly said, "Yes and no."

Leif just stared at me with a puzzled look on his face.

"I will be your wife, but Ralley already has a mom. I will be the best stepmom I can be, but I will not replace her mom."

"I like that," Ralley said quietly.

"That is an acceptable answer," Leif declared and put the lovely ring on my finger. "I'm thinking of a February wedding."

I almost fainted. Miracles do happen. The Snail was moving at a faster pace. My heart thudded even quicker. "Three months, are you serious? Who are you, and what have you done with my Snail?"

Both Ralley and Leif laughed. "Well, your dad and I made a deal. He would teach me some more woodworking, but I had to marry you first. I really want to get moving on those woodworking lessons."

Now it was my turn to laugh. "Alrighty then. Let's get this show on the road."

"I'm kidding, of course," Leif said with a smile. "Your dad and I have no such arrangement. I just want to marry you and not put it off any longer than necessary."

"Was Ralley part of the proposal, or were you afraid I would say no and hoped she could change my mind?" I asked, still joking.

"I was going to leave her with my parents, but she wanted to come, and I figured why not?"

"So, she obviously knew what you were going to do?"

"Yes, she did. She was excited for me to ask you. We even practiced the proposal. It didn't go the way we practiced, but I am glad it's finally done."

I was happy Ralley was excited for the Snail to ask me to marry him. I looked at the ring once more, gave Ralley a huge hug, and then turned to Leif and quietly said, "Yes, I will be your wife. The poem was beautiful."

He smiled and planted a kiss on my lips. "Let's get moving. Everyone will be waiting for us."

I grabbed my purse, and we headed to his car. On the drive

to his parent's house, all I could think about was planning a wedding in three months. We never talked about weddings. I hinted a couple of times about wanting a small wedding, but he never replied when I did. I giggled a little. I thought it was funny that I wanted the Snail to hurry up and marry me, and now that he'd asked me, he wanted to do it in three months.

"What are you gigglin' about over thar?" Leif asked with a slight twang in his voice.

"I was thinking about how I was going to plan a wedding in three months. I have known you were the one for a long time now, and I prayed you would figure it out too. You not only popped the question, but you also set a month for the wedding to happen. You have completely shocked me today Mr. Snail."

"You have mentioned a couple of times that you want a small wedding. That is exactly what I want. We've done the big weddings before, and I was hoping you would keep it small."

I guess he did hear my hints after all. "Wow, normally men don't think of the wedding. The woman plans, and the man sits back and goes with the flow. Since you have been thinking about it, it sounds like you've got it all planned out. Have you picked out the place?"

"I thought we could go up to Pigeon Forge and get married in one of those wedding chapels, and then have our honeymoon in one of the cabins there."

Again I was shocked. I wasn't sure what to think. I wasn't used to someone planning everything out for me. Especially Leif.

"I am perfectly fine with all of that. Getting married is the important thing."

"Yep, and then I can kiss you right proper."

"That too."

We got to his parent's house and walked right in. My parents showed up shortly after we did. My mom immediately noticed the ring. She raised her left eyebrow and looked at me.

I slightly nodded, and she smiled. Leif and my dad were oblivious to the silent communication my mom and I just had.

Ralley was silent and looked first at me than my parents. Later she admitted that she was surprised to see how loud my dad was when he talked to her dad. That's just so funny. We are unique, that is for sure.

We made our way into the living room and kitchen area. All of Leif's family was there. We made all the introductions. Once we said our hello's, the women migrated to the kitchen while the men headed to the couch to watch football games.

As we worked in the kitchen, both Lisa and Dana saw my ring. They just stared at me with their mouths open, and their eyebrows lifted high on their foreheads. I smiled and stayed silent. Dana couldn't help herself; she turned around and went straight to her mom and whispered in her ear. Pam turned and looked straight at my finger.

"Is he going to announce it today?" Leif's mom asked.

"You know, we really didn't discuss it. I would be surprised if he didn't say something."

"The ring is gorgeous," Dana said. Lisa and Pam nodded in agreement.

It was about half-past noon when Pam, announced the food was ready. Everyone scattered and headed to different rooms to wash their hands. One by one, we all made our way to the table. Once we were seated, Lee spoke up and said, "Let us bless this food."

After prayer, everyone started to dive into the bowls on the table. Quickly Leif stood up and said, "Before we dig in, I have an announcement." Everyone froze and looked up at him. "I have asked Dyanna Jo to join me in wedded bliss, and she has deigned to accept."

"Could ya say that in plain English?" Charles son, Charles the second, asked. Everyone started laughing. It sounded funny hearing a six-year-old ask that.

"I asked her to marry me, and she said yes."

"That's better," Charles Two said as he grabbed a roll. I noticed everyone called Charles the second, Charles Two. I have never heard someone call their kid *the second.* I guess all families are unique in their own ways.

Everyone congratulated us and someone, I don't remember who, asked if we'd set a date. Leif told them it would be sometime in February, and we decided on a small, simple ceremony at a wedding chapel in Pigeon Forge.

The train of food bowls made their way around the table, and everyone started eating. Boy did we stuff ourselves. Slowly, one by one, the men made their way to the couch for more football. I noticed a lot of belt loosening as they walked from the table.

Cleanup went quickly. Once the kitchen was clean, and the leftovers were packed in the fridge, the women headed back to the table and sat down. My mom and Pam started up a conversation. I just kept looking at my ring. I found myself looking at my handsome Snail and then again at my ring. I couldn't have planned a better day. Thank you, God, for the gift of family and a man who was everything I had prayed for and more.

LEIF'S JOURNAL

The day I asked Dyanna Jo to marry me, I wasn't planning on taking Ralley. She wanted to go so badly, and afterward, I was glad I took her with me. It was a fun time, and I'm so happy I shared that with her. She's always been more mature than her age. I would like to claim some of the credit for that, but I must give God all the credit. All I've done is pray and made sure to do devotions with her. God's been the one who's turned her into who she is.

I wasn't nervous about asking Dyanna Jo to marry me. I

knew she was ready long before that. I wanted to make it special. It turned out to be special for all of us.

When we arrived at my parent's house, Joe and Pat arrived right behind us. Joe patted me on the back and said, "Good morning, it's good to see your back."

"Good morning," I replied with a laugh. It took me a second to get the last part of his greeting.

As the families met, I could hear Joe saying, good morning, and Happy Ground Hog day to everyone. I could tell that I would hear those phrases often.

All the men and women went their separate ways. Joe hit it off with my dad. They sat telling stories and telling little jokes to each other.

At dinner, I announced that I had asked Dyanna Jo to marry me. Everyone seemed pleased.

As we each started to get up from the table, the women headed to the kitchen, and Ralley started to clear the table. Joe was still sitting in his seat and said, "Hey little lady, why don't you pick up my plate and take it to the kitchen." Ralley didn't hesitate, she picked up the plate, and before she turned to walk away, she stopped and stared at the table. Sitting there was a two-dollar bill. I noticed that Joe had put the two-dollar bill under his plate right before he asked Ralley to help.

"What is that?" Ralley asked

"A two-dollar bill. They don't make many of these. This one is for you."

"Thank you!" Ralley exclaimed. She hurried to the kitchen and showed her Aunt Dana and Lisa the money. They all looked impressed. Joe keeps a wad of two dollar bills in his pocket just for this kind of occasion.

After we visited for a while, Ralley and I took Dyanna Jo home. Ralley fell asleep in the car. Dyanna Joe and I talked quietly. "Did you have a good day?" I asked.

"Are you kidding! This was the best day ever. When Ralley told me you had something to give me, my heart thuddered."

"Thuddered?"

"You know, like thundered and thudded but both at the same time. I just threw the two words together."

I need to remember not to delve too deeply into her thought process. It can be scary. Her talent for picking the wrong word keeps rearing its head. She tries her best, so I should cut her some slack. Plus, most of the time, it's funny.

When we got to Dyanna Jo's house, I walked her up to the front door. We prayed, and then I hugged her and kissed her on the cheek. She sighed. I have such an effect on women. What can I say? Seriously, I knew she sighed because she wanted a humdinger on the lips. She would get more of that in time. Remember, we are in snail time. It was driving her crazy, and I enjoyed that.

I left her pining away on the front porch and took Ralley home. She fell asleep in the car, so I carried her into the house and put her in bed. I wasn't worried about changing her clothes. She was exhausted from playing with her cousin, so I was just going to let her sleep. I sat on her bed and thought about all she'd been through in her short life. Almost dying in utero, losing her mom at a young age, and putting up with a dad that's clueless a lot of the time. It's a good thing God is watching over us and keeping things together. I know I sure couldn't do it on my own.

Ralley's Journal

When my dad finally got off his duff and asked Mom to marry him, I was thinking; it's *about time.* I had already decided I'd be okay with it if he did ask her. I even told him so. He accused me of being pushy. I told him someone needed to be.

Then he was going to drop me off at Grandpa and Grandma's and go ask her without me.

"I want to go with you," I declared.

"You do?" he asked and shrugged. "Why not?"

So, I went with him. I could tell Dyanna Jo was surprised. I was glad when she told me she wouldn't be my mom, but she would be the best stepmom she could be. I called her mom anyway because it was the easiest thing to call her. It seemed strange at first, and I felt like I was doing something terrible towards my real mom, but Dad assured me it was okay.

"Your mom would understand," he assured me. "She told me right before she died that I should get married again. You would need a mother. She prayed that God would lead me to the woman He wants you and me to be with."

"He did, didn't He?"

"He certainly did."

I was glad Dad took me when he proposed to Mom. It was fun to see her reaction. It was also fun when we got to Grandma and Grandpas. Soon I would have a Nana and Papa. My biological mom's adoptive parents died before I was born. I wish I could have met them. I heard they were loving people.

All the women noticed Dyanna Jo's ring when we got to Grandma and Grandpa's. I went and played with Charles Two. He was nine months older than me. He was very goofy. Funny but goofy.

I missed having Dad's twin and his family at Thanksgiving. The first time I saw Anders was when I was about thirteen months old. Dad said I kept looking from Anders to him and back and forth a few more times. He said I buried my head in his shoulder. I peeked a few times and then buried my face again. Dad said it took me a while to get used to Anders.

I liked Philip and Katherine, my other cousins. Whenever Charles two, Philip, Katherine, and I got together, we always had a good time playing. But Thanksgiving was good that year despite Anders and them not being there.

At lunch, Dad made the announcement, "I asked Dyanna Jo to marry me, and she said yes."

All the adults said, "It's about time."

Dyanna Jo wholeheartedly agreed.

Yes, it was a good day, and I am so thankful.

9

THE WEDDING

Dyanna Jo's Journal

It was a tradition to celebrate Christmas Eve with my parents. As a kid, I was able to open one present on Christmas Eve, but this new tradition didn't start until I bought my first house in Tennessee. My mom was always the one to make a perfect meal for Christmas. Now it was my time to take the reins. I would make a bunch of finger foods, hot apple cider, and we would open presents.

Mom and Dad never got Christmas gifts for each other. They had everything they wanted or needed, and so they didn't bother. They just focused on celebrating the real meaning of Christmas. They did, however, exchange one gift on Ground Hog Day. That was something Dad started years ago just to be different, and they had been doing it ever since.

This would be the first year Leif and Ralley would be part of the festivities. They both came to help me set everything up. Ralley mainly stayed in front of the TV watching some Disney Channel show.

"A watched pot never boils," Leif said while we were in the kitchen.

"I'm not sure what you mean," I replied

"You've heard that expression before, haven't you?"

"Yes, I've heard it, and I know what it means, but I'm not sure how it relates to this situation."

"You keep thinking about it and keep it in front of you all the time," he said and pointed to a calendar on my fridge. I had numbered the days until the wedding and was marking off each day. "It's like you're watching the pot."

"You don't think about it?" I asked

"I think about it all the time."

"Yet, you're telling me to stop thinking about it all the time."

"I'm not the one who has a problem with how fast time is moving. I think it's going at a great pace."

"It's moving at a palatial pace to me."

He chuckled. I waited for him to finish and tell me what word I used incorrectly. I put my hands on my hips in disgust when he'd gone a little too long with the chuckling.

"It's glacial, not palatial," he finally managed to say.

"Oh," was my super-intelligent response. What else could I say? Sometimes I wondered if he was marrying me because I was an unwitting source of humor for him. He continued to giggle every now and then and find ways to insert palatial into the conversation. Fortunately, my parents showed up and saved him from having hot apple cider poured on him.

"Good morning," Dad said to Ralley.

"It's not morning, Papa," she laughed.

"It's not?" He acted surprised. Mom ignored him and came into the kitchen. She had brought the dessert, a cheesecake, and some strawberry syrup to drizzle on if anyone wanted that. We don't normally eat cheesecake on Christmas, but the Snail loved cheesecake, and I could tell he was becoming mom's favorite.

We all got our plates and filled them with little finger foods. Our plates were far from small. We all filled them as high as we could get them. Leif prayed and thanked God for the palatial spread we had laid out. I groaned. I would hear about that for a while. After he prayed, we all dug in.

Dad and Leif talked about woodworking. They were cooking up another project. Mom and I sat with Ralley, and we talked about dolls and the wedding. Mom was glad it was going to be low key. My first wedding was huge, and the cost was way over the top. This time around, they agreed to pay for the dinner after the wedding.

We were all sitting in the living room eating, and I noticed Dad and Leif get up and go into the kitchen. I assumed they were getting more sausage or cheese and crackers. When they came back, they each had a massive piece of cheesecake.

"You're not going to wait for us?" Mom asked.

"No," Leif said. "You all are eating at a snail's pace. Downright palatial."

"Isn't that the kettle calling the pot black," I retorted.

They both chuckled. I didn't bother to ask. I was sure I had mangled some word somewhere. Mom, Ralley, and I went into the kitchen and got some cheesecake. The guys kept looking at us, making sure we didn't eat it all.

After stuffing ourselves, we managed to open gifts. Mom and Dad got Ralley a cute Barbie dollhouse. I got a gift certificate to a spa, but when it came time for Leif's gift, Dad told him to go outside. They put their coats on and went out to Mom's car. I peeked out the window and noticed a few snowflakes meandering around, lazily falling, in no great hurry to land. It was so pretty.

Dad opened the trunk, and they both pulled out this huge box. They were huffing and puffing by the time they got in the house.

"What on earth did you do?" I asked Dad.

"You'll see," he said with a bigger smile than usual.

Leif tore off the wrapping paper and revealed a box with a radial arm saw pictured on it. My mouth hit the floor. Dad was enjoying having a son who liked woodworking.

"I know," Mom said when she saw my reaction. "I did the same thing when he came home with that. You should have seen him trying to get that in the car to bring it over here."

"He put it in the car by himself?" I asked incredulously.

"Bill, our neighbor, saw him struggling and helped him," Mom answered.

Leif looked shocked but, at the same time, like a kid in a candy store. We got Mom and Dad gift cards to their favorite restaurants. After the gift exchange, we sat around and drank cider and talked. Ralley started to fall asleep, so Leif took her home. Dad helped him get the saw in his car, and then Mom and Dad left. I stared out the window, watching the snow flurries. There wasn't going to be any snow accumulation—just flurries.

It seemed funny calling them flurries when they were anything but a flurry of activity. They lazily floated around and were in no hurry to go anywhere. I had felt like that until God put Leif in my life. He was a leaf that was firmly attached to the Tree of Life. I was a Christian, but I didn't feel like I had a purpose. I had been asking God what my purpose was, and then I met Leif. When I met Leif, I felt like I had a purpose. I had this feeling as if God was going to do something big in my life. Possibly even our lives.

We spent the next day at Leif's house with his parents and Dana. Charles and Lisa were spending the day with Lisa's family. Mom and Dad wanted to spend the day to themselves, so they didn't come over. We got a ham from Honey Baked Ham, green beans almandine, potatoes au gratin, apple pie and ice cream for lunch and dessert.

After lunch, we opened presents. Leif's parents got Ralley a bicycle. She had outgrown the one she had. They got us gift cards, and we got them gift cards. That's what we wound up doing just about every Christmas after that because it was easy and straightforward. They left a little while later.

Leif, Ralley and I put her bike together. She went outside and rode it for about ten minutes and then came inside.

"It's too cold," she said with rosy cheeks. The rest of the day, we grazed on the leftovers. I went home when Leif put Ralley to bed. When I got home, I realized how lonely and empty it felt. I started to daydream about sharing a home with my new family. It didn't take me long to get ready for bed. I was exhausted. In two months, Leif and I would be married. Please, Lord, make this time pass quickly.

THE DAY of the wedding finally arrived. All in all, time did seem to pass quickly. We rang in the New Year together, and completely skipped Valentine's Day. Now let's get this wedding started!

Leif and Ralley showed up at my house at 2:07 p.m. He was late by seven minutes. I came busting out of my garage and got in his car.

"Anxious, are we?" he asked, amused. "Been pining away for me, have you dear?"

"Yes, I've been looking out the window and looking at my watch and back and forth. And you're late."

"I'm not late," he protested. "I arrived precisely when I intended to."

"I don't doubt that." I didn't doubt that. He probably was late on purpose because he knew it would drive me bonkers. He takes a perverse joy in doing that to me. You know what they say about payback. I was nervous, and it showed, and he seemed like a stone. We checked in at the cabin rental place, put our stuff in the cabin, and went to some outlet stores that were all over Pigeon Forge. I'd finally had it with his nonchalance and asked him if he was nervous. He admitted he was and thought it was rather obvious. Ralley and I didn't think so. We told him to work on it, and he tried, but after a few miserable attempts, we told him to forget it. His face just wasn't capable of showing emotion.

By the time we got to the wedding chapel, everyone was there. We talked to the minister for a few minutes and spoke with our guests. We didn't have many. Both of our families were there and just a couple of friends. We had the ceremony, signed the marriage certificate, took a few pictures, and were out of there in about thirty minutes. Now that was my kind of wedding. Fast, simple, and cheap.

Our families joined us at a restaurant called Conners. We enjoyed an excellent reception dinner, and then we headed back to the cabin while Ralley went home with Leif's parents.

We were now husband and wife. I was looking forward to what lay in store for us. For our adventure to begin, our purpose.

RALLEY'S JOURNAL

After Thanksgiving, the time seemed to speed up and slow down. Sometimes it seemed like it was flying by, and Christmas was here and gone, and then it seemed to take forever for February to roll around. They decided on February 27, 2004, a Friday. They were going to spend the weekend at a cabin in Pigeon Forge, and I was going to stay with Grandma and Grandpa.

"I think you're more excited about the wedding than I am," Dad said one day when I had been talking about it a lot.

I was excited about it, but with Dad, it was hard to tell. He never showed his emotions. He said he did, but no one could ever tell. I helped with planning the wedding, such as it was. There were no formal invitations, just phone calls or emails. No photographer was hired. Dyanna Jo was going to bring her camera and ask someone to take a few pictures. She and Dad were going to wear jeans and nice shirts—nothing fancy. I had never been to a wedding, so I didn't know how they were supposed to be. Dressing casual sounded good to me.

The night before the wedding, I asked Dad if I could sleep in his room. He said I could and got out both of our sleeping bags. He made popcorn, and we watched Lady and the Tramp. I'm glad he let me do that.

The wedding day finally arrived, and the ceremony was scheduled for 5 p.m. Afterward, we were going to dinner. Papa was paying for it. By that time, I was regularly calling Dyanna Jo's parents Nana and Papa. I was referring to Dyanna Jo as "Mom" all the time too, and it felt comfortable.

Dad and I slept in and were sluggards until we ate lunch. Then we got ready and went to pick up my soon-to-be o-fficial mom. I clung to Dad the whole day. I knew things would be different, and I just wanted to stay close to him. I was happy about the changes, but it was the unknown. I knew we'd be fine; I just needed Dad's reassurance.

Mom seemed antsy. When we got to her house, it seemed like she'd been waiting by the door all day. We had barely pulled into the driveway, and the garage door opened. She came out with her bag and got in the car.

"Been pining away for me, have you, dear?" Dad joked.

"Yes, I've been looking out the window and looking at my watch and back and forth. And you're late."

"I'm not late," he protested. "I arrived precisely when I intended to. Patience, my dear, patience," Dad said and patted her on the back.

She gave him a look of scorn. I remembered hearing something about a woman scorned but couldn't remember exactly what it was. I just knew it didn't bode well for the man. But Mom and Dad were all the time going back and forth with each other, so I knew Mom wasn't upset.

The trip to the cabin rental place was uneventful. Check-in for the cabin was at 3 p.m. It took about an hour to get there. The weather was typical of East Tennessee in February. The temperature was in the forties, and a light rain was falling. We got there a little after three. Mom and Dad got checked in and got the key to the cabin. We had to drive up around a hill to get there. When we finally found it we got all their stuff and put it in the small living room. It was a charming log cabin. I wanted to stay, but Dad said he and Mom needed their alone time this weekend. Besides, I would have more fun with Grandma and Grandpa.

We drove to some of the outlet stores in Pigeon Forge and bummed around until it was time for the wedding to begin. Mom still paced and looked at her watch. Dad seemed entirely at ease, a fact that was unnerving Mom to no end.

"Are you nervous?" she asked when she could take no more of his nonchalance.

"Yes," was his curt reply.

"Oh, really," Mom exclaimed. "Gee, silly me. I don't know why I didn't notice."

"I think it's fairly obvious," Dad stated matter of factly.

"He thinks it's fairly obvious," she blabbed to me. "Is it to you, Ralley?"

"No, can't say that it is."

"There," she said triumphantly. "It's two against one."

"Okay. You can't tell I'm nervous. And we've accomplished exactly what?"

"That you need to be more expressive with your face."

Dad tried to put on a nervous face, but it wasn't quite right. He looked like he had taken a bite of a very sour lemon. After a few tries and a few laughs, Mom told him to forget it. "Apparently, you're incapable of showing emotion," she said disgustedly.

I think that helped Mom. She seemed to relax and start joking with us. Up until then, she'd been very serious. By the time we got to the wedding chapel, she and Dad were trading barbs and laughing. When we walked into the wedding chapel, everybody was there.

"I see we're late for our own wedding," Dad quipped. They both laughed along with everybody else. Papa told them good morning and said we weren't late; everyone just got there early. It was four forty-five, and the ceremony was minutes away. The minister took Mom and Dad aside and went over a few things, and then they went up front and took their places. I stood beside them since I had the rings.

The minister was talking, and when it was time to give them the rings, Mom not only gave Dad a ring, she turned to me and said, "This wedding isn't only for Dad and me. You are a part of this too. We are a family, and I vow to always be there for you no matter what." She took a necklace and placed it on my neck. I really liked that.

When it came time for Mom and Dad to sign the marriage license, they had me sign as their witness. I really didn't have a signature, but I printed my name the best I could. After a few pictures, we took off for the restaurant. Once everyone arrived, Papa wished all the guests a Happy Ground Hog Day. From what I learned a couple of weeks ago, he wasn't far off the mark.

It was about eight o'clock when we were done. Mom and Dad had opened some gifts, mostly gift cards. They didn't do a registry because they didn't need anything. They were going to have to downsize. Mom put her house up for sale a few months ago. A few people had looked at it, but no one had made any offers. If it had sold before they got married, she was going to live with Nana and Papa until they were married. It still hadn't sold; they were praying it did soon. They didn't want two houses to look after.

I went with Grandma and Grandpa when it was time to go home. It didn't take but a couple of minutes, and I was fast asleep. When we got to their house, Grandpa carried me in and put me in bed. I woke up the next morning to the smell of bacon, eggs, biscuits, and gravy. My seven-year-old stomach was growling ferociously. I came into the kitchen, and Grandma told me I had perfect timing; it was all ready. She fixed me a plate, and I devoured it.

We spent the weekend playing and having fun. I talked to Mom and Dad a few times, and when they picked me up on Monday afternoon, they seemed all silly. They were all lovey-dovey, holding hands and giving each other kisses. They did manage to break apart long enough to give me a hug. Now they were Mr. and Mrs. Leif Baskin.

10

LOSS

Dyanna Jo's Journal

My heart was completely shattered. How was this possible? I didn't have the words. All I could do was cry. I know that Leif was hurting too, but I just couldn't compose myself enough to console him. Pain was no stranger to me. I had been through a lot of pain throughout the years, but this pain was completely different.

When we got home from the ultrasound appointment, I went straight to our room, got in bed, hugged my stuffed giraffe, and looked out the window. It was a bright sunny day in May 2007. The day started so hopeful and joyous. Now there was nothing but awful pain. *Lord, how am I going to get through this?* I asked God in my mind.

Leif and I had been trying to have a baby for close to three years. When you try for that long and nothing happens, you start to believe that it isn't in God's plan. Selfishly, you want it so badly; you continue to pray to the point of begging.

I begged, and when He finally gave us our baby, I just knew it was from God. As soon as I found out I was pregnant, I ran to the store and purchased: *The Pregnancy Journal: A Day-to-Day Guide to a Healthy Happy Pregnancy by Christine Harris.* Each day I would read and document what I did throughout the day. I was so faithful. I was obsessed with being pregnant and having this gift that God had given us.

Nine short weeks later, a doctor was telling me my baby had no heartbeat. I was numb.

"Can the machine be wrong?" I asked. All I could picture was the ultrasound machine and the tech clicking the mouse and typing on the keyboard. I should have asked if the tech could have made a mistake or if the doctor read the data incorrectly, but no, all I could see was that machine.

"No, Dyanna Jo, there is no doubt. There isn't a heartbeat," the doctor replied. "I'm sorry……." from that point on; I tuned everything out. I could hear the doctor talking and pointing to a photo on her desk, but I couldn't focus enough to listen to her words.

I don't even know what was said from that point on. We left and drove home. When we got home, I headed straight for our bedroom. As I lay there staring out the window, holding my little giraffe, my mind was completely blank. Not surprising, this is how I dealt with all pain. Stuff it deep down, and don't face it. I cried, but my mind was blank.

At some point, I called my mom and cried with her. My mom was always the first person I ran to. She was my rock, my primary source of logic, tough love, in your face, no-nonsense friend, Mom. Today she just loved and consoled me.

The three days leading up to the D&C were a complete blur. I still had to be a wife and mom to Ralley, but emotionally I was dead. I remember thinking the same thing over and over. *What if I'm putting all my faith in a machine and doctors when I should be putting my faith in God.* If I truly believed that this was God's plan, how could I go through with the D&C? I didn't have any signs of having a miscarriage: no bleeding, no pain in my stomach, nothing. After questioning my faith, I would pray, *God, if this is true and the baby is gone, please give me a sign so I can have peace?* I must have prayed that same prayer a hundred times those three days.

THE DAY OF THE D&C arrived. I still had no signs to tell me the doctor was right. Leif drove me to the hospital while Ralley stayed with my mom. We arrived at the hospital and registered. We were told to sit in the waiting room, and we would be called back shortly. I was a nervous wreck. I kept thinking; I *can't do this! This can't be happening. My body feels great. God, please tell me what to do.*

As I sat there agonizing, I felt the urge to use the restroom. I went to the reception desk and asked, "Do I have time to use the restroom?"

"Definitely, honey, it's straight back on the right."

I slowly walked back, and as I entered the bathroom, I immediately saw my reflection in the mirror on the opposite wall. I didn't even recognize myself. I made my way to the toilet and sat. When finished, I wiped and looked down at the toilet paper. Blood! I was bleeding. There was no pain, but I was bleeding. Tears filled my eyes, and in a winded breath, I talked to God aloud, *Thank you, God! You answered my prayer. I can do this. Thank you for being here for me. I need your strength. Please hold me and guide me through this procedure.*

I continued to cry as I washed my hands. By the grace of God, I could do this. I walked back to my seat with tears rolling down my face.

Leif immediately noticed my tears and threw his arms around me. "Are you okay?"

"God answered my prayer. I needed proof that this was the right thing to do, and He gave me the sign I needed in the bathroom. I'm bleeding." I replied quietly with my eyes focused off into space and a faint smile on my face.

The nurse came and brought me back to the procedure area. I undressed and got onto the hospital bed. I felt like I was meandering through each of these actions. My body wasn't my own. The nurse administered my IV, and before I knew it, the doctor was looking down at me, trying to wake me.

I whispered up into her ear, "It's okay, God was here for me, and He gave me the sign I needed to believe that I truly had a miscarriage. God loves me, and He is so faithful."

The doctor left, looking confused. I got dressed, and Leif helped me to the car. We were silent the whole way home. At some point after the procedure, they asked me if I wanted to know the baby's gender. I told them I didn't. Knowing the gender made it all too real. Later, I regretted that decision.

May 2007 was a month of painful memories, but we also had peace. God was there! In one of the worse times of my life, God carried me, and no one could say there was no God.

LEIF'S JOURNAL

A few days after the D&C, Dyanna Jo was still struggling with the pain. We all were. After one of her daily naps, she came downstairs and said," I want to do something as a memorial for our baby," Ralley and I were downstairs watching TV. I couldn't tell you what was on. I was still in a daze.

"Do you have something in mind?" I asked.

"A tree in the front yard, but I don't know what kind of tree to get."

"We will have to do some research on it."

She nodded and went back to bed. Ralley and I continued watching TV. I think she was watching Hannah Montana. I decided to get my laptop and do some research on trees. It would have to be something that could handle our winters.

Winters in Knoxville are mild, but it does get into the teens and single digits on occasion. It would also need to be a tree that wouldn't get too tall. I don't want a forty-foot monstrosity in my front yard. I thought about a dogwood, but our neighbors had gone through a couple of them and didn't seem to have any luck. I finally zeroed in on the Eastern Redbud. It was rated to be able to withstand our planting zone and zones farther north. It had a slow-to-moderate growth rate and grew to twenty to twenty-five feet. It also would get pretty pink or red blossoms on it in the spring.

Dyanna Jo slept for the rest of the day. That's what she did when she was depressed. She slept a lot. I, on the other hand, sat and thought. I didn't pay much attention to what was going on around me. I just sat, almost in a daze, wondering how could this happen to us? What's the purpose of it? This happens to other people, but not us.

I didn't blame God or get mad at Him, but I was confused and just didn't understand. I knew there were times in my walk with God that I wouldn't understand. Things were bad right now, and He allowed this to happen. I also knew that what appears terrible can have good come out of it if I kept my trust and faith in Him. I've never been disappointed in that. He's always faithful.

The next day was Saturday, and Ralley and I got up at about 8 a.m. Dyanna Jo slept until about ten. That didn't surprise me because she was so depressed. Ralley and I had breakfast, and she watched some morning shows and the Disney Channel while I surfed the internet.

"I know something else I want to do," Dyanna Jo announced when she got downstairs.

"Good morning to you too," I responded.

"I want each of us to write notes to the baby and put them in a plastic bag under the tree when we plant it," she said, ignoring me.

"Speaking of trees, I think we should get an Eastern Redbud."

"Why?"

I told her what I found during my research, and she said that sounded good.

After we all got ready for the day, we got in the car and headed to Home Depot to look for the Redbud. We found one that was in bloom and liked it. We got it home, and I set it in the driveway. We then went inside and privately wrote our notes. Ralley and I wrote our notes to "him." Our boy, who was never meant to be. We said things about how we were sad we wouldn't be able to see him, and we loved him. One day we would see him in heaven.

Dyanna Jo couldn't bring herself to refer to the baby as him. She wrote her note privately; it was her way of coping. After we wrote the notes and put them in individual Ziploc bags, I dug the hole in our front yard. Dyanna Jo and Ralley watched quietly. We each put our bag in the hole, and I put the tree on top. After I got it set, we watered it. We stood there staring at the tree, thinking about the baby we never met.

The trunk was thin, and I noticed it swayed quite a bit with just a little wind. I decided I should do something to brace it.

After we got the tree planted and went back into the house, Dyanna Jo headed back to bed. She was overwhelmed with emotions. Her normal, these days, was lying in bed and staring off into space or napping. No matter which, she held the little stuffed giraffe in her arms.

Since it was a sunny spring day, Ralley and I went to a park and played. The park had a substantial wooden playset with big slides, bridges, rock-climbing walls, tire swings, and rope climbs. She was all over that thing. We played together for a while, but when she saw the other kids playing, she ran off to play with them. I made my way to a bench and watched her play and laugh. It was nice to see her happy.

While she was playing, I thought back to when we almost lost her. Janet was six months pregnant when she started having severe complications and was put on bed rest. My mom helped me a lot while Janet rested. Janet was able to make it to the eighth month before having a C-section.

When Janet made it to the eighth month, Dr. Michaels did a C-section because she felt they had stretched it out as far as they could. She wanted to get Ralley out before it got worse.

Thankfully, she was here and was such a sweet girl. She saw me daydreaming and came over.

"Whatcha thinkin' about?" she asked playfully.

"A certain girl who gave us a proper scare when her mom was pregnant with her."

"A proper scare. I didn't know scares could be proper."

"If they're like the one you gave us, they are."

"Since we're on this topic, I've been thinking."

"Uh, oh."

"Daaaaad. Why did you and Mom name me Ralley?"

"We named you that because we thought we had lost you when your mom was six months pregnant, but you pulled through. It was like you rallied and made it to the eighth month. At that time, it was okay for Dr. Michaels to do a C-section and have you make your grand appearance. It was a right proper one, at that."

"What did I do to make it a right proper one?"

"You were crying and had quite a set of lungs on you. All of the family waiting in the room down the hall could hear you. Oh — and after you were cleaned up and wrapped in a receiving blanket, they handed you to me. You promptly peed on me."

"I did?"

"Yes, but I didn't realize that. I thought the blanket was wet because of the nurse cleaning you. Dr. Michaels wanted to hold you after finishing up with Mom. She came out of the OR and held you. She let me know you had peed the blanket and in turn on me. It was obvious I was a new dad. I didn't know what I was doing."

"That's funny. So why did you name me Ralley with an E?"

"We wanted your name to be different."

She was silent for a little bit, and I could tell she was thinking.

"Whatcha thinkin'?" I playfully asked.

"I'm glad you put that E in my name."

"Yes, we had to make sure it was right proper."

"Like Anne with an E."

"I'm glad it meets with your approval in some approximation."

She rolled her eyes but let a little laugh escape. I got a text message from Dyanna Jo asking where we were. I told her we were at the park and were about to leave. She wanted us to pick up something for dinner. Chick-fil-a was our choice. After picking up our dinner, we headed home.

11

———

THE ADOPTION OPTION

Leif's Journal

I work from 6 a.m. to 2 p.m., Monday through Friday at the Y12 National Security Complex in Oak Ridge, Tennessee. It's a Department of Energy facility that houses the nation's stockpile of highly enriched uranium. I work in security.

I got off work on Tuesday and drove home to pick up Dyanna Jo so we could go to the fertility specialist Dr. Swanson recommended. Dyanna Jo's mom came over to stay with Ralley while we were gone. The drive over was quiet. We were lost in our thoughts. I didn't know what she was thinking, but I felt that it was all in God's hands. If we were meant to have a child, this would work out.

Dr. Kennedy's office was more like a living room than a doctor's office. It was about fifteen feet by twenty feet with a desk on one end. In the middle of the room sat a couch and a leather club chair facing the couch, with a coffee table in between. A floor-to-ceiling bookshelf stood opposite the desk, and on the wall behind the couch was a gas fireplace. Since it was May, the fireplace sat idle, but even so, the office had a cozy, homey feel to it.

Dr. Kennedy shook our hands and directed us to sit on the couch. He sat in the club chair and asked Dyanna Jo specific questions about her cycle, going back to her first period. He talked to her for about a half-hour about her feminine issues, and then said he wanted her to do a Clomid Challenge Test. He said Clomid is a drug that stimulates ovulation.

The test is done by having her take the drug, and then on certain days, she would come to the office to draw her blood. The test is used to determine her ovarian reserve. If she had a poor ovarian reserve, it could help determine what kind of fertility treatments could be used. He wrote a Clomid prescription and gave her a sheet of instructions.

"So, what do you think?" I asked Dyanna Jo as we drove to Walgreens to drop off the prescription.

"I like him," she said. "He's nice and relaxed and amiable. I have a feeling, though, that the results of the test will be bad."

"Why do you say that?"

"My age, my history of hormone problems, how long it took me to get pregnant, and then having a miscarriage. I just don't have any hope that it will be a positive result."

"I can see that I've had similar thoughts too. I don't seem to be too optimistic either."

"That's unusual. You're usually the more positive of the two of us. What's wrong with you?" she asked.

I glanced quickly at her to see if she was serious or playing with me. Her smile told me she was playing with me. I liked that because she'd been down in the dumps for too long. I started to worry about her falling into a deep depression.

About three weeks later, she had finished the test. Dr. Kennedy's office called on a Friday and scheduled a time to talk to him about the results on Monday. We tried to keep busy over the weekend so that we wouldn't dwell too much on it.

I got a tree staking kit because the Redbud was not doing very well due to the winds we'd been getting from recent thunderstorms. The kit had three stakes, similar to tent stakes, and three pieces of rope, as well as three quarter inch lengths of garden hose. I threaded the rope through the garden hose. I put the stakes equidistant from each other around the tree. I tied the three pieces of rope to each of the stakes, and then wrapped them around the tree and then tied them to the stakes again. One rope for each stake—this ensured the garden hose was touching the tree so the rope wouldn't rub and eventually cut into the tree. Once that was done, I mowed the yard.

Dyanna Jo and Ralley worked on cleaning the house and doing laundry. They also played games on the PS2. I think it was more games than housework, but they stayed busy, and that was the important thing.

We drove to see the doctor Monday afternoon. Dyanna Jo's mom, Pat, once again watched Ralley for us. Dr. Kennedy didn't waste any time telling us Dyanna Jo had a meager ovarian reserve.

"So, what does that mean?" Dyanna Jo asked.

"It means your eggs are in sad shape. You can get pregnant, but the chances of you carrying the baby to term are bleak."

"Is there anything that can be done to help that?"

"There are some things I can do, but they are expensive and would only increase your chances by two or three percent."

"What are the chances now?" I asked.

"About four percent that she'll carry the baby long enough for it to have a reasonable chance of surviving."

"Doesn't seem like it would be worth it to go that route, since I'm thirty-nine and have a hard time getting pregnant, to begin with," Dyanna Jo commented.

"I agree," Dr. Kennedy said matter-of-factly. "Have you all thought of adoption?"

"No, we haven't thought of that," I replied.

"I think that would be a good option for you."

"We'll have to go home and think about that," I said.

"I'm sorry I couldn't be more helpful to you. If you were younger, I would probably recommend trying another option. Still, I think it's good that you're facing the fact that your age makes it difficult."

"I'm not happy about it, but I try to face things as they are and be realistic," said Dyanna Jo.

"I think that's an excellent approach."

"It also could be God shutting one door and opening another door that leads us to adoption," I chimed in.

"Yes, sometimes the road He takes us on isn't the one we were thinking of, but it turns out to be the best one," Dr. Kennedy agreed.

WE LEFT the office and went home to relieve Pat. Dyanna Jo gave her the scoop on what the doctor said.

"What are you going to do?" Pat asked.

"We really haven't talked about it, but the doctor suggested adoption."

"You need to be careful with that, Dyanna. I have heard of a lot of people doing that, but the cost is expensive, and it could take a long time to get a baby."

That was typical of Pat. She was a worrier, especially when it came to Dyanna Jo.

"I know, Mom. We haven't even talked about that yet. We don't know what we are going to do."

Pat left, and we had dinner. Dyanna Jo went to bed early, and Ralley and I watched a movie.

I couldn't keep my focus on the movie. My mind wandered back to the conversation with Dr. Kennedy. Whenever I thought of adopting, it made me nervous. It made me wonder if that was a little bit more than we could chew. Whenever I was faced with something I didn't know anything about, I researched. Once I got all my research together, I prayed and asked God to show me what He wanted me to do. Now, it was time to research adoption. I grabbed my computer and started my search online.

As I sat on the couch doing my research, my thoughts wandered to how funny it was that God put Dyanna Jo and me together. Could you find two more opposite people? She's loud, impatient, passionate, determined, funny, and she flies by the seat of her pants ninety percent of the time. I'm a man of few words, quiet, patient, snail-like, cautious, and I research things ad nauseam. That's why it took me so long to decide to get serious about Dyanna Jo.

I knew that in a few days, she would bring up the adoption options. I was glad that I would have some research and solid information available to give her. Her idea of research was talking to all her friends, and every person she could get to talk to her. Once she bought into the idea, I better hold on because she will start flying as fast as she can.

DYANNA JO'S **Journal**

I knew we weren't going to get any good results from Dr. Kennedy. Things just didn't feel right after the miscarriage. I knew my desire to have a child was strong but at this point I just didn't see it happening.

After Dr. Kennedy gave us the results, he mentioned a couple of options that we might consider. He recommended adoption, but I piped up and said we could never afford that. He told us that there were a couple of ways to adopt. The first was International adoption; the second was becoming foster parents and adopt through the foster system.

On the drive home, neither of us talked about the adoption idea. My mom was at the house watching Ralley, and when we arrived, I gave her the rundown on the results. Mom shared her concerns and left us to eat dinner.

I was too overwhelmed to talk about the appointment with Leif. I said good-night and headed to bed.

12

FOSTER CURIOUS

Leif's Journal

Have I mentioned that one of the things I like about Dyanna Jo is her funny habit of picking the wrong word for situations? As an example, we were in church one Sunday. Before the service started, she saw one of the ushers, who usually dresses very casually. Our Sunday services are very casual attire. On this particular Sunday, however, Bob was all decked out in a three-piece suit.

Dyanna Jo told him he looked extinguished.

He kept a straight face and thanked her, saying it was precisely the look he was going for. I'm glad Bob has a sense of humor.

Dyanna Jo was clueless. I laughed and told her what she said. She groaned and turned as red as a fire extinguisher. She immediately defended herself and said, "Man! My dad has said that all my life! Now I sound like him."

As I was thinking about that, Dyanna Jo came into the room. I was happy to see that she was up and ready for church.

"Good morning," I said, getting up to give her a hug and a kiss on the cheek.

"Good morning to you."

She seemed to be in good spirits. I called for Ralley to get her Bible and bag for church. We headed out the door.

Today was a really good church service. After we walked out into the lobby, I noticed Dyanna Jo walked away to talk with some ladies across the room. I went to get Ralley, and we met Dyanna Jo back in the lobby. She seemed to be talking to just about everyone today. We waited patiently, and when she was ready, we headed home.

"You were a talker today," I mentioned with a smile on my face.

"I sure was," she replied, smiling back at me. She immediately turned her head back to the car window, and we drove the rest of the way home, listening to Ralley talk about her lesson at church.

We arrived home, changed our clothes, and had lunch. As soon as we finished, Ralley took off to play outside.

Dyanna Jo and I headed to the living room to get comfortable and relax.

"Have you thought any about the appointment on Friday?" Dyanna Jo asked.

"I have, I thought I would wait till you were ready to talk about it. I know it was difficult for you."

"What did you think about the adoption option?"

"Funny you ask, I did some research and learned a couple of things."

"Of course you did," she said with a chuckle.

We began to talk about all the things I had learned. Most of my research showed that adoption costs depend on race. The reason for this is all over the board.

First, I found an article that stated that it wasn't because any specific race was inferior to the other; it was based on the availability of children. A private adoption cost for a Caucasian couple to adopt a Caucasian child is approximately twenty to thirty thousand dollars. The same would be said for an African-American couple adopting a child of their race. However, fewer African-American families are looking to adopt. The number of eligible African-American children is higher and would cost approximately ten to fifteen thousand dollars, which is considerably less. Asian and Hispanic children are rarely available for adoption. The cost to adopt a child of either race would be higher and would take a substantial amount of time to find a child.

A 2002 ABC News report pointed to everything from "supply-and-demand" to Medicare's payment of birth mothers' prenatal expenses, to the length of time adoptive parents were willing to wait for a child as reasons for the different costs of adopting babies of different races.

A final site I viewed stated that despite the possibilities I listed above, the factor still remains race. No matter how far we've come, the truth is, we haven't come far enough. Racism is still a horrible reality. Across racial lines, fewer adoptive families seem to want black babies. We were disgusted by that. No one should be judged by the color of their skin.

We knew that we couldn't afford to adopt privately. In researching foster parenting, I found the website www.adoptuskids.org. There are so many children in the foster system that need homes now. It seemed like a no brainer, but we still needed to learn more before we jumped in.

Immediately Dyanna Joe interrupted me. "I talked to Carol at church today, and she told me she has some friends who are foster parents. She said she would get their phone number for us, but first, she wanted to make sure they were comfortable with her passing it out."

"That sounds good."

We spent the rest of the afternoon talking, watching TV and laughing together. It was nice to hear the Lunatic laugh again.

ON TUESDAY, after work, I was sitting on the deck waiting for Dyanna Jo to get off the phone. She had been on it ever since I'd gotten home. She sure could talk.

"Leif, where are you?"

"Out here on the deck," I yelled.

"Oh, there you are! Carol called me today and gave me her friend Anna's phone number. She recommended that when I call Anna, I invite her and her family over for lunch one day. Carol said we would have a lot to talk about," Dyanna Jo said without taking a breath.

"Hello to you too," I said, laughing. "Sounds good to me. I would like it to be on a day when I can be here too."

"Well duh! I already called Anna and invited them over on Saturday. She was so nice, and we talked for about 45 minutes. Her husband's name is Fred Mussina. I mean, both of their last names are Mussina."

Here we go again. Dyanna Jo was so excited and couldn't stop rambling. "Oh no, I need to check my calendar, I think I have plans on Saturday," I said with a serious face and jumped up as if to go check.

"WHAT! No no no no, you can't. Man! You're teasing me, aren't you?"

"Yes," I said, laughing and hugging her at the same time.

"That's just wrong!"

Sometimes it seemed like we were moving fast, but then I would stop and think about it and realize we weren't going quickly at all. I still wasn't sure what I thought about foster parenting. We had Ralley, and it took such a long time for Dyanna Jo to get pregnant. But, when she got pregnant and miscarried, it made us realize how much we wanted another child.

She continued to tell me all about the Mussina family. Fred and Anna had two biological children, Melissa and Adam. Melissa was thirteen, and Adam was eight. They had adopted Samuel from the foster system, and he was four. Finally, they had Cody. He was ten-months-old, and they were in the process of adopting him.

BEFORE WE KNEW IT, it was Saturday. Dyanna Jo spent the week shopping and got enough food to feed an army. She planned a BBQ style lunch with hamburgers and hotdogs. With all those kids coming, she made sure to have a bunch of kid-style foods like chips and cookies. She wanted everything to be perfect.

The Mussina's arrived right on time. All the introductions were made, and the kids became fast friends. Fred and I manned the grill while the ladies hung out in the kitchen. Amazingly enough, foster care didn't even come up until after we had eaten, and all the kids were off playing. Cody slept in his carrier while the adults talked. He looked like he was busting out at the seams.

"So, what do you want to know about foster care?" Fred asked as Anna and Dyanna Jo returned to the table with coffee.

"We don't know where to begin or what questions to ask," I replied.

"First, before anything else, you are required to take classes. PATH classes - PATH is an acronym for "Parents as Tender Healers." You can look online to see where they're holding classes and who you need to contact," Fred informed us. "There are multiple steps you have to go through before you even think about taking children into your home. Once you're approved, the fun begins."

Fred and Anna shared a look and smiled.

"What age range are you comfortable taking into your home? Kids that is," Anna asked.

"I don't really care, but Leif told me he doesn't want any children older than five," Dyanna Jo said. "I just hate to limit it."

"Leif is actually on the right track. You don't want to take in children who are older than your own. You want Ralley to feel comfortable. If you took a child older than her, the foster child might start bossing Ralley around in her own home. That never works well. Choosing children who are at least two years younger is a good start. You can tell DCS you don't want children over five," Fred told us.

"You can really do that?" Dyanna Jo asked

"Yes, you also don't have to take a child either."

"What do you mean?"

"When placement calls you about taking a child, you can tell them no. You don't have to take every child," Anna interjected.

"That's good to hear," I said. "I thought you had to take them whenever they called. I'm glad you don't. That would be overwhelming."

"You can also have a child moved to a different home if it's not working out for them in your home," Fred said. "I wouldn't do that unless it was absolutely necessary because it doesn't help the kids to move them a lot. But, you can ask to have a child moved if needed."

"I'm glad we're talking to you," Dyanna Jo exclaimed. "We sure didn't know any of this."

"There's a lot of things you'll pick up on as you go, but you can call us if you need any advice," Fred offered.

"Thank you," Dyanna Jo replied. "What are some other things we should know?"

"There are all kinds of caseworkers. Some are really good, some are really bad, and some are in between. In fairness, though, they are very overworked and underpaid. They have a lot put on them. It's also a heartbreaking job. Some of the decisions DCS, Department of Children Services, makes will leave you scratching your head. Most of the children come in to care with a Walmart bag or less. You will learn all that during your PATH classes," Anna said, shaking her head back and forth.

Fred jumped in, "The steps are normally in this order: when DCS is notified of a situation, they will send a CPS, Child Protective Service, worker to investigate. If the CPS worker decides the situation calls for immediate removal, they will remove the child or children. If the situation doesn't call for immediate removal, they will keep the case open and continue to monitor things until they feel the child should be removed. If there is no longer any concern, the case is closed. If the child or children are removed, they will be placed in a foster home. Within seven days of the child being taken, a Child and Family Team Meeting—that's CFTM—will be held. At that meeting, a permanency plan will be made. That sets the goals the parents have to meet to get their child or children back."

"Do the foster parents have to go to the meeting?" Dyanna Jo asked.

"They don't, but it's good to go because you can find out more information about the parents and the whole situation. It helps you have a better idea of how to help the children and the parents. I know you all want to adopt, but the foster care system's goal is to help the parents and children get back together. Unification is always the top priority. Sometimes, that doesn't work, and you can adopt, but it might be years before any child becomes available to adopt. There will be a lot of meetings, home visits, court dates, and visitations. It's best to be as involved as possible."

"It sounds so overwhelming. How are we going to learn or do all that?" Dyanna Jo said with a voice that sounded as if she was about to cry.

Anna immediately touched her hand and, in a reassuring voice, said, "It sounds so scary and overwhelming, but we have been at this a long time. We wouldn't change a single minute of this journey. It's obvious you have a heart for children. God has lead you to this point, and you now have resources. Fred and I would be happy to help in any way possible. I wish we had a couple to help us when we were getting ready to take this step. God is your strength, and through Him, you can do anything."

Lunch turned in to dinner. Thankfully we had a lot of food left over to eat another meal. The rest of the evening went quickly. When the Mussina's left, they said they wanted us to come over to their place sometime.

Dyanna Jo and I finished cleaning up the mess. I stopped and pulled her close. "Did they say anything to discourage you or make you think twice about pursuing foster care?"

Immediately she answered, "No, it just opened my eyes a little more and helped me to be more realistic about it. Did it cause you to have second thoughts?" Dyanna Jo looked up at me worried.

"No, I'm glad to know we don't have to take every child, and we can have a child moved to a different home if it's not working out for us, the child or Ralley."

"I was glad to hear that too. Tomorrow after church, I am going to look online and find out who I need to call Monday to get us signed up for PATH classes." She broke free from my arms and finished up the kitchen. "I can't believe how well behaved Cody was. He just went with the flow. Melissa was such a huge help throughout the day. I can't believe how long they stayed. I loved it!"

Before I could say anything, she headed to Ralley's room to help her get ready for bed.

RALLEY'S JOURNAL

What a fun day! I made some new friends. Melissa was older than me, but she didn't act like she was forced to hang out with me. Adam was closer to my age, and Samuel was four. It didn't seem to matter how old they were; we all played together and had a great time.

Cody was so cute. When Melissa would help her parents with Cody, she would bring him out to play with us. I couldn't help but think about my brother and how fun he would be to play with.

Mom and Dad were thinking about becoming foster parents. That meant I would be a foster sister. I wasn't quite sure how I felt about that. Today I learned that there were a lot of kids who needed good homes. Samuel and Cody were foster kids. The Mussina's had adopted Samuel and would soon adopt Cody. They all acted like brothers and sisters. I would have never known.

Melissa and Adam talked about what it was like to be a foster family. They loved it! I think it would be weird having kids in and out of my house, but it isn't something I can't get used to. Mom and Dad have given me so much love. I know they can give love to other children who need help and a home. I should be willing to share what I had with children in a dire situation. It wasn't that I wouldn't be a good foster sister; I just needed to get used to it.

I guess that's why it's best to pray about it and let God be in control of what child gets placed in our home. He knows what we can handle. Dad says that a lot, but then he says he doesn't know how God thinks he can contain Mom. I don't think anyone can handle Mom. Sometimes, I have to agree with dad; she is a lunatic. But she is a fun lunatic.

One day we drove to the mall and listened to music on the radio. The song *Funky Jesus Music* by Toby Mac came on. Mom said she loved that song and immediately started dancing in the driver's seat. She was busting the moves as much as she could in the driver's seat. People driving by gave us some interesting looks. It's usually an adventure when I go out with her.

I was sure everything would be fine once the foster kids arrived. I was just nervous about how mean they might be. I needed to stop worrying about it. I would need to be patient and loving and pray for them. At least that was what Dad always said. "If someone is mean to you, walk away and pray for them."

"What are you constipating?"

I jumped. Mom was standing in the door watching me.

"I'm sorry, you look like you're lost in thought," she said.

I giggled.

"What did I do now?" she asked, exasperated.

"You asked me if I'm constipating. I think you meant contemplating."

"That is funny. Why do I do that?" she asked and shook her head.

"To answer your question about what I'm constipating," I began, and she rolled her eyes. "I'm thinking about how fun it was today. I was also thinking about what it would be like to be a foster sister. Melissa made it look easy."

"I think you'll be an excellent foster sister. I know you'll be a good example for them. Today I think we all made some new friends. Melissa's mom said that if we ever had questions, we could always call them. I bet Melissa would love to help you."

"I hope so."

"I have no doubt," she just stood there looking at me with that special mom look.

"I'm tired; time for bed."

She closed the door and headed down the hall.

13

PATH CLASSES

Dyanna Jo's Journal

Our lunch/dinner with the Mussinas went great! By the end of the day, I could tell that we had become fast friends, and our families would be spending a lot of time together. I won't lie; I was overwhelmed by all the information we discussed. Hearing the stories about the children they fostered was heart-wrenching, but seeing how their family worked together to help those children was so inspiring.

In regular Dyanna Jo fashion, I didn't waste any time. As promised, I went online and found out who I needed to call. The following Monday, I called DCS to sign up for PATH classes. Unfortunately, the classes didn't start until September. This being the end of July, we would have to wait.

PATH is an intensive introduction to the world of child welfare. We had two class options, both requiring thirty hours of instruction. One was every Thursday from 6 p.m. to 9 p.m. for ten weeks. The other option was on Saturdays for six hours a day for six weeks. The hours were from 9 a.m. to 3 p.m. with a one-hour lunch break from twelve to one. Because of Leif's work schedule, I signed us up for the Saturday classes.

One Sunday in August, while in church, I found myself getting distracted. It seemed like all the people sitting around us had babies. Strollers lined the isles. As I worshiped, I would look down at each of those precious faces. So small and innocent. *Why? Why not me?* I found myself asking God. Tears slowly came, and a couple escaped my eyes. I was sitting next to Alexis, one of my good friends. She knew our struggles and knew that I was still hurting from our loss. As I stood there, staring at the babies, I could hardly move.

After worship, the Pastor asked us to sit. As he began to pray for the sermon, Alexis leaned over, put her arm around my shoulders, and quietly whispered in my ear. "During worship, I felt this incredible impression that God wants you to know that you will, one day, have a baby." I began to sob quietly. I couldn't tell you what the sermon was about; I just sat there hearing those words over and over again. *God wants you to know that you will, one day, have a baby.* Was God really telling me I would have a baby? I was afraid to hope. The loss had been more than I could handle, so I stuffed it deep within and tried not to think about it.

August couldn't pass fast enough. Just like the count down to my wedding, I would mark off the days on my faithful refrigerator calendar. I was beyond ready when September finally arrived.

Our first full day of classes was held the first Saturday in September. There were six couples, including us, an older woman, and a couple of single women in attendance. The first half-hour was spent going around the room and introducing ourselves.

The couples were a mixture of young and old. One of the younger couples had wanted to become foster parents because the wife had grown up in a foster home and was adopted into a loving family. They wanted to pay it forward. Another couple had a family member who had fostered, and they saw how rewarding it was to help children in need.

Leif and I were in the middle of the age range. After we briefly shared our story, the next couple spoke. They were a little older than we were. They were going through the process of becoming foster parents because their niece and nephew had been removed from their home. The husband's brother and sister-in-law were heavily addicted to drugs and refused to get clean. The children were already living in their home, but they had to take the PATH classes to keep them and possibly adopt them in the future. Another couple had a story similar to ours. I couldn't help but feel a little connection to them.

The oldest couple had their grandchildren living in their home. Their daughter had a boyfriend who was abusing the children. She refused to leave him and so the grandparents intervened. In order to keep them at home with them, they had to go through the process.

The older woman was in a similar situation as the couple with the grandkids. However, she was a widow, and her son and his girlfriend were addicted to drugs and were in a facility trying to sober up. Because she too had a history with DCS, she had to go through the process and be monitored regularly. The two single ladies were professional women with no children and no husbands. They had no desire to marry but knew they wanted to have kids. Although they didn't know each other, they had the same reason for becoming foster parents. Over the six weeks, I noticed that they became fast friends.

Leif and I had no idea there were so many different reasons to become foster parents. We were shocked that the grandparents had to go through the process to keep their own grandkids. I also didn't realize that a single person could become a foster parent. Shows how naive I was.

The class instructor was a DCS worker named Julie Board.

She was barely five feet tall and maybe a hundred pounds. She was a tiny little thing. She had beautiful, naturally curly red hair, glasses, and an abundance of freckles. The class also had a foster parent representative. Her name was Michelle Watkins. She was about five nine and had brown hair. She had a look that said she'd seen and experienced a lot.

The first two hours, Julie taught Child Development. It was interesting, but it didn't teach me any more than I already knew. The compelling part was Michelle telling us stories of her experiences.

Michelle and her husband had two biological children, ages eighteen and twenty. They also had five children who they adopted through the foster system. There were also two foster children in their care, a total of nine kids in all. All their adopted and foster children had come from neglect and abusive situations. Two of their adopted children were fifteen-year-old girls. They weren't related, but each had a parent who had sexually abused them. The other three were siblings, two boys and a girl, eight, ten, and twelve. Their parents ran a meth lab in their home and completely neglected the children. The parents were sent to prison. When CPS removed the siblings from their home, it was evident they hadn't bathed in a long time. All three children had health issues from being exposed to all the meth ingredients. The two foster children were identical twin boys. They had been severely beaten by their parents and had brain damage that caused physical and mental disabilities.

Leif and I left our first class tired and emotionally spent. It was a real eye-opener hearing Michelle's stories about her children and the things they all went through. Michelle told us that it was also difficult for both her and her husband, but they knew that God had called them to ministry. These children were their ministry. They wouldn't have it any other way. I'd heard stories about things that happened to children but have never been around a child with that much trauma. It was sobering and made me think more about the heart and commitment it took to foster these poor children.

"One down, five to go," I declared. We were getting in the car to drive home.

"I'm tired. It was interesting, and I liked listening to Michelle," Leif commented.

"I know. She's really taken on some tough situations with those children."

"Do you think we would be able to handle children who have been through those situations?"

"I don't know," I responded after a moment of contemplation. "I've prayed that God would only give us what we can handle. So, I guess we will leave it up to Him."

The rest of the drive home was spent in silence. There was so much to process. I usually talk to get my anxiousness out, but today, I didn't want to rehash all the sad cases we heard. Leif was processing it too. I could see that look that he gets. He has to think about things, mull it over in his mind and pray in silence. Most likely, he wouldn't talk about it much. Today I completely understood.

I knew that listening to Michelle was giving us a dose of reality and helping us better understand the challenges of being foster parents. She was letting us see the condition most of the kids would be in when they were placed in our home. I knew it was difficult, and the kids were in a situation they had no control over, but I didn't realize how bad it could be. I knew we'd really have to trust God.

THE SIX WEEKS WENT QUICKLY. I can't believe I am saying that. Usually, things go way too slow for me, but those six weeks were a whirlwind.

The first time Anna and her family came to our house, she told us that many of the children who go into the system, don't come with much. Most would come with nothing. Michelle also mentioned this in one of our first classes. She suggested that we get various clothes in different sizes. We needed a couple of items for both girls and boys in those sizes if we were planning to take in children who were five and younger. When a child was placed in our home, we would get an allowance to help the child get what they needed. However, that could take up to a week or more, and it wasn't very much. Michelle recommended going to thrift stores or yard sales looking for clothes.

As I was driving home one day, I noticed a big neighborhood yard sale sign out in front of the subdivision next to ours. The sign read: Large Neighborhood Yard Sale, Friday - Saturday from 7 a.m. - 2 p.m. I decided on Friday I would go through the neighborhood and see if I could find some clothes. The neighborhood was huge, so I decided I would drive over, park the van, visit a few houses, and then drive down a little ways and do it all over again. Unfortunately, not many people were out on Friday. Most of the houses I visited said that there would be a lot of homes participating on Saturday. We had PATH classes on Saturday, how on earth could I shop then? I still went to every house that had children's items. I was surprised to see that there were a lot of homes that had clothes, swings, cradles, blankets, decor, rockers, and toys. By the time I reached the end of the subdivision, my mind was racing. What would all these people do with the items they didn't sell? I turned the van around and headed back through the subdivision. As I did, I stopped again at every house with things that would be perfect for children five and under.

The first house I came to, I went to the homeowner and asked, "What do you plan on doing with all the things you don't sell?"

The lady replied, "Most likely take it to Good Will or another thrift store and donate it."

Without hesitation, I said, "We live in the neighborhood next to this one." I pointed and continued, "We are becoming foster parents and have been told that most of the children who will be placed in our home will come with nothing—no clothes, toys, or necessities. I drove around today, trying to find a few things to buy. When I saw how many homes had children's items, I thought I would ask what people planned to do with the items they didn't sell."

"Almost everyone will tell you that they plan to donate everything," she informed me.

"If I return tomorrow after the sale is over, would you be interested in donating the remaining children's items to me? I would be happy to come pick everything up."

"Sure, I can do that. What time do you think you will come by?"

"We have our foster parenting classes tomorrow, so it would be a little later in the day. Let's say closer to 4 p.m."

"How about I just leave everything on the driveway, up against the house, and you come after your classes?"

"That would be great! Thank you!" I was so excited, I could have hugged her, but I wanted to respect her personal space.

I went around to all the houses telling our story, and almost everyone agreed to donate their leftover items. Each one agreed to leave the items on the driveway.

The next morning we woke up extra early so I could visit some of the houses who weren't open on Friday. PATH classes were at 9:00 a.m., so I knew I had to start at 7 a.m. Leif would take a separate car so he could drop Ralley off at my parent's house and then meet me at the DCS office. I was thankful that I had that extra time to go around the neighborhood.

I had perfected our story the day before, so I was able to move quicker. Many people agreed to help and said they would be happy to leave the items on the driveway. Some, however, thought I was out of my mind and just looking for a handout. They told me they couldn't help us. The first house that told me that really embarrassed me, but I brushed it off and kept going. This was for the children, and that is what mattered. It wasn't about me.

After PATH classes, Leif went to pick up Ralley. We agreed to meet at our house and then go to the subdivision together. When we turned on to the street, we saw a couple of homes with clothes on the driveways. The further down we went, the bigger the piles were. There were baby swings, cradles, clothes, toys, bottles, blankets, cloth diapers, car seats, a pack n' play, and so much more. It took us multiple trips to get everything. We were in shock!

God was so good to us! He blessed us in ways we could never have imagined. I know that God placed it on my heart to ask the homeowners for donations the day before. He was in complete control, and He was getting us ready for amazing things.

I spent the majority of the weeks washing clothes and going through everything. The items we got that were duplicates; we took to Good Will. I sterilized all the toys, the swing, cradle, and rocker. We threw out any of the items that were ripped, torn, or stained. We were shocked to see that many items still had tags on them: brand new clothes, bottles, and cloth diapers. I had to continuously run to Walmart to get plastic storage boxes for all of the clothes. I got the kind that could roll under the bed. Every bed in our house had clothes under them. I marked every box with my handy label maker. It was all so over-whelming but so exciting at the same time. I didn't care how much work I had to put into sorting through everything. I was so excited that we could now provide for the children who would come into our home.

LEIF'S JOURNAL

The PATH classes went by fast. Some were thought-provoking, and some were depressing. The worst one was Parenting the Sexually Abused Child. It was useful information, but still hard to sit through.

Michelle shared some of the things they had to go through with the girls who had been sexually abused. It sounded rough. Dyanna Jo and I wondered if we could handle that.

We were still waiting for our home study. Most of the people in the class had already had theirs, and we were impatient to get ours. We busied ourselves with getting things ready for having kids in our home. We found a good deal on a used crib. It was in excellent condition.

We finished our PATH classes at the end of October, and now it was the middle of November. We weren't good at waiting, especially Dyanna Jo. In the years we'd been married, I'd been reminded patience wasn't a gift of hers. She was chomping at the bit, to dredge up a cliché.

Then, it happened. I was at work when I called Dyanna Jo, and she excitedly told me that Ben, our caseworker, had called and scheduled a home study for Thursday when I got home from work. It was Tuesday, and Thursday afternoon was not soon enough for her. Of course, I was excited about the news. Still, my outward expression rarely gives anyone an indication of my true feelings. So even though I was excited, Dyanna Jo wasn't picking up on it. But after several years of marriage, she was used to it.

Thursday afternoon arrived not a minute too soon. I thought Dyanna Jo was going to start chewing on her fingers since she'd already eaten through her nails. Ben came, and we greeted him at the door. He was bald, wore glasses, and stood about five feet ten inches tall. If he had hair once, I could tell it would have been red. We went to the living room and sat.

"Before we get started," he said, "I'll tell you a little about me. I've been working for DCS for eleven years. I was a caseworker for children, and a few years ago, I became a caseworker for families." The way DCS worked, each family had a caseworker, and each child in the home had a caseworker.

"Every month, I have to do a visit. So, before I leave today, I'll schedule a time for another visit. I mainly check to see that there aren't any meth labs on the premises and that there are no dead bodies hidden anywhere."

Hey, he has a sense of humor.

"So, let's get started. I'll let you show me around the house."

We showed him around, and he made sure we had a fire extinguisher downstairs and upstairs. He also checked the layout of the house to see how much room we had. He said he would certify us to have three children at one time. I wasn't interested in having three children at once, but if there was a sibling group, I suppose we could keep them together.

He spent about thirty minutes looking around and then made some notes in his notebook. He had us sign a paper that documented his visit, and then made an appointment for the next visit. He told us that we might get called for placement as early as today.

He wasn't lying. An hour after he left, we got a call from placement. They had a thirteen-month-old boy they needed to place in a home. We said we'd take him. His name was Cameron. Cindy, the lady in placement, didn't know his last name or much about why he was in custody.

An hour and a half later, the social worker showed up. While we were waiting, Dyanna Jo got out some boy's clothes, and we got his crib set up. The social worker, Marvin Sanford, carried him in and showed us his badge.

14

A BABY!

Leif's Journal

I'll always remember our first foster child. He was only with us for ten days, and he was such a happy boy. That amazed me when I considered the circumstances he was in when he entered the foster system. Most of what I discovered about him was gleaned from talking to the couple who adopted him, Geoff and Melody Mason, and his grandmother.

CAMERON JOHNSON WAS A THIRTEEN-MONTH-OLD BOY. His young life had been spent living in squalor. His mom, Susan Johnson, was a prostitute and drug addict. She and her sister, Maria, lived in a run-down seven hundred sixty-four square foot trailer —two bedrooms, one bathroom. The siding on the trailer was missing on one side, and the other side had holes all through it. The roof leaked in a few places, and termites were eating away at the joists. The trailer hadn't been cleaned in forever.

Susan and Maria smoked like chimneys, and it wasn't just

cigarettes. Cameron was left to himself for hours at a time. Susan barely paid him enough attention to make sure he was fed, bathed, or in clean clothes. Most of the time, he was hungry and dirty.

His father was one of Susan's customers. She didn't know which one. Cameron was Hispanic looking, as were many of her customers, so it was hard to say who his father was.

Susan and Maria's mom, Paula, tried to get them to take Cameron to a family at her church that wanted to adopt him, but Susan didn't want to. She thought she was a good mom. Paula would have taken him if her husband didn't have so many medical problems. She had her hands full taking care of him.

Maria had been listening to her mom argue with her sister and thought her mom was right. Cameron should be removed from her sister's care. She knew that she and her sister were hopelessly addicted to drugs, and only survived by selling themselves. It wasn't a good situation for Cameron, and Susan was a terrible mom.

THAT'S when Geoff and Melody Mason stepped in. They got a call from a woman who said her name was Maria. She said she heard they were looking to adopt, and she wanted them to come pick up her son. She said she couldn't take care of him and wanted him to have a better home.

"How did you get our phone number?" Geoff asked. "And how do you know about us?"

"My mom goes to your church. She told me about you. I looked you up in her church directory."

"Who's your mom?"

"Paula Johnson."

"We know her. How old is your son?"

"He's thirteen months, and his name is Cameron."

"Who is that?" Melody asked in the background.

"It's Paula Johnson's daughter," he told her as he held the phone down and covered it. "You remember Paula telling us about her grandson because she knew we were looking to adopt?"

"Yes, I do. Does her daughter want us to come to get her son?"

"Yes, she does."

"Well, let's go get him."

So off they went. It was about a five-mile drive from their house, just off the main road their subdivision was on. Geoff later told me he was glad he brought his pistol as they pulled into a run-down trailer park. Maria's trailer was in the back of the park, and they passed several trailers that had questionable activities going on. They noticed a few people staring at them. Melody's skin was starting to crawl, and she began to wish they had Maria meet them somewhere else. They finally got to her door. It was a sight to behold. Some of the roof was missing, a front window was cracked, and it looked like it was from the sixties.

They knocked on the door, but no one answered. They knocked again, still no answer. Finally, they tried the doorknob and opened the door.

"Hello?" Geoff said.

Again no answer. They took a small step into the house and were overcome by a horrible smell. Melody turned around, stepped back on the porch, and threw up in the bushes next to the house. When she composed herself, she noticed a couple of men standing on the street a few doors down, laughing at her and pointing. Geoff could barely breathe but held his in. The general stench was a mix of cigarette smoke, sweat, dirty dishes, dirty clothes piled up everywhere, and what he could only assume a plugged-up toilet. Cameron was lying on the floor in a diaper and nothing else, even though it was forty-two degrees outside and not much warmer inside. He looked like he hadn't had a bath in several weeks.

"Maria?" Geoff called out.

"Here are his clothes."

Startled, Geoff jumped and turned to see a woman lying on a tattered couch. She threw a backpack on the floor in his general direction. You could tell that Maria had been a very pretty girl at one point in time but now looked vacant and haunted. Like all the life had drained out of her, and she was waiting for the funeral.

"Before you go, can you give me fifty bucks? I need to get some food."

"All I have is a twenty," Geoff said and handed it to her. She snatched it and stuck it in her brassiere. Melody had recovered and was getting Cameron dressed with some torn clothes that were in the backpack. Once she finished, they hustled out to the car. They opened the car door and realized they didn't have a car seat. Melody just held him as they drove home. They just wanted to get out of there as fast as possible.

They had left their twelve-year-old daughter, Elizabeth, and ten-year-old son, Luke, at home while they got Cameron. Back at home, they put the baby straight into the bathtub and scrubbed him from top to bottom. He was a cute little guy once all the crud was off him.

"Geoff," Melody said after they'd been home a few hours. "This whole thing doesn't feel right."

"I know what you mean," Geoff replied.

"Did you notice how Maria didn't even seem torn up about Cameron leaving. I know she's a drug addict, but I still think she should have been more emotional about it."

"I noticed, but all I was thinking about was getting us out of there as fast as I could."

The following Sunday, they went to church, hoping to see

Paula and talk to her about the situation. Paula was nowhere in sight. Melody kept Cameron with her during the service. After church, they got the kids and headed to their car. Immediately, two women ran up to them in the parking lot. Geoff recognized Maria but didn't know who the other young lady was.

"That is my son!" Susan yelled out as she started to grab at Cameron. Maria was trying to hold her back.

"Who are you?" Geoff asked

Maria answered quickly, "Susan is my sister, and she is Cameron's mom."

"Darn right I am!" Susan yelled in Maria's face.

"Susan, calm down! You know we can't take care of him. You're just fighting because you want to prove Mom wrong."

Susan stared at Maria and then at Geoff. "Didn't you say he gave you some money the day they came and got Cameron?"

"Yea, twenty bucks."

"I want some money. I am hungry too, but I want more than twenty lousy bucks."

"I can help you with that. Melody can run to the ATM and get you some money," Geoff told her.

Susan shook her head, "Thats what I want, but I want a hundred bucks."

Geoff put Cameron in the car seat they had purchased and asked Melody to drive to the ATM and get Susan one hundred dollars. While Melody was gone, Maria and Susan stood off to the side, waiting for her to return. Fifteen-minutes later, Melody returned and gave Geoff the money.

Susan grabbed the money, and as she turned to walk away, she stopped, turned back towards Geoff and said, "Don't let my mom have him! I don't want her to have him."

Geoff agreed with a nod of the head. The whole encounter made Geoff and Melody very uncomfortable. They had to take care of Cameron. They couldn't let him go back to them.

Over the next month, the women returned to the church

multiple times, asking for money. Each time asking for a little more. Finally, when Geoff refused to keep giving them money, Susan said she would let them have Cameron and adopt him, but she had to be paid for it. Geoff told her that he would have to contact his lawyer. Susan agreed and told him she would be back next Sunday.

That was the point when Geoff and Melody knew they couldn't continue like this. They went home and contacted DCS. A couple of hours later, a CPS agent came to the house. They explained the whole story to the agent. The agent, David, told them that Cameron would need to be placed in DCS custody and placed in a foster home. There would be a court hearing in three days, and at that time they could attend and petition to adopt. David explained that it would be a long process because they would have to investigate the parents and determine if they should have their rights terminated. He told them the court doesn't like to terminate parental rights until the parents have been given ample opportunities to gain back custody.

Melody collected a few items for Cameron and hugged him tightly before giving him to David. Tears were streaming down her face. Melody and Geoff watched David leave the house and put Cameron in the car seat. They could hear Cameron's cry get louder and louder. He didn't want to leave. He didn't act like that when they took him from Maria. Melody was a basket case and prayed that God would help them get him back soon so they could adopt him.

But before that happened, Dyanna Jo and I fostered Cameron.

～

CAMERON WAS small for his age. He seemed happy and eager to play. I got down on the floor with him, and we played with some blocks. Ralley came and joined us. Dyanna Jo was wringing as much information out of Marvin as she could. She was OCD. She was the type who asked all kinds of questions to make sure everything was covered, and when someone didn't have all the answers, it drove her crazy.

She was going crazy now because Marvin didn't know much about Cameron. She asked about his parents, the prospects of adopting him, and on and on. He didn't know anything about his parents, but he did know that the people he was picked up from were interested in adopting him. He didn't have any answers to the other questions, though. All he could tell us was within seven days of Cameron coming into DCS custody; there would be a child and family team meeting. He told us that we could attend the meeting and find all the answers we wanted to know. Marvin left shortly after that.

Ralley and I continued to play with him while Dyanna Jo busied herself getting clothes from the bins, bottles out and ready, and then finally she sat on the floor and played along with us.

Cameron was very alert and intelligent. He was happy and looked like someone had cared for him. He had thin black hair and small brown eyes. He looked Hispanic.

After playtime, it was dinnertime, and he ate well. Then we played with him some more. He seemed to be getting tired. He wasn't walking yet, but he tried to stand a few times and then got all wobbly and fell on his diaper-padded rump. The last time he fell, he rolled on over and laid down like he wanted to sleep. I scooped him up, and Dyanna Jo and I took him upstairs and brushed the two teeth he had, checked his diaper, and then put him in his crib. He cried half-heartedly for a few minutes and then went to sleep.

He woke up in the middle of the night, and Dyanna Jo and I went into his room and soothed him. He went back to sleep after a few minutes and slept for the rest of the night. I got up at four the next morning and got ready for work. I found myself continuously looking in the monitor at him. We had two monitors, one upstairs and one down. The monitor had a camera that was hung above the bed, and we could watch him on a screen. I left the house at four forty-five. Later that morning, I called Dyanna Jo to see how the morning was going. She told me it was a piece of cake. Cameron woke up about seven, she changed his diaper, got him dressed, and then they had breakfast.

She said he was a finicky breakfast eater. He ate dinner with no problems the night before, but he would hardly eat anything for breakfast. Grapes, no thanks. Toast, not on your life. Frosted Flakes, have you lost your mind? Cream of Wheat, now you're talking. She told me she was surprised. She didn't think he'd eat the Cream of Wheat, but that was the last thing she could think of, and he ate all of it.

The next day was the Saturday before Thanksgiving. We had a great day of playing together, doing some work around the house, and doing laundry. Sunday morning, we went to church and repeated everything we did Saturday. Cameron fit right in.

Monday morning Dyanna Jo got a call from Marvin letting us know that they scheduled a child and family team meeting the following day. We would learn more about Cameron on Tuesday.

15

———

GEOFF AND MELODY

Leif's Journal

Dyanna Jo's mom stayed with Ralley and Cameron while we went to the child and family team meeting. The meeting was being held at the Richard L. Bean Juvenile Court and Detention Center on Division Street in Knoxville. The meeting was significant, for we were meeting with Cameron's potential adoptive parents.

I got off work at 2 p.m. and came home to pick up Dyanna Jo. We arrived at ten till three and parked the car. It was a windy day; thankfully, we didn't have to walk very far to the entrance. As soon as we entered, we spotted a security station operated by Knox County Sheriff's Deputies. We followed a line of people, and as we approached the security station, we were given instructions to put our hand-carried items in a plastic tub and pass them through the x-ray machine. One by one, we walked through a metal detector. Dyanna Jo looked a little nervous around the Deputies and x-ray machine.

Once we moved passed security, we headed down a long hall. There were bathrooms on the left and three courtrooms on the right. At the end of the hall was a semicircular kiosk. Because we had never been there before, we decided to follow the people. Everyone headed to a line right in front of the kiosk. To the left of the line was an extensive, very full waiting area. After a few minutes of standing in line, it was our turn.

The guy at the desk had a nameplate on his desk that identified him as Barry Newsome. He wore a flannel shirt with John Deere tractors on the front, back and arms. He held up his jeans with green and yellow suspenders that said John Deere all over them. He also had several John Deere model tractors on his desk as well as a John Deere calendar hanging on the side. He must have had at least ten coffee mugs with John Deere imprinted on them. He sipped his coffee from one of the tall mugs. His name may be Barry, but in my mind, he was Mr. John Deere.

"Who are you here to see?" he asked.

"We are here for the Johnson child, family team meeting," I responded.

"And you all are ...?"

"We are the foster parents."

As he perused his list, I noticed two glass doors behind the kiosk. Mounted on the wall beside the right door, I recognized a small square box known as an RF reader. I had observed several people put their identification badges up to the reader, listen for a click, and continue through the glass doors. The building seemed to go on forever. Through the glass doors, I could see a long hall that led to the back of the building. Two halls branched off to the right. A person could get lost in this place.

After Mr. John Deere found our names and checked us off his list, we were told to find a seat in the waiting room. That was not going to be easy; the place was packed. We only saw one empty seat. Dyanna Jo sat while I stood. From where we were seated, we faced the double doors and were close enough to the kiosk to hear what people were saying to Mr. John Deere. We watched and listened to see who else would be showing up for our meeting. People just kept coming. I didn't see how they were going to fit all those people in this waiting room. As we looked around the room, we heard a man at the kiosk say that they were there for the Johnson child family team meeting. Dyanna Jo and I immediately turned our heads to see a sharp, well-dressed couple standing at the kiosk, talking to Mr. John Deere.

"Do you think they are the couple trying to adopt Cameron?" Dyanna Jo whispered up at me.

"They might be," I whispered back. "I don't think they're the parents."

She nodded in agreement. Mr. John Deere instructed the couple to sit in the waiting area. They headed to the back of the room and started talking to an older woman that had been sitting there for a while. The woman looked as if she was in her fifties. They seemed to know each other.

At about five after three, Mr. John Deere announced for all those attending the Johnson child family team meeting to come to the kiosk. We got up, as did the other couple and the older woman. We approached the kiosk, and all began to smile at each other. No one said a word. Mr. John Deere pointed to the double glass doors and told us that Marvin would be escorting us to our meeting. In unison, we all walked over to Marvin.

Marvin led us through the doors, all the way to the end of the hall and turned right. As we walked, we could see that there were about ten rooms on each side of the hallway. Marvin stopped in front of the third room on the right. As we entered the room, we noticed that three people were sitting at a rectangular table. Each of them was wearing business attire.

"Welcome, please find a seat, and we will begin in just a moment," one of the ladies, at the table, said.

Dyanna Jo and I sat at the end of the table, farthest from the door. The other couple sat on the right side, closest to our end. The older woman sat on the opposite end of the table facing us. Marvin squeezed in where ever he could find room. The three business-dressed people sat directly across from the couple on our right.

"Hello, everyone, my name is Veronica, and I am the FSW, Family Service Worker for this case. I coordinate the efforts of the team; to ensure that everyone understands their role and responsibility to help the family achieve their long term goals. In the event, the family is not a viable resource for the child; the team will work toward finding a permanent, nurturing home for each child in care. Let's have you all introduce yourselves while you sign the piece of paper that Sylvia," Veronica pointed to her left and continued without taking a breath, "is about to pass around. Foster parents, if you want to keep your names anonymous, just introduce yourselves as the foster parents." Veronica nodded to Sylvia.

"As Veronica mentioned, I am Sylvia. I will be taking notes and making sure everything is documented correctly," Sylvia said, passing a form to her left.

The man to the right of Veronica began to speak, "Thank you, Sylvia. My name is Michael. I am Cameron's guardian ad litem."

We all looked at each other confused. "Excuse me," I said, "what is a guardian ad litem?"

With a smile, Michael answered, "I am an attorney who the court appoints to act as a representative for the minor child. I am to remain objective, impartial, and act in the best interest of the child. In this case, that would be Cameron," Michael said.

Dyanna Jo and I, along with the other couple and the older woman, all said, "Thank you," at the same time. We turned to each other and laughed.

Veronica nodded to the older woman at the opposite end of the table. She cleared her throat and said, "My name is Paula, and I am Cameron's grandmother." She looked down at her lap. The woman who arrived with her husband reached out and grabbed her hand.

"Hi, we are Geoff and Melody Mason. We are petitioning the court to adopt Cameron and ask for him to live with us as we go through the process," Geoff said in a kind but authoritative voice. Melody just smiled, still holding Paula's hand.

Marvin spoke up and introduced himself, "Hello everyone; I believe we have all met. However, for the record, my name is Marvin. I am Cameron's caseworker."

We were the last people in the room to introduce ourselves. I simply said, "We are the foster parents." Dyanna Jo gave a little wave and smiled nervously.

Marvin had informed us that in the meetings, most foster parents don't give their names. It was a safety measure for both the children and the foster parents. If the children's family knew our names, they could possibly find a phone number or address to call or visit without permission. We didn't want that to happen.

Veronica officially began the meeting, "today we will be obtaining as much information as we can about Cameron, the family and any person tied to this case. Our goal is to help the family and this team work together to achieve Cameron's permanency as soon as possible. According to our records, Geoff and Melody Mason contacted DCS and informed them that they had Cameron in their care."

"That is correct," Geoff said.

"Are you related to Cameron," Veronica asked.

"No."

"How did Cameron come into your care?"

"I'll tell you how," Paula, the grandmother, said wearily. "I have two daughters. They are both drug addicts and living off on their own in some God-forsaken place. My oldest, Susan, is Cameron's mom. There's no telling who the father is because she has slept with so many men. She has no idea who it could be. My girls feed their habit by selling themselves to men." She paused, got a tissue then dabbed at her eyes. I felt terrible for her and noticed that Dyanna Jo and Melody had also grabbed tissues.

"I go to church with Geoff and Melody. I've talked to them from time to time and knew that even though they had two children of their own, God had laid it on their heart to adopt another child. When it became apparent, my daughter was incapable of taking care of Cameron; I told her that Geoff and Melody could adopt Cameron and give him a loving home. Susan didn't want to hear about them. Maria, my youngest daughter, came to my house and found the Mason's phone number and called to tell them to come to get Cameron." Paula stopped and struggled to compose herself.

Geoff sat up straight in his seat, cleared his throat, and told the team the rest of the story.

"We want him back home, in our home," Melody spoke up with tears running down her face. "We love him so much."

"You did the right thing calling DCS," Veronica said. "Our records also show that Marvin made a visit to Susan and Maria's house yesterday, and Susan denies ever taking money from the Masons."

Veronica saw the Masons both open their mouths to speak. She put up her hand to hush them. She continued, "Susan's exact words were, *I did not sell my baby! I want him back!*" Veronica's hand remained in the air. "Marvin told both of the girls that there was a child, family team meeting today, and if Susan wanted to fight for her son, she needed to come to this meeting."

The room was so quiet you could hear a pin drop. Veronica lowered her hand and looked at Paula. "Ma'am, do you feel that your daughter has any chance of getting her act together and provide a safe and nurturing home for Cameron?"

"No, I do not," she said definitively. "She's twenty-eight, and for ten years she has been doing this. In the first few years, she told me she would change. But, after it was apparent she wouldn't, she started telling me she couldn't change. I held out a small hope that when Cameron came along, she would change, but all she cares about is getting her drugs. The only way she can do that is to prostitute herself. Susan doesn't want Cameron; she just wants to get back at me. If she did, she would be here. I want Geoff and Melody to adopt him. He doesn't need to be in that environment anymore."

My heart sank, that poor mother. I could feel her pain. I looked at the Masons and noticed Dyanna Jo's head turn towards them at the same time. When Cameron first came into our home, we heard someone was trying to adopt him, and I have to admit, we were concerned. Dyanna Jo and I had briefly thought maybe we could adopt him. Sitting here today, hearing their story, the Masons were Cameron's perfect family.

The team continued to work through all the specifics of Cameron's case. We decided that Marvin and Michael would work with the Masons to get a home study done and work through the steps they needed to take, to petition the court. At this point, it was too soon to talk about adoption, but if they passed the home study, they could ask the court if Cameron could be returned to their care.

"Any more questions?" Veronica asked.

I noticed Geoff and Melody discussing something between them, Geoff spoke up.

"If the foster parents don't mind, would it be possible for us to have a visit with Cameron?" he asked.

"That is something the court must decide. If the court agrees to supervised visitation, we will contact the foster parents and make the arrangements," Michael said.

Everyone began to stand at the same time. One by one,

everyone headed out the door. We noticed the Mason's held back and looked at us with hope in their eyes.

"Hi, I am Dyanna Jo, and this is my husband Leif," Dyanna Jo said without even asking me if I was comfortable with her giving our names. She didn't need to; she already knew deep in her heart. "We would be happy to work with you when the court allows visitation."

Melody reached out her hand and touched Dyanna Jo lightly on the arm, "Thank you! How is he?"

"How about we head out to the waiting area and talk awhile," I said before Dyanna Jo said another word.

We headed to the waiting area and were pleased to see there were plenty of open seats to sit and talk comfortably.

16

CAMERON'S NEW START

Leif's Journal

Another Thanksgiving was upon us. Time seemed to pass quickly these days. We had our traditional holiday lunch with my parents at their house. This year we had Cameron, and everyone fell in love. He was trying his best to walk; he would take a few steps and quickly land on his bottom. We always made sure to stay close; you never knew what he was going to do next. Thanksgiving with a baby was a new experience.

The Saturday after Thanksgiving, we heard from Marvin. The Judge granted the petition to allow the Masons visitation, but only supervised visits until their home study was completed. Marvin said that we would be considered supervisors, and therefore we could meet anywhere we chose. We were comfortable with having them over to our house, and we figured that the Masons would like to see where Cameron has been staying.

Dyanna Jo called Melody to make arrangements for tomorrow after church. The ladies had already been on the call for thirty minutes and showed no sign of ending anytime soon. I decided to park myself on the couch and watch football. Cameron was taking a nap, and Ralley was reading a book. She wasn't much into football. However, she liked watching the Atlanta Braves play during the baseball season.

"Dad."

"Yes, Ralley."

"Did you say the Masons have a ten-year-old daughter?"

"They have a twelve-year-old daughter and a ten-year-old son. Why do you ask?"

"Cameron might be living with them soon, and I just thought it would be nice if I liked them."

"I'm sure you will. I think they have good parents."

"I hope so," she mused and returned to her book.

Dyanna Jo came downstairs and had the imprint of the phone on her left ear and cheek. Ralley giggled.

"What are you giggling about?" she asked.

"You have a mark on your left ear and cheek from the phone ."

"I do?" she asked rhetorically and went to the bathroom to look in the mirror. "How long was I on the phone?"

"About an hour and a half."

"That long. No wonder my arm hurts. I didn't realize we were on that long."

"Well, somewhere in that hour and a half, did you manage to set a time for tomorrow and give them directions? Or did you get sidetracked and completely forget the purpose of the call?" I said, teasing her.

"Ah, man!" Dyanna Jo exclaimed. "I completely forgot about that. I told her the Judge granted the petition, but we started talking about all kinds of stuff and never got around to set the time. Doggone it."

"You didn't do that, did you?" Ralley asked incredulously.

"No, I didn't really do that. We got the arrangements out of the way first, and then we talked about stuff."

After church, we came home, had lunch, and waited for the Masons to arrive. Ralley started looking out the window every five minutes. She started on the couch; she would get up, look out the window, and return to the couch. She repeated the process over and over again. Back and forth, forth and back. It was like watching a tennis match with a long rally. (pun intended)

After about a half-hour of watching the pot boil, the Masons arrived. The kids were miniature versions of Geoff and Melody. I bet childhood pictures of Geoff and Melody would look the same as their children's photos.

They came to the front door, and of course, Ralley already had it open for them. We made all the introductions, and I could see Geoff and Melody looking around and sizing up the place. It seemed as if they approved.

As soon as Cameron saw them, he pointed, crawled over to Melody, and held his hands up to her. She scooped him up and gave him a big hug and kiss. Dyanna Jo went to get a box of tissues. Melody and her daughter had already started to have eye drainage. It didn't take long before Dyanna Jo, and Ralley had the same malady. Geoff, his son, and I kind of looked around and surveyed the area.

"Did you have any trouble finding our place?" I asked after the drainage issues finished.

"No," Geoff answered. "We had no trouble."

"I asked because Dyanna Jo gave directions, and she's notorious for giving bad ones."

That earned me a punch in the arm. They all laughed.

"Actually, I used the GPS app I have on my iPhone. The directions did leave a little to be desired."

"Would you like a tour of the rest of the house?" I asked. I figured they were dying to see it. I just thought they wanted to know in what kind of environment Cameron was living.

"Yes, please. We would like that very much, if it's no trouble," Melody quickly said.

"It's no trouble at all. We've hidden all the booze and buried all the bodies, so you're good."

"That's a relief," Geoff said. "It's nice to know you have good manners."

We showed the upstairs first. We started in the master bedroom then Ralley's room, the bonus room, and Cameron's room. They lingered in Cameron's room.

"His room is perfect. I couldn't have asked for a better place for him to be. Thank you for loving him," Melody said with signs of more eye drainage.

We left Cameron's room and finished the upstairs tour. We showed them two bathrooms and the laundry room. We all headed downstairs and walked through the dining room, kitchen, and ended in the living room.

"You have a beautiful house," Melody said. "We're so thankful that we got to come. We've been so worried about Cameron's environment. You know, you hear stories about foster care, and it isn't always pretty. We also know where he lived before. We can see now that he's in good hands. It's a big weight off our shoulders."

I was beginning to think I needed to get that box of tissues again, but the plug held, and there was no more leakage. The afternoon was still young, though.

We all sat down, and Ralley got everyone some water. The Masons children, Elizabeth and Luke, were on the floor laughing and playing with Cameron. When Ralley returned with the waters, she joined the kids on the floor. Ralley and Elizabeth hit it off right away.

Over the next hour, Geoff and Melody filled us in on how things were going with them getting Cameron back.

"The Judge wants us to take the PATH classes and become foster parents," Geoff explained. "We've never considered becoming foster parents, but we will do anything to get Cameron back. Marvin will have to schedule visitations for Susan; if she misses those appointments and doesn't work the parenting plan, they can move to terminate her parental rights. A classified ad in the newspaper will have to be run every Friday for thirty days. The ad is just a formality. They have to try to find the father. If no one steps up, we must wait six months before they will allow us to adopt."

"Will they let him stay with you while you take the classes?" Dyanna Jo asked.

"We asked if we could, and the Guardian Ad Litem told the court that he felt it would be best for Cameron to be placed back in our home. They want us to have a home study first. We have already gone to get our background checks done. The Judge said that if we passed the background checks and the home study, Cameron could come home. PATH classes count toward the six months."

"Have they scheduled your home study?" I asked.

"Marvin is coming on Friday," Geoff replied.

"You should be good on the background check," I said. "I had an arrest record that was four pages long, but they said since it was under five pages, I was good to go. I can't imagine yours being more than a page or two."

"Well, we all have our secrets," Geoff said. "If they don't look at my juvenile records, I should come in under five pages."

The wives didn't think our attempt at humor was amusing. They rolled their eyes and started a conversation.

They stayed a little over two hours; their visit with Cameron went great. When they left, Cameron did really well. No crying or anything. He seemed so laid back and happy go lucky. I was glad they were going to adopt him. He would have a great home with them.

FRIDAY OF THAT SAME WEEK, Marvin called and told us that the Masons were approved. They passed the home study and background checks. Cameron was going home. He asked if we wanted him to take Cameron to the Masons or if we wanted to take him. Dyanna Jo told him we would take him.

Dyanna Jo called Melody to arrange a time to bring Cameron over. Melody didn't waste any time. She was ready for him to come back today. Melody gave Dyanna Jo directions to their house. We were glad that we were able to take Cameron to the Masons. We wanted to see their home as much as they wanted to view ours.

As soon as I got home, we left. It took us almost an hour to get to their house. It was a sunny day; the drive was beautiful. The temperature was in the thirties, so it was chilly. They lived on the opposite side of town and out in the country. Their subdivision mixed with old farms around it. Those farms would most likely wind up being subdivisions also.

They had a two-story house with a brick front and vinyl siding. We walked up to the front door, it was wide open and they were waiting for us. They'd probably been doing the same thing we did on Sunday, looking out the window every five minutes.

When we walked in the front door, we saw steps, on the left side, leading upstairs. A hall was directly in front of us and led to the kitchen. To the right was a big open living room; on the other end was the dining.

After they got us some water, we went upstairs and toured the three bedrooms and a bonus room over the garage. We settled in the bonus room to talk for a little bit and let Cameron play. They had so many toys waiting for him. Luke, Elizabeth, and Ralley enjoyed playing on the floor with the new toys. Cameron giggled and crawled all over the room. Occasionally he would stand himself up and walk a couple of steps to Elizabeth. Luke immediately got Camerons' attention with the fire trucks and dump trucks. Elizabeth and Ralley tried to play along, but the boys were all over the place, they couldn't keep up. They decided to sit on the couch and talk to the adults.

"We think we are going to have to change our phone number," Melody said.

"Why?" Dyanna Jo asked.

"Cameron's mom keeps calling us and asking for money," Geoff said. "We tell her we can't help her and not to call us, but she doesn't listen. Sometimes her sister calls."

"It's a nightmare," Melody said and sighed. "All day long, they call. We make sure to document every call; we don't want any problems with DCS." Just then, her phone rang. She checked the caller id. "That's her," she said wearily. She silenced the phone. "Yep, we are changing our number, and we will make sure it is unlisted."

"That's why we don't let the parents of the children in our home have our number. We are afraid they would call all the time and maybe find out where we live and start stopping by our house," Dyanna Jo said.

"I wouldn't like Susan stopping by, especially if I'm not there," I said.

"Fortunately, they don't know where we live. Susan probably hasn't thought of looking in the phone book for our address," Geoff said.

"Thank God," Melody said emphatically.

WE LEFT after a half-hour and headed home feeling empty. The car ride home was quiet until Ralley spoke up about halfway through it.

"Is it always going to be like this?" she asked plaintively.

"Like what?" Dyanna Jo asked. She thought she knew what Ralley meant but wanted to hear her say it.

"Hurts. Cameron wasn't with us very long, but I got to liking him and think he's pretty cool, and then he's with somebody else."

"I feel the same way," Dyanna Jo said. "We were told in our PATH classes not to get too attached to the children because it's hard when they leave, but it's hard not to."

"Maybe the longer we do this, the easier it will be," I said. Little did I know, the next few weeks weren't going to be easy. We were silent for the rest of the way home.

When we got home, Dyanna Jo went up to the babies' room, stripped the crib of its sheets, gathered all the dirty clothes and blankets, and started some laundry. She was disappointed Cameron couldn't stay, but she knew she had to be ready for the next call. She busied herself for the rest of the day.

Ralley and I went to the mall. West Town Mall, specifically. It was on the outskirts of West Knoxville when it opened in 1972, but it wasn't really in West Knoxville anymore. West Knoxville was, well, further west.

We went to the mall regularly for our Father/Daughter dates. We enjoyed dinner in the food court. We always went to Asian Chao, bourbon chicken with lo mien noodles for me, and sweet and sour chicken with lo mien for her. After we ate, I got my usual Irish cream mocha from Starbucks then headed out on our jaunt around the mall.

We'd walk around, window shop, go into our favorite stores, talk, and take pictures in the little photo booths. You know, the ones where you made goofy faces and acted silly. Occasionally, I would buy something for Ralley. Sometimes I would consider something for me, and sometimes we both left with shopping bags.

This time, we were subdued. Usually, we joked around,

laughed, and cut up, but tonight our thoughts were preoccupied.

Right past Starbucks stood a circular pool about twenty feet in diameter with a bridge spanning it and a fountain on either side. The pool was littered with pennies from people making wishes. On the bridge was a sign that read, *All coins donated to the Simon Youth Foundation.* Simon Malls was the owner of West Town Mall.

"A penny for your thoughts," I said as we passed the pool. Ralley smiled. That made me feel better.

"Looking to donate to the Simon Youth Foundation?" she asked facetiously.

"Tell me what you're thinking, and I'll throw in a penny."

"Well," she took a deep breath. "I'm thinking that I should be happy for Cameron. He has a good home. God knows what He's doing. Cameron is safe and happy; instead of thinking about myself and feeling miserable and down, I should think about the good things. We were there for him when he needed us. Even if it was just for ten days."

"That's worth a lot more than a penny," I said proudly. "That's very good, Ralley, and it makes me happy to hear you say that. Who knows, maybe those ten days were the difference between him having a Godly life or a destructive life. For those ten days we were a place of refuge for him."

"Yea, you never know when God might use you to help someone rally and get their life straight. Well, as straight as it can be, in this fallen world."

I was proud of her. I took out four quarters; two for Ralley, and two for me. We threw them in one at a time.

"How come you threw in four quarters, Dad?"

"I thought what you said was worth more than a few pennies. So, I thought I would contribute a little more than a few pennies."

We walked a little bit longer around the mall. We found a store for girls Ralley's age. I turned and walked into the store.

"Where are we going, Dad?" Ralley asked.

"Why don't you try on a couple of dresses," I replied.

"Really?"

"You better hurry, or I will change my mind," I toyed with her.

When she tried on the dresses, I could see she wasn't my little girl anymore. She was getting older. She usually liked wearing baggy clothes, jeans, t-shirts or button-up shirts. But, when she put on those dresses and twirled around, she was a young lady. I saw that she was changing. I didn't know if I was ready for that. It didn't matter if I was ready or not—she was changing, and nothing was going to stop it.

Of course, being her dad, I thought she was by far the fairest eleven-year-old in the land. She didn't seem to be too comfortable in the dresses, but she liked wearing them. After she tried on a few, I asked her which one she wanted. I wasn't surprised when she told me the solid navy blue dress was the one she wanted. I thought that one looked the best on her too.

On the way home, I joked with her about getting a shotgun to fend off all the suitors she would have. She rolled her eyes. When we got home, she showed Dyanna Jo the dress. Instantly Dyanna Jo announced that Ralley had no shoes, earrings, or whatever thingamahoochies you're supposed to wear with a dress. Of course, she didn't. The kid hadn't worn a dress in the last three or four years. I told Dyanna Jo she would have to accessorize the dress because I wouldn't have the first clue what to get. She didn't seem too thrilled about it. She hated shopping. But, there's no question, she would do it for Ralley's sake. She would make it a special mother/daughter day.

Ralley's Journal

I guess I was more attached to Cameron than I thought. The only thing that made it tolerable was that he was going to a great family. I liked being a foster sister. I had to get better at managing my feelings and emotions. He was only with us for ten days, and I wanted to cry about him leaving us. What will happen if they are with us for a few months or years and then leave to go to their parents or another foster home?

I enjoyed Liz and Luke. I knew they would be good siblings to Cameron. I hoped I'd see Liz again. She was sweet, and we liked a lot of the same things. I could see us being good friends. Cameron sure liked her, and she was really good with him. Luke was good with him too.

So, that drive home after leaving him with Liz was annoying. I was on the verge of crying the whole time. I don't like to cry. Tears running down my face, nose running, and getting all emotional—yuk! So, I managed to keep from crying. Talking to Mom about it helped. I just wondered how soon we'd get called for another child. Hopefully, I would be better prepared.

I was glad when Dad suggested we go to the mall. It was exactly what I needed. It wasn't surprising that Mom got busy cleaning when we got home. She said we needed to get ready for our next placement.

Dyanna Jo's Journal

It was bittersweet. I liked Geoff and Melody and knew that Cameron was loved and had a safe home. But, in that short period, I fell in love with him. He was so sweet, and those beautiful brown eyes would look up at me and say, *I trust you.* I had hoped that maybe he could stay with us and we could adopt him. I know that the goal of being a foster parent was to be there for the children, give them a safe home, and help the families work towards getting their kids back. That was going to be the hard part. You see where these children come from and how the parents act. It's hard not to be judgmental and think that you would be a better parent. I know that I am not going to get a call and boom, I get to keep the child and adopt them. Leif kept telling me that I had to trust God to put the child He wants us to have in our home. My lack of patience and faith showed its ugly head way too often.

I wondered how Ralley was handling everything. She had helped us a lot with Cameron, changing his diapers, feeding him, and helping us bathe him. I should have checked on her sooner.

I found her in her room, reading a book about Sherlock Holmes. She loved reading and had recently discovered the book series and was devouring them.

"Hey, sweetie," I said cheerily. "How are you doing?"

"I'm okay. Why do you ask?"

"Just wondering if you are upset about Cameron."

"Oh," she said and scrunched up her face. I could tell she was thinking of what to say.

"So, while you're constipating, I just want you to know your dad, and I are here for you if you're upset or need to talk." I purposely chose the wrong word to get a reaction out of her. Maybe a small smile? It didn't work as well as I had hoped.

"I'm not upset," she said after she took a minute to compose herself. "He hasn't been here long enough to get really attached to him. I like Cameron, and it would have been nice having him here."

"I think so too," I agreed. "But I've decided, I'm not going to worry about how attached I get to any foster kids we get. I can handle it when they leave, so while they're with us, I'm not going to worry about it."

"It makes it easier knowing he's going to a good home."

"Yes, it does. I'll let you get back to your book."

I was glad she was handling it well. She was more mature than any eleven-year-old I knew. She was always diligent about helping around the house. When she chose who to hang around with, she chose wisely. She was a loyal, caring, and generous friend. She has taught me many things about being considerate and unselfish. I hope her attitude will rub off on the kids we foster and adopt.

17

—————

AND THEN CAME LARON

Dyanna Jo's Journal

Ralley was growing so fast; she'd outgrown most of her clothes. I knew a trip to the mall was in my future. In an effort to get out of it, I asked Leif to take her. They love the mall; it's their thing. Normally, however, they only come home with one or two items. She needs clothes, lots of them. They're both at the mall right now. Who knows what she'll bring home.

I was enjoying a quiet house. It helped me think and get some work done. I was still trying to process the events of the past few days. Our first foster placement, sweet little Cameron, meeting Geoff and Melody and hearing what they had gone through. We were in a whole new world. Our lives had changed entirely. Praise God! He's been with us every step of the way.

We miss Cameron. I know we shouldn't get so attached, but it's impossible. Children are a gift, so innocent and such a blessing.

"Mom! Mom, where are you?" Ralley shouted as they came through the front door.

"I'm back here! How was your shopping trip?" I asked when she found me.

"It was good. Rejuvenating," Leif said.

"I wouldn't consider the mall rejuvenating," I said with a little scowl.

"Well, some of us enjoy shopping. Strangely, you don't," Leif said. "How is it that the first place the three of us went together was to the mall? If I recall, you invited us to the mall. It's amazing what you'll do to rope in a guy. Oh, the sacrifice..."

"Very funny!" I shot back.

"I'm glad at least one of you likes the mall," Ralley interjected as she sat on the floor in front of me. "Look at what we got!"

She pulled three dresses from her shopping bag and announced she would give us a fashion show. Up the stairs, she scampered to change clothes.

"How are you doing?" Leif asked as we waited for our fashionista to return.

"I'm okay; I am ready for another placement. Cameron was only here ten days, how is it possible that the house can feel so empty," I answered.

"I know."

Suddenly, Ralley shouted from the top of the stairs, "Mom, Dad, close your eyes while I make my grand entrance!"

"Okay!" we both called out.

We heard her bounce down the stairs and slide to a stop right in front of us.

"Now, open your eyes!" she exclaimed.

"Oh, I like it a lot!" I squealed and clapped my hands. The dress was lovely — blue with a tea-length hem and capped sleeves. I see a trend here. Her first two dresses were blue.

Ralley beamed. "Great! Now I'll try on the next one."

As she hurried back upstairs, Leif commented, "I wonder what foster child God will send us next."

"I'm not picky, as long as it's a boy or girl," I quipped.

"Yes, it would be weird if it wasn't a boy or girl," Leif teased. That Snail of mine can be so nerdy sometimes. He loves to try to make me laugh.

Just then, Ralley reappeared.

"Mom, what do you think of this one?"

"Gorgeous!" I responded. She did look cute as she twirled in a denim dress that hit just above the knees. Another blue dress, blue denim, has always been my favorite fabric. Give me a good pair of Jeans, and I am in happy land. Make it into a dress, and you've got perfection. I know, I'm a bit weird.

"You really like our picks? Not too short? Not too long?" Leif asked.

"Yes, so far, so good. Show me the third!"

Ralley bounded up the stairs again to try on her last selection, which gave us a few extra seconds to discuss fostering.

"So, you're open to any child? Handicapped, medical conditions—"

"I trust whatever God feels we're equipped for," I assured him.

"Alrighty, then," he agreed.

We heard the clump, clump, clump on the stairs and down came Ralley, decked out in a pink cotton shift.

"And last but not least ..." she said with another twirl.

"Aww," I stated. "Sweet and age-appropriate. A pink dress for our newly made girly-girl. Oh — but wait a minute. Did you buy shoes or earrings to wear with these dresses, or did you buy any other clothes to replace the ones she has grown out of?"

"Oops!" Leif exclaimed. "That means you'll be taking her back to the mall."

"Me? Did you do that on purpose? Don't do this to me! I'm not the one who forgot everything!"

"Yeah, but you know how bad I am at picking out clothes, shoes, and especially accessories."

"True. You wouldn't have the first clue what to get—"

"So, tag, you're it, Mom," Ralley interrupted, obviously pleased to go on another shopping excursion.

RALLEY'S JOURNAL

Mom finally decided it could be fun taking a quick trip to the mall. When Mom goes shopping, she knows what she wants and where to get it. In and out, that is her motto. She doesn't like going from store to store like Dad and me. Mom says she would rather have a root canal.

Mom didn't want to waste any time. Getting my clothes situation taken care of was her main priority. She grabbed her keys, and out we went. When we arrived, she marched into the mall, went to one department store that had everything I needed, and got us out quickly. Finally, I had everything I needed, pants, shorts, shirts, shoes, and accessories.

Mom decided we would stop and eat dinner at our favorite Mexican restaurant. We love the salsa bar at El Burro Flojo on Kington Pike, right down the street from the mall.

She called Dad to see if he wanted to join us, and he didn't hesitate. We knew he wouldn't and could be there in 10 minutes. We ate dinner, laughed, bantered back and forth, and had a great night. In fact, it was a great day. All of us needed that time together. We missed Cameron, but it was time to clear our minds and move forward.

LEIF'S JOURNAL

The next day we got a call from placement. They had a three-week-old baby who was currently in the hospital. He was born drug-exposed and six weeks premature. He'd spent the last couple weeks in the NICU, Neonatal Intensive Care Unit. The hospital worked towards weaning him off the drugs, and finally, he was ready to be placed in a home.

An hour and a half later, the caseworker showed up with the baby. She took him out of the car, carried him to the house in an infant car seat, and rang the doorbell. When we opened the door, she showed us her ID, and we let her in the house. The name on the ID was Jillian Vargas. She stood approximately five foot eight inches tall with brown hair and brown eyes. We invited her into the living room so we could talk.

Jillian told us the baby's name was Laron Childers. He was African American, tiny and weighed about six pounds. Thankfully, he was doing a lot better after a rough three weeks of withdrawals from the drugs. He was taking his bottle, consistent with his feeding times, and kept his food down.

"Does he have any siblings?" I asked.

"He has three brothers and a sister. They are all in foster care and have been in the system for a couple of years. They are currently in a foster home and thriving."

"What's the mom's backstory?" Dyanna Jo asked.

"The mother is a single woman who is unable to keep a job, stay off drugs, moves from couch to couch, and hasn't been able to care for her children, let alone herself."

"What about the dad?" I asked.

"She won't tell us who the dad is."

"When's the next child and family team meeting?" Dyanna Jo asked.

"Tomorrow at three-thirty."

"Okay, that works with my schedule," I said.

Jillian asked if we had any more questions, and since we didn't, she left. Jillian had brought a couple of items they used at the hospital and some of his formula. Shortly after that, Laron woke up; we changed his diaper and fed him. He took his bottle, burped, and went back to sleep. Dyanna Jo also went to bed, even though it was only 8 p.m. She didn't know how much sleep she'd get and decided to snooze when he slept.

He woke us up at 2 a.m. Dyanna Jo got up and fed him. I got up at four to get ready for work, and Laron was still sleeping like a baby. When I called at lunchtime, Dyanna Jo told me Laron woke up at about five-fifty, she fed him and changed his diaper. He fell back to sleep while she made breakfast for Ralley.

Dyanna Jo broke the news that I'd have to go to the child and family team meeting by myself while she stayed home with Laron and Ralley. Usually, her mom babysat for us, but couldn't that afternoon. I don't think Dyanna Jo was all that interested in going anyway — she was pretty fixated on baby Laron.

WHEN I ARRIVED at the Richard L. Bean Juvenile Court building, I parked, entered the front doors, passed through security, and checked in with Mr. John Deere. After a twenty-minute wait, someone stepped through the double doors and called for anyone attending the Childers child and family team meeting. I got up with a few others, and we all went back to the room.

The same FSW was there, but the other people were new to me. Veronica, the FSW, started the meeting and introduced herself. Just like our last meeting, we all went around the table and introduced ourselves. On Veronica's right was a woman named Clarissa Morris, Laron's Guardian ad Litem. Next to her was Francis, the foster parent for Laron's siblings. On the opposite side of the table from Clarissa sat Laron's mom, Takesha.

Takesha introduced herself and sounded like she was under the influence of something. Her speech was slurred, and she talked slowly like she was having trouble thinking of what she wanted to say. She rested her elbow on the table and put her head in her hand. It was disconcerting sitting across from her because she hardly looked at anyone. However, she was fixed on me almost the entire time, like a tiger sizing up its prey.

"The first issue we need to discuss," Veronica, began, "is if Laron will remain in his current foster home or if he will be moved to Francis' with his siblings. Francis, do you have any input on it?"

Francis was a heavyset woman with a kind face, but underneath I sensed she was in charge and wouldn't tolerate any lip or backtalk. I could picture the children in her home being well behaved and respectful of authority.

"I told Clarissa that I could take him. I work nights at Fort Sander's Hospital. I have a babysitter who is DCS approved to stay with the kids while I'm at work, and I have a sister and brother-in-law who are foster parents. They also watch the kids when I'm at work; we help each other out. So, I can handle having Laron in my home."

"What do you think of that?" Veronica asked Clarissa.

"I believe that would work. We want the siblings to be in care together whenever possible."

"We'll have to get approval to place him with Francis so it might be a few days before he's moved. What do you think, foster dad?" Veronica asked me.

"I think it would be great if he could be with his siblings. It's best to keep them together, if possible."

"Do you have anything you'd like to say, Takesha?"

"I'd like for all my kids to be in one place," she said lazily. "I want their phone numbers; I wanna talk to my kids." She raised her head long enough to look at Francis and back to me.

Francis shocked me when she said, "Takesha, you have my number. You call it all the time."

"Oh yeah.... right," she slurred. "What about him?"

"Would you like to give Takesha your number?" Veronica asked, looking right at me.

I was dumbfounded. I couldn't believe she asked me. At Cameron's child and family team meeting, we discussed the standard practice of foster parents not giving out personal information.

"I'd rather not," I said after I got over my disbelief.

"Why can't I have your number? You don't want me checking on my baby?" Takesha asked.

"That's not the reason," I replied. I was perturbed with Veronica at that point; she put me on the spot. "I don't give personal information to anyone, and if you want to know how Laron is doing, you can call Jillian."

She just kept staring at me like a lion sizing up its next meal. It was getting extremely awkward.

"Takesha," Francis broke in, "most foster parents don't give out their phone number. I gave you mine because I've had your other four kids for a long time now. I've been working with you for some time, so I feel comfortable doing that. Usually, I don't give out my phone number, either."

I was glad Francis said that. The meeting wasn't very long. This meeting was nowhere as long as Camerons. As I was leaving, Veronica tapped my arm, and we stepped out into the hallway.

"I want to apologize for putting you on the spot. I know better than to mention giving out phone numbers. I don't know why I asked you."

"I was definitely caught off guard, but everything is fine. I'm not mad, and I appreciate your apology. No one's perfect, and I've done stuff like that too; I'm not mad."

"Thank you for accepting my apology and for your forgiveness. By the way, I think you handled it well in there."

"Thank you."

Francis also took this opportunity to share more of Laron's backstory. It was terrible, and my heart ached for the little guy.

I'd be sharing the details with Dyanna Jo just as soon as I got home.

As I left the building and walked to my car, it felt like someone was watching me. Sure enough, I saw Takesha and those tiger eyes boring holes through me while she smoked a cigarette and leaned against a car. She was a few rows over from where I was parked. She turned and got in her car. When I left, I kept checking my rearview and side mirrors to see if she was following me. She wasn't.

~

D**YANNA** J**O**'**S** **Journal**

Laron was easy to care for and only got fussy when he was hungry. He drank his bottles just fine and didn't seem to have any problem with his plumbing. Ralley enjoyed helping me and liked holding him on the couch. It was so sweet to see how nurturing she was with a baby in her arms.

When Leif returned home from the child and family team meeting, he filled me in on everything I'd missed. Ralley was out playing in the back yard on the playset. Hearing Takesha's story broke my heart. I wonder if she knows Jesus. God sees the broken. He loves her so much that He sent His Son to die on a cross for her and her children. My heart was heavy. I walked over to the Pack n' Play and stared down at Laron's little body. *God loves you too, little guy.*

Jillian called shortly after dinner to let us know that she would be coming in an hour to pick up Laron. Francis was approved to keep him with his other siblings. When she arrived, Ralley was getting ready for bed. She had already said her good-byes to Laron and knew that her dad wanted to speak with Jillian privately. Leif told Jillian the story about Takesha watching him when he was walking to his car.

"She's done that before," Jillian admitted. "Francis is the

third foster home her kids have been in because she's been aggressive and threatening to the other foster parents when they show up for team meetings."

"I wish I had known what I would be walking into before I went to the meeting," Leif said with agitation in his voice. "Thankfully, Dyanna Jo wasn't there."

"I'm sorry you weren't aware of the situation," she replied. "Takesha really is more bark than bite. She is aggressive and threatening with words. She thinks that showing us she is willing to fight for her kids, will make us more sympathetic. We've told her it only hurts her case, and the only way she can get her kids back is to work her parenting plan and get off the drugs. She isn't willing to fight that hard. Many new foster parents aren't prepared for that, and therefore they decide it would be best to have the children moved elsewhere. You need to understand that there will be times when you don't know all the circumstances of a case. We will always do our best to protect you, and if there is danger, you will know right away. This will not be the last time you will be in this kind of situation, but truly, we will not have you attend a meeting or court hearing where you are in physical danger."

"Thank you. We appreciate your honesty. We will be more alert with our future placements. If we are uncomfortable with any of the parents or families, we will let DCS know right away."

Jillian took Laron and put him in her car. We walked out with her and gave her all his stuff. After she drove away, we went into the house and got ready for bed.

This case wasn't as emotionally challenging as Cameron's. We learned a few new things and found that a baby was just as fun as the toddlers. Yet again, we would wait for the next placement.

18

BRITTANY AND BRIANNA

Leif's Journal

Often, when I reconstruct our foster children's backstories, I try to put myself in the shoes of the biological parents. The more I learned, the more it helped me understand what the children had gone through and the special care they might need. Nothing I learned could help me understand why parents would abuse, abandon, or neglect their own offspring in the first place. Usually, I was left speechless. George Bernard, his wife Constance, and their two little girls were one such case.

GEORGE WANTED TO HIT SOMETHING. His wife, Constance, was within striking distance, and it had been a while since he popped her. He refrained, though. He was mad because those government agents had taken his two girls. Brittany, a fifteen-month-old, and Brianna was six-weeks-old. They said his girls were neglected and malnourished. He had never heard such nonsense in his life.

"We had a complaint," the DCS caseworker said.

That fat, ugly DCS woman, George thought. He would have hit her if that cop hadn't been with her.

The daycare had called DCS because every morning when Constance dropped them off, the girls were filthy, hungry and had heavily soiled diapers. It didn't look as if their diapers had been changed since they left daycare the day before. The daycare talked to Constance about it, but the girls kept showing up dirty, soiled, and hungry.

When the government agents showed up at the daycare and took custody of the girls, George thought about burning the daycare down. Instead, there was a showdown at the DCS office. The fat, ugly women — Sydney Hopkins — had been a caseworker for more than twenty years and could tell George was capable of violence at the drop of a hat. She was glad Deputy Morris was with her.

"Brittany and Brianna are malnourished and have severe diaper rash. Brittany's diaper rash has turned into an infection, and she has pneumonia. They've been neglected and need medical attention. Once they are well enough, they will be placed in a foster home until you two can show you can take care of them," she told angry George and timid Constance.

"We do take care of them," George said slowly and sternly. "They're clean enough."

Constance never said anything. She sat quietly beside George and stared at the ground. Sydney had seen enough battered women to know when she was looking at one. Unfortunately, there was nothing she could do if the woman didn't ask for help. This did not look like a good situation.

"I'm not going to argue with you," Sydney said. "You have a court hearing in two days, and you can plead your case to the judge."

"Where are the girls now?" George asked.

"They're getting the medical care they need," Sydney replied.

"You took them to Children's Hospital! You can't do that," George yelled.

"Mr. Bernard, I am going to have to ask you to calm down," Deputy Morris said with authority.

George popped up out of his seat; the Deputy stood up as well. Constance continued to look intently at the floor. Sydney stared at George. She'd seen his type before. She doubted the girls would be going back any time soon, if at all.

George sat down after about a minute. "We want to see our kids," he said with a tiny bit of menace.

"I am sorry, sir, you are not able to see them at this time," Sydney told him.

"Why can't we see them? We will just go down to Children's and find them."

"Sir, as I have told you. You have a hearing in two days, and you can speak to the judge."

"I'm just going to go down there right now, and I will see them. I pity whoever gets in my way," he snarled.

"Your children are in DCS custody, and therefore, hospital security will not allow you to see them," Deputy Morris informed him.

Sydney could see the steam coming out of George's ears. He was fit to be tied. Constance was staring so intently at the ground it looked like she was digging a hole. She probably wished she could dig a hole and crawl into it. It stayed that way for about thirty seconds, but it felt like several minutes to Sydney.

"Let's go, Constance!" he barked and got up so forcefully that his chair fell over and hit the floor hard. He stormed away. Constance rose slowly, pushed her chair up to the table, and bent over to pick up the chair. She got it upright and pushed it under the table. She moved faster when she heard George yell, "Constance! Come on!" She walked like she was carrying the weight of the world on her shoulders.

Deputy Morris got out his cell phone and called the hospital to alert them that George and Constance Bernard were most likely on their way to the hospital to find their kids.

IT WAS A FRIDAY AFTERNOON, and I had just gotten home from work. Laron had left the night before. Dyanna Jo and Ralley were finishing their homeschooling for the day and were putting the school books on the bookshelf.

"There's my girls," I said affectionately. The home phone rang, and Dyanna Jo reached over the kitchen counter to answer the phone.

"Hello," she said into the receiver. "Yes... this is....I see...." there was a long pause. "Can you hold a moment?" Dyanna Jo covered the mouthpiece, looked at me, and said, "Its DCS, they have two girls in custody. One is fifteen-months-old, and the other is six-weeks-old. They are in the hospital due to malnutrition and neglect. They asked if we would be willing to come to the hospital and stay the night with the baby. The baby should be able to come home tomorrow, but the fifteen-month-old will remain in the hospital for another week. They would like to place both girls in our home. We would need to head over to Children's Hospital now."

"What do you think? You would be the one to stay the night. I would have to bring Ralley home to sleep," I replied.

"I am okay with that, but I want to know that you are comfortable with the situation."

"I'm fine with it, but I would like all three of us to go to the hospital, and once you're settled, Ralley and I will come back home."

Dyanna Jo uncovered the phone, lifted it to her ear, and said, "Yes we would be happy to help. Where do we need to go? Yes... I understand... we're on or way. Thank you. Bye." She turned to look at me, "let's go, we'll talk in the car."

I grabbed the keys, Dyanna Jo ran upstairs and got a few overnight items, and we all headed out the door. On the way to the hospital, Dyanna Jo gave us the details.

As instructed, we entered the hospital, went to the reception desk, and asked for Sydney Hopkins. The lady at the desk turned, nudged the lady next to her, and nodded her head. She turned back to us and immediately rushed us to a side door. Once we got through the door, she said, "right this way."

We were taken down a long hall and asked to wait once we reached the elevators. A few minutes later, the elevator doors opened, and a security officer asked us to step in the elevator. We all looked at each other confused.

"Hello, sorry for the confusion. I am taking you up to meet with Sydney," he explained. "Brittany and Brianna's parents are in the main lobby. They arrived just before you got here. When they heard the girls were taken to the hospital, they came and demanded to see the children. We want you to use this elevator and the employee entrance, which I'll show you when you leave. We want to be sure to avoid any confrontation."

The elevator doors opened, and a woman stood right outside in the hall. "Hello, Mr. and Mrs. Baskin, I am Sydney Hopkins. I apologize for the drama. We didn't realize the parents would be here when you arrived."

"Thank you for ensuring the safety of our family," I said to both Sydney and the security guard. "Dyanna Jo will be staying with the baby tonight, and my daughter and I will return tomorrow when she is ready to leave."

Sydney nodded, "We're going to ask that you take this elevator and exit through the employee entrance when you leave. We will be sure to show you that entrance. You will be given a special passcode to use when you enter the same door tomorrow."

"Thank you. We appreciate it," I said. Sydney and the officer stayed with us. I noticed that Ralley's eyes were wide. This was undoubtedly an experience for her, and I didn't want her to feel scared.

"Wow! Armed security, a secret elevator, and a special code. There's no need to worry," I quipped. "It's the secret agent life of a foster family"

Ralley eyes relaxed. She smiled and said, "what an adventure."

Sydney and the security officer chuckled. Dyanna Jo and I quietly breathed a sigh of relief, knowing our remarkable preteen was taking things in stride.

When we got to the baby's room, a nurse was changing Brianna's diaper. Dyanna Jo gasped. The nursed turned and said, "are these the foster parents? You came at just the right time. I can show you how to care for Brianna's diaper rash."

Dyanna Jo walked over to the nurse and listened carefully as she gave instructions.

"That's terrible!" Ralley exclaimed. "Poor baby."

"The girls were taken into custody because of neglect," Sydney explained.

"I believe it, her poor little bottom," Ralley said.

Ralley and I sat and listened to Sydney while she talked to Dyanna Jo. During the night, Brianna will need feedings, diapers changed, and breathing treatments. The nurses will check in multiple times throughout the night to check Brianna's vitals. They will take care of the first breathing treatment so they can show Dyanna Jo how to do them.

"Well, I guess we got it from here," Dyanna Jo said. "If we need to know anything more, we'll ask the nurses."

I left Ralley with Dyanna Jo and followed Sydney down to the employee entrance. She gave me the code, showed me the keypad and gave me her business card. She said she would back tomorrow when it was time for Brianna to be discharged. After we said our good-byes, I headed back up the elevator to Brianna's room.

"I'm glad," I said after the nurses left, "that we were told about the family and given an alternate way up here."

"I know. This whole experience has been crazy," Dyanna Jo replied.

"It's like something out of a movie," Ralley marveled.

Ralley and I went down to the cafeteria to get dinner. We all ate together in Brianna's room. When it was time to leave, we hugged Dyanna Jo, and I made sure she understood that I wanted her to call me if there were any problems. She can be extremely independent at times and insist on doing things on her own. Ralley and I headed home. On the car drive home, Ralley was unusually quiet.

"Are you thinking about something?" I asked.

"Yes, I'm trying to understand how parents could treat their children the way they do."

"I know. It's hard to think a parent could do that to their child. Don't be too judgmental, though. If it wasn't for the Grace of God, I might be just like that. I'm thankful my parents raised me in church and taught me about God. Brittany and Brianna's parents might not have had loving parents to guide them when they were growing up. Or they could have had a great childhood, but they rebelled. Maybe they got caught up with the wrong people and messed themselves up. We don't know why people do the things they do, but we can pray that they turn from their wicked ways and turn to God."

"Thanks Dad, I am so thankful that I have two great parents who love me and keep me safe."

DYANNA JO'S Journal

The night was rough. Brianna had multiple lead wires that connected her to the machines that monitored her vitals and breathing. Whenever a lead wire got disconnected, an alarm would go off. The nurses showed me how to reconnect the wires; once they were reconnected, the alarms would go silent. No matter how hard I tried not to touch a wire when I fed her or changed her, a wire always came loose. The alarms went off all night. I worried that I was doing something wrong or that I was hurting her.

I quietly prayed, "God be with these precious girls. Help me to care for them properly and give them a love that they have never known. Heal them, Lord. I need you, God, I need your strength."

The night slowly passed. The nurses came in and out at shift change; each one would tell me I was doing great. God answered my prayers; He got through the night. It was time to take Brianna home. Leif was on his way. I never saw Brittany. Sydney arrived to check in on the girls. She told us that she would call us when Brittany was ready to be discharged. Sydney would bring her home.

On the drive home, I told Leif and Ralley the story of my night. Leif looked concerned, but I reassured him that I was fine, he didn't need to worry. The important thing was to care for Brianna until Brittany came home.

About an hour after we settled in at home, Brianna started to sneeze, and her nose started running. Her lungs sounded congested, so I gave her a breathing treatment. It didn't seem to help. She was so fussy. I held her and rocked while I sang.

"Jesus loves you this, I know, for the Bible tells me so. Little ones to Him belong, they are weak, but He is strong. Yes, Jesus loves you. Yes, Jesus loves you. Yes, Jesus loves you; the Bible tells me so."

Her sneezing and runny nose continued throughout the

night. I couldn't understand, she didn't sneeze at the hospital. Her lungs didn't even sound this bad. Something wasn't right. The difference between last night and tonight was completely different.

I cried out to God, "Please, God, show me how I can help her. I need you, Father, I need you." As I sat there praying, I felt one of the cats rub against my leg. We had two, Bonnie and Clyde. They were my babies. Immediately it hit me. The cats, she must be allergic to the cats. "Thank you, God, Thank you."

Leif and I took turns rocking, feeding, and changing Brianna's diapers. When morning finally came, I called Sydney and told her about our night. Unfortunately, Brianna had to go, and we would never meet Brittany. Sydney asked me to bring Brianna back to the hospital. She would have to find a new home for the girls. We were so disappointed. We wanted to help these girls. It was frustrating.

We took Brianna back to the hospital, kissed her little cheek, and said goodbye. We left and drove home in silence.

Now it was a matter of waiting for the next call. Little did we know, the next child would almost cause us to quit being foster parents.

19

CHRISTIAN

Sometimes, we can only guess what goes on in the lives of children who end up in foster care. Reports and written documents are one thing, but the real-time moments of poor parenting choices, dangerous situations and damage inflicted, are left to the imagination. We have to piece together what occurred—and when and how—to best serve these physically and emotionally traumatized children.

I learned as much about Christian's backstory with the clues available and envisioned the following scene. I could see it in my mind as vividly as a movie.

MARTIN BURPED SO LOUD the windows in his truck rattled. He had been drinking and had just chugged a twelve-ounce can of beer. He tossed it out the window as he drove down the road. He was on his way to visit his son, Christian, who was staying with his grandmother, Martin's mom, Betty. Martin and his ex-wife Cindy were in the middle of a messy custody battle made worse by the fact that neither parent could have custody of Christian. They were only allowed supervised visits for a few hours a couple of days a week.

Christian just turned three, and he cussed enough to make a sailor blush. His dad's chances of getting full custody of him were practically nil. Showing up drunk to visit your son doesn't help matters. But no one ever mistook Martin for a very smart feller. Some said he was about as sharp as a bowling ball.

Cindy wasn't much better. She was as sharp as a dull knife and unemployed. She smoked as if cigarettes would be banned at any minute. She couldn't keep a job to save her life. Cindy considered the perks of staying on welfare permanently, but the only drawback was she couldn't have custody of Christian if she didn't have a job.

Martin was driving from Tennessee to Georgia, where his mom lived. He turned into her neighborhood and almost took out a mailbox. He parked crooked in her driveway and walked up to the front door.

"Are you drunk?" his mom asked when he came through the door.

"No, I'm not drunk," he snapped, not bothering to hide his annoyance.

"You're just not sober," she said sarcastically.

Martin wanted to throw a few F-bombs and slap her. He didn't like women talking to him that way, even if it was his mother.

"You don't need to be a smart aleck," he said.

"I don't want you to see him when you're drunk. Come back when you're sober."

"I am sober," he snarled as he pushed his way past her. She almost fell.

Martin grabbed Christian and his sippy cup filled with juice. He started walking to the door.

"Where are you going? You know you can't take him. You have to have supervised visits."

"I'm taking him to the park, and if you want to come then, I suggest you get in the truck. I'm taking him, and that's all there is to it."

"Just go," she sighed deflated.

Betty had enough; she couldn't take this roller coaster anymore. She watched her son drive away. If Martin brought Christian back, she was taking him to DCS. The toddler was just as bad as his dad, maybe even worse. Christian routinely cussed her and threw screaming fits. She had given up on disciplining him because none of it worked. The only way to shut the kid up was to give him a sippy cup of juice. Betty kept the refrigerator stocked with juice. The only way to get Christian to sleep at night was to put him in the crib, with a sippy cup in his mouth, and another in the crib for later. Today was the last straw. She couldn't do it anymore; she was so tired.

Dyanna Jo's Journal

On Monday evening, we got a call from placement. They said they had a three-year-old boy named Christian who had been living with his grandma in Georgia. His mom and dad were in the middle of a messy custody battle. That was about as much as placement knew. I was told that when the caseworker dropped him off, she could give us more details.

Leif was on his way home from work. I asked if I could call her right back. I wanted to call my husband to confirm. After I called Leif and gave him the information, I called placement and told her we would be happy to take him.

A few hours later, Lisa Matthews showed up with Christian. He was big for his age. He looked like he was closer to five. He had short blond hair and hazel eyes. Christian followed Lisa through the door. He held a sippy cup in his hand and began to explore the house. Ralley followed him around.

"Please, have a seat," I said to Lisa.

"Thank you."

Lisa put her purse on the floor and looked in a manilla folder in her hands. "Christian just came into custody," She began. "His grandma lives in Georgia and after a fight with her son, who came and took Christian out of her home, decided she couldn't take the stress anymore. She contacted Georgia DCS and asked them to come and get the child. Because both of Christian's parents reside in Knox County, he was transferred to Tennessee. Neither parent qualifies to keep their son; they will need to work through their parenting plan in order for a judge to grant either of them custody. When DCS arrived at the grandmother's house, she gave them a few jugs of juice, a couple of sippy cups, and very little clothing. It's obvious she gave Christian way too much juice. I would recommend weaning him off the juice."

As Lisa left, she gave us the date and time for the child and family team meeting. She didn't bother to say goodbye to Christian.

Christian needed a bath badly. We took him upstairs, showed him his room, and walked him into the bathroom. While Leif started the bathwater, he proceeded to get Christian ready for his bath. I went and pulled out a pair of pajamas from our stash. When I returned to the bathroom, Christian was already in the tub.

"Dangerous," he said and pointed at the water.

"The water's not dangerous, Christian," I said.

"Dangerous," he said again.

"It's not dangerous," I said as I swirled my hand through the water.

Christian cursed.

Leif and I looked at each other. Ralley was standing in the

doorway. She was ready for bed. All I could think was, *What'd he say?* I decided that maybe I didn't hear him correctly. I started washing his body and could hear Christian growling. As I looked at his little face, I could see that his little teeth were almost completely rotted out of his mouth. I tried to comfort him as he continued to growl.

"Dangerous."

"No, Christian, you are doing great," I reassured him. "You are safe. The water is not dangerous." I realized I needed to finish this bath as quickly as I could. Once we got him out of the tub and dressed, we headed downstairs to fix dinner.

Lisa came right at dinner time, so we hadn't cooked or eaten anything. Leif grabbed a couple of things out of the pantry and quickly threw something together.

I lifted Christian into the highchair. Actually, let me rephrase that; I tried to put him in the highchair. He fought and kicked. He didn't want anything to do with that chair. Leif jumped in to help, but he couldn't get him in the chair either.

"Dangerous," he repeated with a few f-bombs added to his phrase.

We did everything we could to reassure him that he was safe. We finally gave in and put him on one of the dining chairs. He grabbed a piece of food and put it in his mouth. Immediately he spits it out. He grabbed another item, put it in his mouth, and spits it out. After he had tried everything on the table, he just started grabbing food and throwing it on the floor. He got off the chair and proceeded to stomp all over the food that was on the floor. He kept saying the word "dangerous." We didn't know what to do. Ralley did so well with him when he first got to the house. She thought he might be more comfortable with her. She tried to help him, but he threw his arm back and hit her in the face. Ralley stood there, stunned. It was time to remove him and all of us away from the situation. We would eat dinner later.

Christian cursed after Dyanna Jo announced that dinner was over. I looked after Ralley to see if she was okay. She seemed to be, but I could tell she was trying not to cry. He popped her good; Dyanna Jo looked mortified.

An hour later, we took him back upstairs and put him in bed with a watered-down juice cup. We hated to give him anything to drink in bed, but to try to give him some sense of normalcy, we gave him the sippy cup. We covered him up, and he raised the cup to his mouth. Immediately, he threw the cup and began to say the F-bomb over and over again. It was disconcerting to hear a three-year-old say such words.

I walked Ralley to her room, kissed her goodnight, and prayed for her.

"Dad."

"Yes, Ralley."

"My heart is breaking. I have never seen a little boy, so mean and hurting at the same time."

"I know Ralley. We have no clue what that poor boy has been through."

I could hear a loud banging noise coming from the room Christian and Dyanna Jo were in. I apologized to Ralley, told her I loved her, and ran down the hall.

Dyanna Jo was sitting on the bed, holding Christian as tight as she could while he banged his head against the wall. She was trying to pull him away from the wall and just continued saying, "Please stop Christian; I know, honey, you're okay. Please stop, you're hurting yourself."

I jumped in and took Christian from her arms. We tried for hours to get him to sleep without the juice. Finally, the poor guy wore himself out and fell asleep. Dyanna Jo was an emotional wreck. She went to our room and got ready for bed. I needed a shower desperately. Fighting to protect Christian was like wrestling Hulk Hogan. I was covered in sweat.

When I got out of the shower, I went into Christians room to check on him. When I returned to our room, Dyanna Jo said, "I have checked on him at least a hundred times while you were in the shower. That poor little boy. How could anyone do this to him?"

"I'm calling Lisa in the morning," I announced. "I'm going to tell her he needs to go to a home that is equipped to handle a child like him. He has issues that we've never been trained to handle."

"I think you're right," Dyanna Jo agreed. "I don't like that he hit Ralley. I can't imagine that he did that on purpose, but either way, we have to protect Ralley first and foremost."

"I am calling work and taking a personal day. I don't feel safe leaving you and Ralley home with him."

Dyanna Jo just sat there, nodding her head. Tears began to fall from her eyes. I held her until we both fell asleep.

I woke up the next morning hearing Dyanna Jo speaking to someone. I got out of bed, headed down the stairs, and found her in the kitchen talking on the phone. Christian was sitting on the floor, eating mini donuts.

"Lisa, you need to find him a home and come and get him now. This poor child is addicted to sugar. He only calms down if he has juice or some other sugary treat. We need to protect our daughter. He needs someone who is trained to handle a child with this kind of trauma."

Ten minutes later, Dyanna Jo hung up the phone and informed me that we would be meeting Lisa at Fellowship Church on Middlebrook Pike in two hours. She walked upstairs, leaving me standing in the kitchen, staring at Christian eating. A couple of minutes later, she was back down with clothes for Christian. She changed him in the middle of the floor while he ate his donuts. Dyanna Jo was done; she could not take this anymore.

We met Lisa in the parking lot of Fellowship Church. She told us that she found Christian a home for children who are sometimes violent and have behavioral issues. The foster parents had been given specific training on how to handle them.

"Seems like he shouldn't have been in our home, to begin with," I told Lisa.

"Your right," she replied. "We didn't have all the facts. We don't always get all the details, but I am truly sorry, he should never have been placed in your home."

We drove home once again in silence. Every placement we'd had, in three-weeks, had left us bewildered. Was it always going to be this hard? Did we do the right thing? I didn't have the answers.

RALLEY'S JOURNAL

We made the drive to meet Lisa and hand over Christian. We were exhausted physically, but a lot more emotionally. We didn't think our foster experience would be like this. I'm fairly sure Mom and Dad assumed we'd have one or two kids for a few months or more, and either we'd adopt them, or they'd go back to their family. Boy, were they wrong? Later that afternoon, we were all resting in the living room. Mom was sound asleep on the couch.

"Not much of a refuge, are we?" Dad piped up.

"What do you mean?" I asked.

"You know, we named you Ralley because we thought we had lost you when your mom was pregnant with you. I thought I'd lost her too because she was in bad shape. But both of you rallied and pulled through. I see being a foster family the same way—a rally point for these kids. Kids who are broken and hurt and need something stable with firm love. A place of refuge."

"Aww. That's nice, Dad. I feel that way too," I said.

"A rally point is a term the military uses for a designated place to go to if you're attacked and need to disengage, or something happens, and your unit gets scattered. You can all go to the rally point and get the accountability of people and equipment. Get reorganized and tend to any wounded. So, I see that as how our foster home can be."

"Five kids in less than four weeks," Mom said quietly. It looks like we woke her up, or maybe she just couldn't sleep.

"Maybe we should call the Mussina's," Dad said.

"I thought that too," Mom agreed.

Later that evening, I could hear Mom on the phone with Anna. She cried into the phone, she felt like a failure. It made me feel bad for her; honestly, I felt bad for all of us, especially the foster kids.

"How are we helping these kids when they are allergic to our cats, and we couldn't keep one from slugging Ralley?" she sniffled. She continued to tell Anna all about the whirlwind of having five kids in less than four weeks.

When she got off the phone, Mom said that Anna hadn't experienced anything close to what we had in the nine years they'd been foster parents. They had a few kids that only stayed for a day or two, but never back-to-back to back-to-back. She did say Christmastime was the worst time of the year for foster kids, and maybe this year was particularly bad.

Mom felt better after the call. We had Ben coming tomorrow for his monthly visit. We were going to ask him about it.

~

LEIF'S JOURNAL

Ben, our caseworker, showed up on time. We greeted and welcomed him into the living room. As foster parents, we have a caseworker that will visit the home once a month. Ben is who we would call if there were problems.

"So, how's everything been going?" he asked cautiously.

"Glad you asked," Dyanna Jo said dryly. "We have something to bounce off you. We've been foster parents for three weeks and have had five children placed in and out of our home. Well, actually, one of the children never made it to our house. We didn't think we would be a revolving door when we got into this."

"I know what you mean. We've had meetings about it because it seems bad this year. It's always bad around the holidays, but this year has been especially bad. Other foster families have gone through similar situations. Hopefully, it will slow down after the holidays."

"Well, we've thought about putting ourselves on hold until after the holidays," I said. "We want to think about it more to see if we still want to do this. We've had some difficult cases."

"I understand. It's tough for everyone having kids moved around a lot. Do you have any other concerns?"

"No. Just that."

"Okay, I'll let placement know not to call you until you tell me you'll start taking kids again."

After he left, we went out to dinner with Dyanna Jo's parents. They were treating us to a Christmas dinner even though it was over a week before Christmas. We went to Connor's Steakhouse in Turkey Creek.

"So, what did you tell Ben?" Pat asked after the waiter took our order. She knew we had been thinking of taking time off from fostering.

"We told him we were taking a month off," Dyanna Jo answered.

"What did he say?"

"He said that was fine. It's been crazy this year, and he doesn't blame us for wanting to decompress."

"Well, it seems like a good idea to me," Joe agreed.

The waiter brought our food. We made small talk for the rest of the dinner. When we were done, the waiter asked if we wanted any dessert. I immediately spoke up and told him I wanted the Bananas Foster without the bananas. He looked at me funny.

"Are you kidding me?" Dyanna Jo asked incredulously.

"What? You know I hate bananas."

"You did that at our wedding dinner. We went to Connors up in Pigeon Forge. I remember, our end of the table thought you were so weird."

"Well, that's the weirdest thing I've ever heard," Ralley opined.

"Does it drive you bananas?"

"Oh, brother!" Ralley, Dyanna Jo, and Pat all groaned at the same time, shaking their heads. Joe and I just laughed.

The waiter took the rest of the dessert orders with a baffled look on his face. He had a slight smile on his face when he came back a few minutes later with our desserts. I think he had gone from befuddled to amused.

"Here's your Bananas Foster sans bananas," he said when he put it on the table. He still looked amused. Pat, Joe, and Ralley seemed amused as well. Dyanna Jo was still shaking her head. I didn't waste any time; I started shoveling it into my mouth. It was good.

20

DECOMPRESSING

Ralley's Journal

I can't seem to get Christian off my mind. Writing about it helps, mainly because he was such a challenge. I couldn't believe how messed up he was. It burned me up when I saw those rotten teeth in his mouth. I knew kids were treated poorly, but being a foster family opened my eyes to how badly they were treated.

Mom said the whole night with Christian was very troubling, and she felt inadequate. She didn't think we could meet his needs. He needed a home where the foster parents had some training to deal with his behavior. I was glad when Lisa and Ben told us he shouldn't have been placed in our home. I didn't feel like such a failure and was relieved they were putting him in a house that was more capable of meeting his needs.

Dad looked drained, and Mom said I looked like I was put through the wringer too. She was mostly worried about me and didn't want the experience to make me resentful.

"You are such a good kid, and I don't want you to be miserable in your own home," she said. "You look really frazzled, and I'm worried."

"I'm drained, Mom," I replied. "Can we talk later?"

A week later, she knocked on my door as I was reading my Sherlock Holmes book. She said I was a book worm if there ever was one.

"You're only eleven, but you're a lot smarter than me." She started. "I had to beg my teachers to pass me in the twelfth grade. My grades weren't good enough, but I begged and pleaded, and they passed me with the lowest' D' they could, even P.E. I told them I wasn't going to college because I knew I would drown in that environment. I already had a job working in the office at my dad's accounting firm. I also wanted to go to Cosmetology school. I think they passed me because they knew another year wasn't going to help anything sink into my brain."

"What is Cosmetology school?" I asked.

"Beauty school, I wanted to do people's hair and nails. Make all the ladies look and feel pretty."

"That sounds fun."

"It was, but I made a lot of poor choices, got in trouble, and hung around a lot of bad people. I dropped out of beauty school. Yep, I am a beauty school drop out; but that's a story for another day."

A beauty school drop out. I heard that saying before and the way mom said it made me think it was supposed to be funny. I smiled and hoped that would appease her.

"Well, are you going to get to the point," I blurted out, "or are you going to keep standing there looking like death warmed over? Do you want to talk to me about Christian?"

Mom smiled and said, "You're not just smarter; you're also a smart Aleck. And I don't look like death warmed over. I'm an epidemic of health."

Oh, my goodness. I love her unintentional funny-isms and started belly laughing.

"What. Is. So. Funny?" she huffed.

"When you said 'epidemic,' I think you meant to say, 'epito-me,'" I explained. "You know, *the epitome* of health."

Then we both started giggling.

"Well, I'm glad I could give you a good laugh," Mom said. "I came here to talk to you about the whirlwind our fostering experience has been, and to see how you're doing."

"Are you over the whole fostering thing?" I asked.

"Only if you are," Mom said. "We're in this together or not at all."

"No, I'm not over it. I'll be fine if you decide to continue," I assured her.

"I'm sure we will. I just need to catch my breath. There are so many children who need homes."

"I need to catch my breath too. I think I lost most of it laughing at you."

Mom stuck out her tongue to demonstrate what an excellent example of maturity she was.

"I like you, kiddo. You are always so resilient. Sometimes it's hard to remember that you're eleven. I have an idea."

"What's that?"

"I'd like to spend some time with the Mussina's over the holidays. You know, socialize and pick their brains about fostering and stuff."

I thought that was a great idea! "Yeah, I'd love to see Melissa, Adam, and Cody."

"Then it's settled. I'll call Anna now."

Mom hurried out of the room, and I'm sure she made a beeline for the phone. I must admit, I felt better after talking to her. It was nice that she included me in the decision-making process and that my opinion mattered. No one said fostering would be easy, and it wasn't. But I knew in my heart that if we could help even one child, it was worth it.

LEIF'S JOURNAL

On December 22, we had the Mussina's over for an early Christmas dinner after a few weeks off from fostering. Whew— what a whirlwind. We looked forward to talking to Fred and Anna about the five kids who were placed in our home in just three short weeks.

They arrived at 5:03 p.m., precisely three minutes late, which was twenty-seven minutes early for them. Fred told me they are usually a half-hour late to most things due to the chaos of trying to get everyone out the door.

They have a twelve-passenger van, and Ralley was watching for them. They all piled out and came up to the house. Anna carried Cody, and Ralley had the door wide open by the time they reached our porch. Once they were all in, Ralley and Melissa disappeared upstairs to Ralley's room. I figured it would be a while before we saw them again.

Anna put Cody on the living room floor so he could crawl around while Adam and Samuel played with him. He had turned a year old a few days prior and was close to being able to walk. He kept using our coffee table to pull himself up and cruise around it.

Anna and Fred brought dessert—an apple pie and a cheesecake. I called first dibs on the cheesecake. Fred and I sat in the living room while Dyanna Jo and Anna finished getting dinner ready.

"So, tell me about these first few weeks," Fred said.

"Well, we had five children in three weeks. The first stayed for ten days, but the others were only here a day or two. One sibling group was two girls; Dyanna stayed at the hospital the first night and brought the baby home the next day. Her sister never made it to our house. I guess we technically only had four kids, but they felt like a lot more than that. "

"We've never had that happen to us. Our's usually stayed for a few months or longer."

"We asked one of the social workers why it's been like that, and she said it usually isn't. This year has been unusual."

"So, when are you going to reopen?" he asked.

"After the new year," I said. "Do you think we're wrong for taking a break? I worry that we're being wimps."

"No, I don't think you're wimps at all. Anna and I have done that a few times over the years. Sometimes, you need to do that if not for you then for the children you will take in the future. Those children need you to be one-hundred percent all the time."

"I know, but we just started, and we are already taking a break. The last two placements physically drained us, but all of them wore us out emotionally."

"That's the hardest part of it."

Dyanna Jo hollered at Ralley and Melissa to come down for dinner. They ran downstairs, and we all went into the dining room. I prayed for the food, and Fred and I inhaled it.

The cheesecake was outstanding. The apple pie was good too. By the time we got done, there wasn't much food left. The ham, turkey, dressing, yams, corn, green bean, and desserts were pretty much gone. Dyanna Jo, Anna, Ralley, and Melissa cleaned up the mess.

After dinner, the plan was to open presents, but we were all so stuffed that we sat around hardly able to move. The kids recovered more quickly than us old folks, and after a half-hour, they were chomping at the bit. Melissa and Ralley led the gift exchange between our families. The tree looked as if Santa visited us twice, if not three times over. There were presents to open tonight, and there were even more for Christmas Eve and Christmas Day.

After the kids opened their presents, Ralley and Melissa sat down.

"Aren't you going to bring the adults our presents?" I asked.

"No," they said in unison.

"Might I inquire as to the reason?"

"No," they said in unison once again.

"Apparently, they have a limited vocabulary," Anna said.

"Quite," I agreed. "Perhaps I will amble over to the tree and secure our presents."

"No," they said again. But cracks were forming on their stern faces, and those cracks took the form of smiles.

"Okay," Ralley said. "We'll get your presents."

They brought us our gifts, and we each took turns opening them. Gift cards, yep, you can't argue with that; always the easiest thing to purchase and everyone can use them. We visited for a while longer, and then the girls hugged and said their goodbyes. I was glad Ralley got to spend time with Melissa. We enjoyed having them all over, and I'm happy I got to talk to Fred. He was an immense help. Hopefully, Anna and Dyanna Jo got to talk while they were in the kitchen.

Dyanna Jo's Journal

I was thrilled that the Mussina's would be joining us for a Christmas celebration. They have become such great friends. I don't think we could have made it this past three weeks without their encouragement and support.

Anna and I were busy in the kitchen. The men and kids were all off doing their own thing. We could freely talk and not hold anything back.

"We've been foster parents for over ten years," Anna began, "and we've had about twelve children in our home."

"See, that's what I assumed would have happened for us. Instead, it's been a revolving door!" I exclaimed.

"That wears me out just thinking about it. Pretty overwhelming, huh," Anna said, sympathetically.

"Yeah, it seems to be happening a lot lately. I've spoken to a few of the foster parents we met while attending the PATH classes, and they said they've been experiencing the same thing. They can't keep a kid in their homes for more than a day or two."

"I can't blame you for taking a few weeks off," Anna said. "Hopefully, after the new year, it will settle down, and you'll get some consistency."

"You don't think we're being unreasonable?" I asked. "I mean, we've only been doing this for three weeks, and we're already taking a hiatus."

"Let me put this in perspective for you. After six years, we had our fifth child placed in our home. You've had five kids in three weeks, and don't tell me the girl who stayed in the hospital didn't count. She counts; the possible threat from the parents, the hospital stay, the alarms, and the baby's allergic reaction. Everything you did was to bring both of those girls home safely. You can't discount that. So, no, I don't think you're unreasonable. It's completely up to you how often you want to take children. Whenever you think you need a break, take it. If you have a placement, but it's emotionally challenging, take advantage of respite."

"I remember them talking about respite in PATH. What is that again?" I asked

"Respite care provides you with a temporary break, whether it is to address an emergency, care for a family member, or take a quick break. It's necessary for reducing foster parents' stress, and it promotes the stability of the children in your home. You're not giving the children back; there are people who have been approved by DCS who can watch the kids for a couple of days."

"We need to keep that in mind," I replied. "If we have a difficult, long-term placement and we need a break, I wouldn't feel guilty taking advantage of the services that DCS provides. It makes total sense as to why they offer it."

I was grateful for her encouragement. Sometimes, I felt like I was getting in over my head. Leif and I wanted to be good foster parents, but we weren't off to a promising start. I also worried about how all this turnover was affecting Ralley. She seemed to be handling it well. I just hoped things settled down after the new year.

When we sat down at the table, there was plenty of food—enough for leftovers, or so I thought. Boy, was I wrong? All the boys, that includes the adult boys, packed the food away. Leif wasn't shy about it either. By the time we got done, there was hardly anything left.

We were thankful when Ralley and Melissa helped us clean; that made it go a lot faster. We needed to digest all that food before we opened presents, so we sat around and talked. I enjoyed Fred and Anna. It was nice having a couple who could help us learn how to navigate this journey we were on.

ON THE 27TH, we had to go to a continuing education class. Unfortunately, DCS didn't take a break for the holidays. The training was held every three months on the last Thursday of the month; we had to be sure to attend. The class was in the evening from six to nine p.m. The Mussina's told us they usually consisted of reviewing what we learned in the PATH class. Sometimes they covered something new.

However, tonight, they discussed respite and had families there to tell you how important it is to take a break if needed. *Thank you, Lord!* I thought. It was confirmation that we were doing the right thing.

It was nice to meet other people who were also struggling

during this season. The stories we heard were heart-wrenching but at the same time heartwarming. The ones who struggled but came out on the other side were so encouraging. Some of the parents had experienced the same problems and were as frustrated as we were. We all hoped the New Year would be different.

21

DEVIN AND MATTHEW

Leif's Journal

Discovering the back story for Devin and Matthew was easy. The parents attended all of the child and family team meetings, court appearances, and visitation. They cooperated—what a breeze. Devin and Matthew were the first children we took in who made us feel like foster parents.

BRIAN AND WANDA had been married for three years. They had a son named Devin, who was eighteen-months-old. Brian was a redhead, freckles to spare, and had pasty white skin. Devin took after his father. Brian was so happy when he found out that Wanda was pregnant again.

Just a few weeks ago, Wanda gave birth to a beautiful boy; she named Matthew. He had brown eyes, brown hair, and caramel-colored skin. It was apparent Brian wasn't the father. Matthew looked nothing like Brian. Wanda broke down and admitted that she had an affair, but she promised she'd broken it off.

Pedro was single and owned a new construction business. When Pedro met Wanda, he was immediately attracted to her. He didn't know Wanda was married. He was devastated when she told him. She broke off the relationship and refused to see him. When Matthew was born, there was no question that Pedro was the father.

Brian tried to make the best of it, but he couldn't get past the affair. It didn't help that Wanda was taking off every night and leaving him with the kids. Brian and Wanda lived with Thelma, Brian's mom. Thelma was not thrilled with the arrangement.

To deal with the situation, Brian started to fall back into some of his old habits. His drug of choice? Cocaine. With Brian getting high and Wanda disappearing at all hours of the night, she was left to care for the kids. Not just her grandson but another man's baby. She couldn't blame Matthew for his mother's choices. The question was, who was his father.

Between her son's drug habit, and her daughter-in-law abandoning her kids every night, Thelma was getting tired of the drama. She loved those boys; she didn't care who Matthews's father was. She knew it was time to contact DCS.

Thelma and her husband, Bill, had their share of problems over the years. Bill and Thelma were both recovering alcoholics. When Brian was younger, DCS came and removed him from their home. They got sober and worked their parenting plan to get him back. Even after Brian had returned, Bill and Thelma had to meet specific requirements, or they would lose Brian again.

Thelma knew she had to call. She had to follow the rules if she had any hope of helping her son or keeping the kids herself. She took the risk and called DCS.

DCS removed the boys, and Pedro was notified that he had

a son. Unfortunately, Pedro had his own problems with alcohol. He just started his construction business but couldn't keep a job because he would show up drunk. Losing Wanda was difficult for him, and he drank to take the pain away. It never worked.

They all had a long road to travel, but they knew that it was time to get their act together for the sake of the kids.

DYANNA JO's **Journal**

The holidays were over, and we had a month to decompress. It was the middle of January, and we decided to start retaking kids. As soon as we contacted Ben, they called about a brother and sister who were fourteen and sixteen. They were with a foster family that was going on vacation but couldn't take the kids because they were going out of state. We declined; we didn't feel comfortable having kids that were older than Ralley, even if it was only for a week.

An hour later, placement called again and said they had two boys, an eighteen-month-old and a six-week-old. We were given the specifics. Placement had far more details about this case. DCS truly believed that the family was going to work the plan. If the parents didn't, grandma was going to do all she could to get legal custody. However, due to her past, she had to meet specific requirements to get them home with her.

We felt good about this case. We knew most of the story, and we knew that the boys would be with us anywhere between a month to six months. We accepted the placement.

About three hours later, at 7:22 p.m., they arrived. We hadn't met the caseworker before. We opened the door, she showed her ID, and we invited her and the kids into our home. The caseworker, Madison Taylor, was tall with beautiful dark brown, almost black, eyes. They showed a kindness that made us relax immediately. Her face was round with a medium shade of ebony, which was beautifully enhanced by her shoulder-length black shiny hair.

"Hello, this little guy is Matthew," she said as she handed me the baby carrier. She gently turned and lifted a little boy who was hiding behind her, into her arms. "And, this is Devin." She gave him a tight squeeze.

We walked into the living room and got comfortable. Ralley went over and touched Matthew's hand. She looked up at me with the sweetest face and smiled. She then walked over and sat on the floor by Madison's feet. Madison put Devin down next to Ralley, and immediately they began to play with the toys sitting close by.

Madison began to tell us all about the case. She told us about the boys' parents and grandmother. The child and family team meeting was already scheduled for two days from today. Unfortunately, Leif would be at work and unable to attend. Madison told us that Matthew needed breathing treatments. She had a nebulizer with her, as well as the medicine we would use. He was having some breathing problems, due to his parents and grandparents smoking. You could smell the strong smoke odor on their clothes.

After Madison left, we gave both of the boys a bath. Devin was tired, so we put him in the crib. Devin was such a good little guy. Ralley fed Matthew his bottle and burped him; he didn't act sleepy. Leif had to go to bed because he had to get up early for work. Ralley and I put Matthew in the baby swing and sat on the couch, just staring at him. We were both lost in our own thoughts. When Matthew was fast asleep, we turned off the lights, got him out of the swing, and headed to bed. I walked Matthew up to our room and placed him in the cradle, which was right by my side of the bed. I felt safer keeping such a small baby right next to me.

Two days had passed, and the kids were still in our home.

We were thankful for that, no revolving door with these kids. On the day of the child and family team meeting, I called Mom and asked her to stay with Ralley and the boys. Once everyone was settled, I headed to the meeting. I went through security and checked in with Mr. John Deere. You could always count on him being there to greet you. Once they were ready to start the meeting, Mr. John Deere made the announcement, and multiple people got up and headed over to Madison, who was waiting by the double glass doors. We were led down a hallway that Leif and I had never been down. Madison arrived at our destination, turned, and invited us to step into the room. The room was much larger than any of the other rooms we visited. We all piled in and found seats around a large oval table. It was a crowded room. All the key players were there: FSW, DCS caseworker, Guardian ad litem, foster parent, three parents, and two grandparents. That's a lot of people representing the family.

The meeting was cordial, no fighting, and no arguing. Everyone had the children's best interests at heart. The parents were still struggling with their demons, but they truly loved their children. Everyone agreed that the goal was to get the children safely in the care of the grandparents. Brian and Wanda needed to get jobs, sober up, and move into their own apartment. The grandparents had a few things they needed to take care of: home studies, PATH classes, and background checks. All the steps that foster parents take. We set a visitation schedule that would allow all the family members to have one-on-one time with the kids. They must be in a supervised environment. I was to drop the kids off at the DCS office and leave them for two hours. There were three visitations a week. One day for the grandparents, another day to Brian and Wanda, and the final day belonged to Pedro.

The children were behind on their vaccinations. I need to call and schedule an appointment at the health department.

They provided me with information about WIC, a federally-funded program designed to provide supplemental food assistance and nutrition education to low-income pregnant, postpartum, and breastfeeding women, infants, and children until age five. Foster parents also qualified for WIC. WIC would allow us to get Matthew's formula and additional food for Devin. We would be given a specific dollar amount to purchase necessities for the children—a one time allowance. The money would not be given directly to us; Madison was required to schedule a time to meet at a specific store, and after I shopped, she would pay the bill. We would only be able to purchase particular items like bottles, clothes, blankets, diapers, and bedding.

It would take time before I could get scheduled with WIC, so Madison gave me a couple of cans of formula to get me through until my appointment. I learned so much from this meeting.

There was only one last thing to take care of, homeschooling. I spoke with Madison and explained the difficulties of homeschooling Ralley with Devin and Matthew underfoot. She informed me that I could put both of the boys in daycare. DCS had a list of specific daycare centers that qualify to take foster children. I would complete all of the paperwork, but DCS would pay for it up to a specific rate. If the daycare exceeded that rate, we'd have to pay the difference. My head was swimming when I left.

I drove home overwhelmed, but it was a good overwhelmed. There was so much to do to help this family heal and move forward. We would be there for them. There was so much I needed to do; appointments with the Health Department, meeting Madison to shop, getting the kids to visitations, getting the boys in daycare, and getting an appointment with WIC. Thank God I was a bit OCD when it came to this kind of stuff. I always keep my planner with me so I can write notes, make To-

Do lists, and then plan. Thankfully, I brought it with me and could refer to it to get everything done.

I got home, walked through the door to a room full of family. Leif was back from work, Mom was holding Matthew, and Ralley was rolling around on the floor with Devin. A happy home. I am so thankful for the gifts God has given us.

"So, was it a good meeting? Who was there from Devin and Matthew's family? What's the story?" Leif asked, not letting me answer a single question. I couldn't help but notice the smile on his face.

"Well, hello to you too, dear," I replied.

"Hello, now answer my questions," he said facetiously.

I began to fill them in on everything that happened: every key player, family members, and a bit of history.

"So, Wanda had an affair with Pedro?" Mom asked. "Was it awkward having Brian and Pedro there?"

"I could tell that there was some tension, but no one got in each others face. There were glances, but they handled everything well. Keep in mind, Pedro just found out he had a son two days ago. Brian knew for six weeks that there was another man. In my opinion, it shows a lot of character when all these people can sit in a room, keep their drama out of it, and focus on helping the boys. They've done a paternity test on Pedro, but it could take a few weeks to get the results. Looking at Pedro and Matthew, there is no doubt Pedro is the father."

22

———

SETTLING INTO A ROUTINE

Having a six-week-old and an eighteen-month-old in the house was nice. After a week, we were starting to feel comfortable.

"So, how did it go with homeschooling now that Devin and Matthew are in daycare?" I asked

"It went great. I was able to get the lessons taught, and Ralley could work on her homework without interruptions or distractions."

"What time are you picking them up?"

"Since you're home, I'll go get them now."

"I'll go check on Ralley."

I traipsed up to the bonus room. We had turned it into her bedroom and schoolroom. It was 21 x 13, big enough for one end to be her bedroom area, and the other end to be her school work area. We had put a desk there for the MacBook she used for schoolwork.

"Hey, Ralley."

"Hey, Dad."

"Are you done with your homework?"

"Yes. I was just doing some surfing on the internet."

"Anything interesting?"

"No, not really."

"I thought we could have a father-daughter date. It's been a while since we've done that."

"Now, Dad, that's an excellent idea."

"The mall?"

"But of course! Where else would we go?"

I called Dyanna Jo to make sure there wasn't anything planned for dinner and to see if she was good with Ralley and me having a date at the mall. As always, she told us to go ahead.

We left and went to the mall. We got our Starbucks and walked around. While we browsed around Sears, she saw a pair of jeans she liked. She took the jeans off the rack and went to try them on. I wondered if she'd ask me to buy them.

She came out of the room and said, "I'm ready to go now."

"Are you going to put the jeans back?" I pointed to the jeans in her hands.

"Nope, I'm going to buy them," she declared and smiled.

"With what?"

"Well, you see Dad, they make this stuff called money, and when you have enough of it, you can buy a pair of jeans." She replied with a tilt of the head and a smirk on her face.

"Where did you get this stuff called money? Did you rob a bank?"

"No, I did some things around the house, and Mom gave me some money for helping her."

"What did you do?"

We started walking toward the nearest cashier. "I cleaned the bathrooms and vacuumed."

"And she paid you for that? I thought that was just part of doing your chores around the house."

"She wanted to pay me for it, so I could start learning how to manage money."

"Oh, okay," I said. When did she become miss independent?

When we got home, Ralley had to model her jeans. Dyanna Jo thought they were adorable. She loved the fun patterns, but mainly she liked the jeans in particular. The jeans had some designs on the back pockets and had a stonewashed look.

"Where on earth did you get those?" Dyanna Jo asked. "I want a pair!"

"You can't buy a pair. We would look stupid as twins. Leave that to Dad and Uncle Anders."

And with that, Ralley headed upstairs. She wasn't angry, but the thought of her mom dressing like her was just too mortifying. Dyanna Jo and I had a good laugh over that.

"We have a preteen in our midst." Dyanna Jo said as she laughed.

I could see Devin lying on the floor surrounded by toys, but the poor guy was asleep face down. Dyanna Jo had just fed Matthew his evening bottle right before we got home. She placed Matthew in the baby swing while I picked up Devin and started to walk towards the stairs.

"Would you mind giving Matthew a quick bath when you return?" Dyanna Jo asked.

"Sure, I'll be right back."

I came back downstairs and gently took Matthew out of the swing. He was starting to look tired. I gave him a bath, and before I could get his pajamas on, he fell asleep. As he slept, I got the nebulizer, added the medicine, and held it close to his mouth and nose. I made sure the mist covered his nose, and he breathed it in. After his breathing treatment, I kissed him on his forehead, prayed for him and his family, and put him in his cradle.

DYANNA JO'S Journal

Today I had to take the boys to the Health Department for their vaccinations. Honestly, I wasn't looking forward to the busy waiting room or the long wait. Madison agreed to allow the boy's parents and Grandma to be at the appointment. The wait would give them time to visit with the boys. Brian, Wanda, Pedro, and Thelma were all there. It's was impressive how the family was working their parenting plan.

The wait wasn't as long as I'd expected. Devin was glad to see his parents and squealed when he saw Thelma. Pedro spent all of his time with Matthew.

After a twenty-minute wait, Wanda and I went back with the boys. The checkup and vaccines took about thirty minutes. They were both doing well, and the doctor wanted Matthew to keep having breathing treatments. She prescribed more of the Xopenex. Everything else looked great.

After the appointment, Devin and Matthew's family said goodbye with hugs and kisses. It was so nice to actually visit with the family. They were open and honest about their situation. I headed to Walgreens to get the Xopenex. The boys fell asleep in the car on the way home. When the boys and I got home, Ralley helped me get them in the house, and then she went up to her room to finish her school work.

"So, how did the visit go?" Leif asked.

"It wasn't bad. The boys are doing great. Matthew still has to do breathing treatments."

"Were the parents still playing nice with each other?"

"Yes, they were. Brian and Pedro didn't talk to each other, but I didn't sense any animosity between them either. I don't suppose they would have much to say to each other. It's not like they are going to be friends or anything. Wanda talked to Pedro because of Matthew, but I don't think she wanted to talk to him much. It's a strange situation. It was obvious that Pedro loves his son."

IT FELT good being in a groove with the boys. We had a set schedule, and the kids fit in so well. We were all getting attached, but we knew that they would be leaving us one day. Seeing the family working so hard made it bearable.

We received a call on March 10th, letting us know that the boys would be going home with Thelma the next day. It will be quiet around here. Although, I don't believe our home will stay quiet for long. Placement called us multiple times over the last couple months. We decided that we would focus on Matthew and Devin and their family. They deserved our undivided attention. I am truly going to miss these sweet boys.

RALLEY'S JOURNAL

Shopping with Dad or Mom is fine, but it sure feels good to buy stuff with my own money. I loved the look on Dad's face when I bought those jeans. He seemed quite perplexed. I'm glad Mom pays me for vacuuming and cleaning the bathrooms. I take ten percent and put it in the offering at church and take ten percent and save it. The rest I use, any way I want. So, I saved it until I had enough to buy the jeans.

I'm glad I'm learning to handle money. Mom and Dad told me they hadn't been very smart with money when they were younger. They had learned some hard lessons. They wanted me to benefit from their experience and the lessons they learned from the school of hard knocks.

Being a foster family is a lot of work. Devin and Matthew are fun, but they are a handful. Even with all the hard work, it's rewarding being able to help them and provide a stable home for them while their parents got their act together. Some of the kids come from sad situations, and I am thankful for the family I have.

I was glad we decided to continue fostering. We wanted to adopt, but in the meantime, we could be a place for these kids to have stability and maybe sow some seeds of the gospel in them. Mom and Dad were good about that. We always prayed for the kids when we put them in bed. Hopefully, someday those seeds would sprout into something.

The next six weeks went by fast. Brian, Wanda, and Pedro were able to visit with Devin and Matthew quite a bit during that time. We gave them our phone number so Brian and Wanda could call and say good night to Devin. Pedro called a few times during the weeks for updates on Matthew. They never abused it or came to our house.

On March 11th, Madison came and picked up the boys. She was taking them to live with their grandma, Thelma. Brian and Wanda moved out of her house, and they were trying hard to get clean. We asked if Pedro was going to get to have any kind of custody of Matthew. Madison told us that there were a few things Pedro had to figure out, but the paternity test came back a match. Matthew was Pedro's son.

Mom said it finally felt like we were a real foster family. With all the initial turnover, it just didn't seem like we were doing any good. But this time, it felt different, like we had made a difference. We gave Devin and Matthew a stable place to rally while their family got things worked out.

23

CARRIE

Ralley's Journal

I t wasn't too long before we had another placement. As always, we gathered the child's backstory in bits and pieces. I was somewhat older, and I was allowed to listen in as Mom and Dad discussed the troubling details, rehashing it verbatim. Some of this information came from our foster baby's birth family. Here's what we learned about newborn baby Carrie.

IN DECEMBER 2007, Gwen stood in the doorway of her daughter's apartment and surveyed the filth. It wasn't anything she hadn't seen before. Her daughter, Stephanie, was thirty-two years old and had been doing drugs since the age of seventeen. She lived in the Adam C. Clark housing project in downtown Knoxville.

Gwen didn't go to her daughters very often. For safety, she always carried a gun in her purse. It was disconcerting to see her daughter living in a pigsty and such a dangerous place. She was used to it, but it still was difficult to understand.

Stephanie had tried multiple rehabs; the last was eight years ago. She never stayed clean. Stephanie had four children in addition to Carrie. Gwen had adopted the oldest two, an eight-year-old boy named Jaron and a six-year-old girl named Jaylee. Stephanie's sister, Candace, adopted the other two, a four-year-old girl named Marsha and a two-year-old boy named Marcus. All of the children had different fathers, and a couple didn't know who their father was. It was a mystery.

Gwen perilously walked through the living room. There were clothes scattered everywhere. They looked and smelled as if they hadn't been washed in years. Gwen walked past the kitchen and saw the sink was overflowing with dishes that hadn't been cleaned in ages. Dried food was caked on the dishes. Ants were crawling on the counter and in the sink, and flies had called dibs on the table and overflowing trash can.

Thankfully, she reached her daughter's bedroom without seeing the bathroom. She didn't even want to see the waste or filth. The last time Gwen was at Stephanie's apartment was a year ago. At that visit, she tried to clean the apartment, but she couldn't believe how bad it was when she got to the bathroom. Just thinking about it made her feel nauseous.

Her daughter was in bed, sound asleep. Not surprisingly, a man laid beside her. He woke up with a jolt.

"Hey, old woman," he said unkindly, "you make it a habit of barging into people's apartments?"

"When it's my daughter's apartment, I do," Gwen snarled with equal disrespect.

His mouth formed the word 'oh,' but he didn't make any attempt to move.

"I need to talk to my daughter; can you please leave?"

"I don't have any clothes on."

"You don't have anything I haven't already seen."

He shrugged, got out of bed, bent over, and snatched up his clothes off the floor. He did not attempt to cover himself as he went into the bathroom. Gwen kept a watch on the bathroom while her hand rested on her pistol. The .22 wasn't big, but she liked it because she could handle it, which made her feel secure. Sometimes she wondered if that feeling was an illusion in this neighborhood. She was wary of rough-looking dudes—most of the guys her daughter had over wouldn't be mistaken for choir boys. Thankfully, this current guy finished dressing in the bathroom and left quietly.

Through all of that, Stephanie still slept. Gwen tip-toed toward her daughter, walking over clothes, shoes, beer bottles, syringes, and some things she couldn't identify. Her shoes were contaminated—she'd have to throw them away, along with her outfit when she got home.

"Stephanie?" Gwen tapped Stephanie on the shoulder. Her daughter moaned and then quieted. Gwen tapped her harder.

"Stop it, Gerald," Stephanie said, and then went back to sleep.

Gwen hauled off and punched her in the arm. That finally got through to her pickled brain. Stephanie's eyes opened, and Gwen could tell she was having a tough time focusing. When she did focus, her face registered surprise and then defiance, Gwen expected that. Stephanie had always been defiant when it came to her and her husband, Stanley. She was always taking up with hoodlums, dirtbags, anyone she knew her parents would hate.

"What do you want?" Stephanie snapped.

"I've been trying to call you. When I didn't get an answer, I came to tell you that your father died two days ago. He had a heart attack. The funeral is two days from now. Tomorrow will be the receiving of friends at Rose Mortuary on Western Avenue at 6 p.m. Can you remember that, or do I need to write it down?"

"I can remember if I want."

But you don't want to, Gwen thought. "Well, I just wanted to let you know he's dead."

Stephanie got out of bed, and Gwen noticed her abdomen had a small bulge.

"Are you pregnant?" she asked, afraid of what the answer would be.

"Yes."

"Well, don't expect me or your sister to take it. I can't, I'm fifty-four, already have two of your kids, and Stanley just died. I don't know how I am going to handle what I have. Candace can't either; she has her hands full with her three kids and your two. She's also taking Marcus and Marsha to physical therapy a couple of times a week because of all the drugs you did while pregnant with them."

"Maybe I'll keep it."

Gwen laughed. "The minute you go to the hospital, DCS will take custody. Your last two were born drug-exposed, and you're on their radar."

"What do you care?"

"I care because I've seen what drugs do to these babies. You keep getting pregnant, popping out drug-exposed babies, and you never know who the father is."

When there was no response, Gwen asked, "Do you know who this one's father is?"

"No."

That didn't surprise Gwen. *Stephanie slept with so many men; it would be hard to know. It's a wonder how she hasn't picked up a disease,* Gwen thought.

"I'll leave now."

Stephanie just walked into the bathroom, shut the door, and turned on the shower. Gwen left, and when she got to her car, she sank into the driver's seat and sat for a minute. A small tear escaped her eyes and lazily ran down her cheek. It had been years since she'd cried after visiting her daughter. She'd become numb. She was crying now because her Stanley was gone, and their prodigal child couldn't care less. "Will she ever return to you, God," she pleaded.

LEIF'S JOURNAL

I'm not sure I'll ever get used to taking care of children who are born drug-exposed. Carrie was placed in our home one week after Devin and Matthew left. March 11, 2008, after a harrowing birth, a premature baby girl of thirty-six weeks, was born. The baby was addicted to marijuana, cocaine, and barbiturates. The mother had no prenatal care.

According to DCS, Carrie's birth mother arrived at St. Mary's Hospital as high as a kite. A nurse wheeled her straight up to the maternity ward, but before they got off the elevator, Stephanie asked for an epidural.

PATTY, one of the nurses in the maternity ward, turned towards Donna and said, "I'm going to call DCS, that woman is as high as they get. Did you hear she asked for an epidural even before she got off the elevator?"

"Shannon told me when I came in for my shift," Donna replied. "She's definitely in outer space. Have you checked the computer yet?"

Patty pulled the keyboard closer and started to type; she entered the social security number, and the screen flashed a warning to contact DCS if the patient was admitted to the maternity ward. It also listed four children under Stephanie Wilson's name, two were drug-exposed at birth.

"I can assure you that the one she's about to deliver will test positive as well. She was floating around the room earlier," Patty sighed.

"That's sad! I wish they could tie her tubes while she's here," Donna said.

"Oh, don't get me started! As angry as I get, I'm glad she didn't have an abortion. She's giving her baby a life."

"That's true, at least she's doing that," Donna agreed.

Stephanie gave birth later that day. As soon as the doctor had the baby in his arms, the baby was in distress — no heartbeat was detected.

After a few minutes, the neonatal pediatrician resuscitated the baby girl. She was breathing, but not as good as the doctor would like. Stephanie was still being sewn up when the baby was taken to the Neonatal Intensive Care Unit, NICU. A sample of the baby's blood and meconium was sent to the lab. Meconium is the first fecal material excreted by a newborn. It's a depository in which the drugs are exposed. There was no surprise when the tests came back positive for marijuana, cocaine, and barbiturates.

The NICU nurses, unfortunately, had plenty of experience with drug-exposed babies. This particular baby weighed six pounds, one ounce, and measured twenty inches long. Considering all she'd gone through in utero, that was a decent weight and size. They hooked her up to all kinds of monitors and were especially concerned about her breathing. It had worsened since she got to the NICU. They put a nasal cannula on her to help her breathing. So far, things hadn't improved.

Stephanie announced that the baby's name was Carrie. She hadn't seen nor asked about the baby. CPS informed her that DCS had taken custody of the baby, and she'd have her first court date in two days. She said she didn't care and walked right out of the hospital.

At 2:41 a.m. on March 12th, Carrie stopped breathing. Her pulse was feeble. The nurses began treating her and paged the on-call doctor who arrived in a few minutes. Before the doctor could get there, the nurses had already gotten her breathing again. Her pulse was better. The baby screamed and cried for several hours. She had barely touched any of her bottles—not enough to gain weight. After many hours, she went to sleep.

Poor little Carrie experienced withdrawal from all the drugs her mom did. They say that drug withdrawal is extremely difficult for a grown adult who knows exactly what is happening to them. Imagine a six-pound baby enduring that kind of stress not only during utero but after they were born. Carrie was agitated most of the day and slept fitfully as her vital signs kept fluctuating. Her situation was tenuous the first few days in the NICU, but by the fourth day, she started to eat more and wasn't as anxious. She slept more as a newborn should.

Over the next few days, Carrie grew stronger and stabilized.

Dyanna Jo's Journal

"I can't believe we haven't gotten a call from placement yet," I observed. "It's been four days since Devin and Matthew went home."

"I know what you mean," Leif agreed. "I thought for sure we'd have another child by now."

"Well, even though we want another child, it is nice to have a break."

"It's kind of like recharging our batteries."

It was Saturday afternoon, and we were hanging around the house when the phone rang. It was placement, they had a baby girl they'd like to place in our home. I accepted and hung up the phone. I told Leif about the call.

"So, when are they going to bring the baby over?" Leif asked when I told him about the call.

"The baby's at St. Mary's right now. She was born drug-exposed, and they aren't sure when she'll be leaving the hospital. They just wanted to have a home lined up for when she can leave. Get this; she was born on March 11th."

"That's the day Devin and Matthew went back to their family."

"I know, it's amazing how we were saying goodbye to the boys on the same day, this baby girl was born, and she would be living with us in the coming days."

I continued to tell Leif all about the call. He had so many questions. It cracks me up when he does that because I'm usually the ten thousand questions lady. Leif isn't very excitable, but when we get a call from placement, he becomes a different man.

"Linda, the lady in placement, said one of us could go to the hospital to meet Carrie, but only one."

"Are you wanting to go see her right now?" he asked.

"Yes! I would love to!" I exclaimed.

"Well, go ahead. Ralley and I will see what kind of mischief we can get into while you're gone."

The excitement came over me. I didn't say another word. I ran upstairs, cleaned myself up, and took off to meet Carrie. I wasn't sure what to expect once I got there. After I found out where to go, the person managing the desk had to call DCS before I was authorized to enter the NICU. Thank goodness I didn't forget my ID.

After I was officially approved as the foster parent, the nurse took me to an area where I had to follow specific instructions: 1. place all personal items in the locker provided. 2. wash hands for at least two minutes following the six steps of hand washing allotting at least 20 seconds for each step. The six steps were palms/fingers/web spaces, back of hands, fingers/knuckles, thumbs, fingertips/wrists, and forearm up to the elbow. 3. Do not touch anything after hand washing. 4. The nurse would put on my hospital gown, mask, and hat. I was told that at least one-third of all annual deaths in the NICU are caused by infection. They took all precautions to fight against infection.

It was all so overwhelming, but when I walked into Carrie's room, and looked down at her beautiful face, all my anxiousness went away. I looked up from the baby's bed and saw two women standing on the opposite side of the room. One of the ladies was a nurse and the other was wearing a DCS ID badge. Most likely, she was the caseworker. Introductions were made, but we weren't allowed to shake hands with each other.

The caseworker spoke up, "Hi, my name is Thyme McBroom. Thyme, as in the herb, and not the clock?"

"I like that. I've never heard anyone named that before, I love unique names," I replied.

"Well, people have come up with all kinds of puns, thanks to my name," she said dryly.

"I can imagine. Just a heads up, the more we get to know you, my husband may be one of those people. He loves puns! I can't stand them, mainly because I don't get half of them, and then I become the butt of the joke." I said, shaking my head.

"This little lady," Thyme said, pointing to the baby, "is Carrie Wilson."

"Has the mom been by to see her?" I asked.

"No," she said sourly. "I don't think she will. I've dealt with her before. She has four other children who have been adopted by family members and in each case she didn't come to meetings, court hearings, or show any interest in the children. She left the hospital a day after Carrie was born and expressed no interest in spending time with her; doesn't surprise me."

"I can't imagine that. Having a baby girl and not wondering how she is. I had a miscarriage almost a year ago, and I was a mess for months. It still hurts."

"Unfortunately, she's a drug addict, and that's all she cares about."

"At least she had the baby. She could've had an abortion."

"That's true," Thyme agreed.

Thyme left a few minutes after we talked. She told me about the child and family team meeting set for next Friday the 21st. I stayed for a few hours, helping with feedings, changing Carrie's diaper, and holding her. I loved holding her and watching her sleep. Her chest rose and fell so peacefully, and her beautiful ebony skin was so pretty. Her hair wasn't as curly as I thought it would be. It was so soft and straight with random curls around her head. I counted a total of five. I would have to look into caring for her hair; I knew absolutely nothing about that.

When it was time to leave, I felt impatient. I wanted to take Carrie home with me, but they weren't sure when she could leave the hospital. At least I knew she'd be coming to our home. I felt such peace.

24

WELCOME HOME, LITTLE ONE

Dyanna Jo's Journal

Finally, Thyme called me on a Tuesday, exactly seven days after Devin and Matthew went home. She told me that Carrie was ready to be discharged and wanted to know if I could pick her up from the hospital. Without hesitation, I called my mom to stay with Ralley and headed straight to the hospital to pick up the baby.

When I arrived, the nurses were gathering all of Carrie's belongings. I was surprised that they were packing two blankets. One was hand crocheted using a beautiful baby pink yarn. The other was made of satin and had Carrie embroidered on the corner.

"Where did these come from," I asked the nurse.

"Oh! Those are pretty, aren't they?" the nurse said. "We have volunteers who make blankets for the babies in the NICU. These two were specially made for Carrie."

My heart was full, thinking of those precious volunteers doing such amazing things for these sweet babies. The nurse finished packing the bag and put Carrie in the baby carrier that

I brought from home. I grabbed the bag and threw it over my shoulder, then I picked up the carrier and headed for the van.

Both Leif and I were cautiously optimistic about our chances of adopting Carrie. But, deep down inside, I just couldn't get my hopes up too high. I had dreams of having a baby in the past, and it was taken from me. Going through that pain, I can't get my hopes up and have them break on the rocks of disappointment. No, I would be careful not to get too emotionally attached.

We had a newborn, and this time we knew she would be staying for many months if not longer. Another case that wasn't a revolving door. That made me happy. Leif got home from work before I returned from the hospital. He tried to relieve my mom of her duties, but she wouldn't hear of it, she was staying until the baby and I returned.

When I got home, I noticed that Leif and Ralley were riding bikes up and down the street. I hollered for them to come on home. When they rode up, I asked why my mom's car was parked on the street. Leif just laughed and told me she refused to leave. Yep, that sounds like my mom.

While they were putting up their bicycles, I took Carrie out of the van and inside the house. Before I knew it, they were right behind me carrying diapers and formula the hospital sent with me. Carrie was sound asleep, but that didn't stop Leif from taking her out of the car seat and inspecting her.

"Hey," my mom said as if she was agitated. "I stayed all this time, and you get first dibs? I don't think so, hand her to me."

Mom was sitting in the rocker when I walked in the door; it was apparent she was waiting for a baby to hold.

"She's so cute," Leif gushed. "She has the cutest round face."

I could see that he was torturing my mom on purpose. He smiled at my mom and finally handed Carrie over.

"Thank you," she said sarcastically.

"Did she seem like she was having withdrawals?" Ralley asked, concerned.

"The nurses said she was awful the first three days, but today was the first day she has been halfway normal. She's taking her bottle and isn't nearly as fussy," I replied.

"I'm glad to hear that," Ralley said, relieved.

"I also met her caseworker. Her name is Thyme McBroom. It's Thyme like the herb, not the clock."

"That's a unique name," Leif commented.

"Yes, and she's heard all the jokes and puns about it. So after you get to know her, keep your puns to yourself," I insisted.

"Ha! Well, I never," he said as if I had utterly offended him.

We settled in, and Carrie opened her eyes to look up into my mom's face. That sure made her day. The wait was worth it. My mom just rocked Carrie forwards and back, forwards and back. It was a beautiful sight.

My mom is my heart. She has been there for me my entire life. She's given her faith, wisdom, love, criticism, knowledge and mainly support. She doesn't always agree with my crazy decisions; she will let me know exactly what she thinks, but I can always count on her to stand by my side no matter what I do. She was nervous about us becoming foster parents. Mom was afraid it would be difficult, heart breaking and stressful; but when we said "We are doing this" she supported us and has been there to care for Ralley and all the children who came into our home. She bought clothes and necessities whenever we needed them. She babysits when we need to go to child and family team meetings, court hearings, and I can always pick up the phone and call her to cry or laugh. She's my sounding board. I have heard the words "I told you so" hundreds of times, but regardless, she is there.

Ralley and Leif stood behind the rocker, looking over my mom's shoulders.

"Get back! You're suffocating me. If I wanted this kind of abuse, I would have stayed home with Joe."

We all laughed.

"Aww," Ralley said. "She's so sweet."

"Yes, she's a doll," I responded.

"What's Thyme like?" Leif asked.

"She's nice. She's a redhead with lots of freckles, and she's probably five-feet-five-inches tall. I like her the best out of all the caseworkers we've had so far. She's easy to talk to."

"Did she say anything about the mom?" my mom asked.

"When I talked to her on the phone earlier, she didn't say a word. The other day when I went to visit Carrie in the NICU, she said she's dealt with Stephanie once before with one of her other children. She never shows up for court hearings or child and family team meetings. Thyme said that she won't tell DCS who the father is either. She claims he's dead."

"How did it go at the hospital?" Leif asked.

"It went well. The nurses weighed and measured her before we left. She weighed six pounds, which was one ounce less than when she was born. She hasn't gained any weight, but she hasn't lost a significant amount either. The nurses were glad she stayed at her birth weight, considering the rough start she had. The nurses put two blankets in her take-home bag. They have volunteers who make the blankets for the babies in the NICU. They are so pretty. Oh, the nurses also said she was still weaning off the drugs her mom pumped into her. They gave me this stuff we mix with her formula. I have no idea how to pronounce it."

Leif picked up the bottle and read the label. "It's Phenobarbital," he announced. "It says we give it to her for four weeks. Each week we give her a little less than the previous week."

Leif's Journal

After Pat left, I finally got my hands on the baby. I fed and burped her. I have to laugh at that whole concept. We beg a baby to burp, and when they don't we pat and rub their backs tirelessly just to hear that heavenly sound. However, when they get older, we fuss and tell them to cover their mouths or burp quietly. It's such an oxymoron.

Carrie drank about three-fourths of the bottle and had a big burp. She seemed quite satisfied after her bottle. Ralley held her for a few minutes and rocked her to sleep. We put a Pack n' Play downstairs so we could always keep the babies close. It had an insert we put near the top that turned it into a bassinet with a little mobile. Ralley put Carrie in the Pack n' Play and swaddled her, the best she could, with a Winnie the Pooh blanket. I got the camera and took a couple of pictures. We all walked into the kitchen to get a snack.

"I thought up an algae," Dyanna Jo said as I put the camera away.

"You thought up a what?" Ralley and I asked in unison. We were looking at each other confused.

"An algae," she replied.

"What are you talking about?" I asked mystified.

"I was driving home with Carrie and feeling cautiously optimistic about adopting her, but I had to tell myself that I didn't want to get my hopes up and have them break on the rocks of disappointment."

Ralley busted out laughing, and I joined in. We tried to contain our laughing. She was expressing a very personal feeling.

"I guess it's not a very good algae," Dyanna Jo mumbled embarrassed.

We tried harder not to laugh, but it wasn't easy.

"What are you two laughing about," Dyanna Jo asked exasperated. "I'm serious; I admitted my feeling to you, and you both think it's funny?"

"You came up with an analogy," I said. "Not an algae. An analogy. Algae is what grows in ponds or stagnant pools of water."

"Are you kidding me! I was close. You knew what I meant?" she said, defeated.

"At first, we were genuinely confused. But yes, honey, once we figured it out, we knew exactly what you meant, and we're sorry. You have to admit using algae was funny," Leif said apologetically.

"Fine! You two are rotten."

I gave Dyanna Jo a hug and kiss until I knew she wasn't upset with us anymore. I walked back over to the bassinet to check on Carrie. I found myself wanting to hold her, but she was sound asleep.

So, I settled for the next best thing and stood beside the bed and stared at her. I listened to her breathing and watched the rise and fall of her chest. I saw her twitch a few times. No doubt dreaming about her bottle and that big burp she had earlier. Then I tip-toed back to the kitchen and joined Dyanna Jo and Ralley.

I heard some thunder in the distance and looked out the window. It was getting very windy. The Redbud we'd planted in the front yard was blowing around, bent over, and whipping around like a gymnast doing tumbles. It started pouring down sheets of rain, and a big gust blew the tree over. I saw it break and wondered if that would be the end of the tree.

When the rain, wind, and thunder stopped, I went out to the tree. It broke about three feet up the trunk. The trunk was originally about three and a half feet tall before it broke, but now all the branches were on the ground. I got a saw and cut off the top, then came inside and called Thress Nursery Gardens out on Clinton Hwy., to ask if the tree would survive. They assured me that it would start to grow limbs just below where it broke. I hoped they were right. It was a sentimental tree. I would be extremely disappointed if it died.

Dyanna Jo got quiet.

"What's the matter, honey?" I asked.

"Seeing the tree break brought back the memories of my miscarriage," she said, with a distant look on her face. "When that happened, I felt like I had been through a storm and was broken; there were times when I felt I wouldn't survive. I yearned to recover the same way we yearn for the Redbud to recover and survive. Helping these foster children is, in a sense helping me."

Carrie woke, and I scooped her up, immediately smelling a scent that sent me straight to the changing table. I threw her up on the table and changed her diaper. I made a new bottle and fed her. Unfortunately, I forgot to put a burp cloth on my shoulder, and when I burped our sweet girl, she got some spit up on my shirt and a little on my neck. I was officially christened. Carrie has given me her approval. Dyanna Jo was ecstatic that I finally got some food on my shirt.

I burped her again when the bottle was finished. She spit up again, but Ralley made herself useful and procured me a burp cloth. After Carrie finished her dinner, I held her. She looked at me while I talked to her. She was so incredibly cute. Those deep brown eyes of hers were like pools of obsidian.

As I'm writing this journal entry, Ralley is sitting next to me and asking if I would share what I talked to Carrie about. I spoke to her about the solar system and the planets. I talked about how big the Sun is and how it has an immense gravitational pull so that the planets orbit it. I like science fiction, space, and space travel. All I can say is that Carrie hung on my every word. She understood the gravity of what I was saying. Ralley rolled her eyes and groaned.

I handed Carrie off to Ralley and went into the kitchen. Dyanna Jo was making dinner.

"Do you think we will change her name if we adopt Carrie?" I ask.

"Carrie is a beautiful name, but I don't feel like Carrie is the name she is meant to have. It's just a feeling I have. We can't change her name at this point since we have no clue where this will go, but I pray that if and when that time comes, God will give us a name. Her special God-given name."

25

BITING OUR NAILS

Dyanna Jo's Journal

On Friday, March 21, we had a child and family team meeting. My mom stayed with Ralley and Carrie. Mr. John Deere was manning the check-in. Thankfully, there wasn't much of a line, and we got checked in quickly. We saw Thyme come in; she came over and sat with us.

"How's everything going?" she asked.

"Really good! Carrie's doing great," I announced proudly. "She sleeps and eats really well. If she is experiencing withdrawal, we haven't noticed. She's never fussy."

"Good, that is a good report to bring to the meeting," Thyme replied.

We headed to the double glass doors and down the hall to our meeting room. As we entered the room, Thyme introduced us to Shelly Winters, the FSW. She smiled and nodded her head. She came across, shy, and reserved. The Guardian ad Litem, Michael Fortner, stood and introduced himself. He was impeccably tailored and a big stout guy. None of Carrie's family members were there. We sat at a small rectangle table, and Shelly passed around the sign-in sheet. This meeting didn't seem as formal as the others we'd attended.

"I guess it's just us," Michael said.

"Doesn't surprise me," Thyme said. "Stephanie never shows up for these meetings. I've called her, but she doesn't answer the phone. My boss told me to go to her apartment, but I let her know that I would need a police escort to go with me. An officer was assigned, and we headed to her home. She didn't answer so I left a notice on her door."

"I've been Guardian ad Litem for a couple of her children, and I've never seen her or talked to her. Sometimes I wonder if she exists."

"Well, since we're the only ones here, we can review the file and head on home," Thyme said. "Michael, do you want to start?"

"We've decided that we will be charging Stephanie with severe child abuse," Michael said. "Carrie is her third child born drug-exposed. At the court hearing, we will notify the judge of the severe abuse charges and request a termination of her parental rights. I know she will not attend the court hearing. The judge will order that we file all the relevant papers, notify Stephanie, and a new court date will be scheduled."

"What does that mean exactly," I asked.

"She won't be arrested," Michael answered. "It means that if she has any more children, drug-exposed or not, she will not be able to keep any of those children in the state of Tennessee. Now mind you, if she goes to another state and has a baby, this charge does not follow her outside of Tennessee."

"I had no idea that you could do that. Hopefully, Stephanie won't have any more children born with drugs in their system; but if she does, at least she won't be able to keep them. She has hurt so many lives with her drug use," I said.

As we finished the meeting, Thyme and I scheduled a home

visit for April and a time to meet at Walmart to get necessities for Carrie. As we walked out to the parking lot, Thyme reminded me to contact WIC.

So far, I really liked working with Thyme; she seemed more laid back and more experienced. She always answered my questions and took the time to get to know me personally.

Today was the first day that Leif met Thyme. He seemed comfortable and joked around a little. Thankfully he didn't make any puns about her name.

THYME WAS right on time for our April home visit. She picked Carrie up and held her for a little while. Carrie was alert and looking straight into Thyme's eyes.

"Has a court date been scheduled?" I asked.

"No, sometimes these things can take a couple of months to get scheduled and finalized." Thyme said.

"Is there another child and family team meeting scheduled?" I asked.

"No, everything is quiet right now," Thyme replied. "Because Carrie's family isn't requesting visitation or coming to the meetings, we just wait for the courts and follow the process."

"What are the chances of us adopting Carrie?" I asked, hopefully.

"When it's this early in the process, I don't feel comfortable saying one way or the other. Stephanie's history shows that she won't fight to get her back. We still have to notify all the family, even those who told us no in the beginning. We have to notify all the family members near and far. We still don't know who the father is, and we may never know, but we have to do our best to find him, and if we don't, we have to place an ad in the classifieds to see if he will come forward."

Leif and I just looked at each other.

"That sounds like a lot," Leif murmured. "We'd love to adopt her."

"Knowing this case the way I do, I feel good about your chances; however, I don't want to give any false hope. My job is to remind you that our main goal is reunification, but if that doesn't work, we will consider adoption. Just relax, enjoy your time with Carrie and let us worry about the rest."

After Thyme left, I changed Carrie's diaper and laid her in the Pack n' Play. Leif and I talked a lot about how strange the whole system was. At our last child and family team meeting, we learned that they were going to charge Stephanie with severe child abuse because she used drugs while her baby was in utero. But on the other hand, she could have gone to an abortion clinic and killed her baby and walk away with no consequence. How does that make any sense?

Leif's Journal

At the beginning of May, Thyme came for our monthly home visit. There was nothing to report, so we all just sat around and talked. A home visit is required each month, regardless of any new developments. We enjoyed visiting with Thyme, so we didn't mind. The visit lasted about one-hour; we scheduled June's home visit, and she headed out the door.

On Monday, May 12, we took our two-month-old Carrie to the Knox County Health Department for a checkup and vaccines. She got a good health report, and then her vaccines were given. Hearing her cry is so hard. She will never remember this, but it still hurts to listen to her cry.

Our appointment was so late in the day that by the time we left, it was dinnertime. We made a trip to our local Chik-fil-a. We ordered our usual: chicken nuggets with Polynesian dipping sauce, waffle fries and medium drinks. Carrie had chicken nugget flavored formula with a hint of Polynesian sauce. Every time I say that to the girls, I get a double eye roll and a shake of the head. I love it when I get that reaction from them.

Meanwhile, Carrie told me she wanted to continue our discussion of the Solar System. She was intrigued by gravity and orbital mechanics and all that stuff. Since I was so silly, Dyanna Jo informed me that I would be feeding the baby while they ate. She said it would give her and Ralley a chance to discuss the mysteries of me.

I fed Carrie, and we figured out how to achieve the speed of light. Several people came by and told us she was cute. She had some rather loud burps that caused the people around us to laugh, and a few applauded. She smiled at them, and they loved that. Ralley took Carrie, so I could finally eat my dinner. It's not easy to eat while holding a baby in one hand and a bottle in the other. The nuggets were great, even if they were cold.

"Did you figure out my mysteries?" I wryly asked.

"We decided you're as mysterious as a black hole," Dyanna Jo said. She didn't mean that as a compliment. She doesn't know much about science or space, and I really don't know much either, but I know that a black hole is bottomless and has a lot of gravity. I took her comment as a compliment.

"I like that. A black hole is deep and has a lot of gravity, so I'm a deep person, and people are drawn to me. They just can't stay away."

"I'm about to gag," my loving and adoring Ralley said.

After we got home, Ralley got Carrie ready for bed. Dyanna Jo watched while Ralley bathed, dried, put on her diaper, and put on her pajamas. Ralley loved taking care of Carrie.

Dyanna Jo rocked Carrie and sang the same song she sang every night. "Jesus loves you this I know, for the Bible tells you so......" When Carrie was fast asleep, she laid her in the crib and walked out of the room. Dyanna Jo was a nervous wreck when we transitioned her to the crib. She started to relax but only because she could stalk Carrie in the video monitor whenever she wanted.

Carrie was sleeping approximately five to six hours a night for the most part. She was never one of those babies that like a pacifier. We tried giving her one, but she kept spitting it out. She always seemed happy when she didn't have it in her mouth, so we quit trying to give it to her. Ralley had used one, and when she was two or three, we had a ceremony to get her to stop using it. We dug a hole, and she put her pacifier in it. It worked; she never asked for it again.

MAY CAME and went in a flash. June rolled around with another home visit from Thyme.

"On July 19, there will be a court hearing to get a final ruling on the severe abuse charge and to terminate Stephanie's parental rights," Thyme said.

"What about the dad's?" I asked.

"Stephanie still hasn't given us the name of the dad. When we've been able to reach her, all she says is that "he is dead." Women with drug problems will claim the dad is dead because often it's her dealer. They know that giving DCS the dealer's name could cause a lot of problems for themselves. We will place a classified ad in the paper, which will run every Friday for thirty days. It will be addressed to the unknown father of Carrie Wilson, but it will also list Stephanie Wilson as the mother. We will provide the DCS contact information in the event we get a call. I have never received a response from an ad searching for a dad."

"What happens if no one responds to it?" Dyanna Jo asked.

"We will petition the court to terminate his parental rights."

"So, if they both have their rights terminated, how long until we can adopt Carrie?" Dyanna Jo asked.

"Legally, she must be in your home for six months. If DCS has completed all its due diligence, you'll be provided an attorney at the expense of DCS. The attorney will petition the court for adoption. A personal hearing with the judge will be scheduled, and at that time, you will legally be Carrie's parents."

"Will we be able to change her name?" Dyanna Jo asked.

"Yes, you will," Thyme said." Let me guess; you already have a name picked out."

"Actually, we don't," Dyanna Jo answered. "I have prayed that when the time is right, and when we can adopt her, He will give us her name. God has been with us every step of this journey, and I know that He has a plan for this little girl. He should name her."

Thyme smiled and cuddled Carrie for a little bit longer. Before she left, she scheduled our July home visit and informed us that we needed to have Carrie at the July 19 court hearing. July 19, will be our very first court hearing since becoming foster parents.

RALLEY'S JOURNAL

Mom was going crazy. She wasn't thrilled about how long the court process took and wanted to adopt Carrie yesterday. I was glad we could adopt her, but I was starting to have reservations about adopting other kids. I wondered how much time Mom and Dad would have to devote to Carrie as she grew older. We were told that drug babies need special care throughout their lives. There wasn't a book that could tell us how her life would be, or how the drugs affected her brain?

I knew my attitude wasn't right. But it was the one I had. I was used to having Mom and Dad all to myself, and now I had to share them. I thought I could get used to it, but it was harder than I thought it would be. I love Carrie; I really do.

Mom and Dad gave me plenty of time and attention, but it wasn't as much as I was used to, and I was having a pity party. I needed to get over it. I knew I would eventually.

There was so much I had to be thankful for, like being Carrie's big sister. But, there was a significant age difference between us, and I also wondered how much I would have to babysit. I like taking care of her, but as I get older, will I resent it?

I was thinking about school and graduation. If I go off to college, I won't be around, but Carrie will be, and she will be taking up all of Mom and Dad's energy. I wanted to go to college, but would Carrie prevent that from happening? Listen to me, I'm just going into middle school, and I am already worried about college. I'm really messed up today.

On July 19, we will be taking Carrie to court. I have never been to court before. It should be interesting but scary at the same time. What if Carrie's mom comes, would she try to take Carrie back?

I can't imagine being a kid and having my biological parent's rights terminated. How will she feel when she is older and understands what happened to her? Maybe that's what I should do — think about how I would feel if I was a foster child. Perhaps that will help me get over the funk I'm in. Maybe it will help me to be more understanding of her situation. I'm intellectually aware of how it is for foster children. Still, I need to internalize it more and feel it more with my heart.

I want to be a good foster sister and be a conduit for God's love to flow to Carrie and other kids. The more I think about it, that's what God did for us. We needed redemption so he could adopt us. We were foster children. We had run away from Him and were still running from Him, and He sent Jesus to open a door for us to come back to Him. It doesn't matter how far away we think we've gone. The door is always right there. All we have to do is open it and invite Him in. He's standing there knocking, waiting for us to invite Him in.

26

PATIENCE AND PEACE

Leif's Journal

"Today's the day," Dyanna Jo chimed. "July 19, court day."

I took the day off from work so we could go to the court hearing. The hearing was at 9 a.m. in the main courtroom at the juvenile detention center. We arrived at 8:45 and saw Thyme outside the courtroom.

"Hello, you guys. How's it going?" Thyme asked.

"Nervous, we don't know what to expect," Dyanna Jo answered.

"Well, let me fill you in on a couple of things. I believe that I told you that when I talked to Stephanie on the phone a month ago, I told her that when I came to her house, I could hear someone on the other side of the door, but no one answered. She responded by saying that she doesn't answer the door to white people. We needed to be sure that she was notified about this hearing today. We sent Shari Klein, an African American caseworker, to Stephanie's apartment, and Stephanie actually opened her door and talked to Shari. Shari gave her the notice of today's hearing, and she was required to sign a paper stating that she was notified. None of us expect her to be here today, but at least we can say she was notified."

At 9 a.m., we were called into the courtroom and instructed to sit on the front bench. Carrie's Guardian ad Litem, Michael Fortner, Thyme, Shelly Winters, and a few other DCS workers, we didn't recognize, were present. As predicted, Stephanie wasn't there.

The DCS lawyer, Mandy Turner, submitted a motion to charge Stephanie with severe child abuse, along with the request to terminate Stephanie's parental rights. The judge asked for the DCS representatives to plead their case, and when they were done, he asked Michael Fortner if he agreed with the motion. Michael agreed. The judge asked if the mother or her lawyer was present. Not a peep was heard.

I could see Dyanna Jo sitting there nervous as she could be. Her eyes were wide, and her shoulders were tense. As we waited for the ruling, I could see her staring holes straight through the judge. When he finally ruled in our favor, I could see her mouth say '*Thank you*' with no sound.

We were at the four-month mark. The first step on this journey was over. DCS still needed to work on terminating the father's parental rights. We needed to wait until we reached the six-month mark in order to petition the court for adoption.

We went home and had lunch. Ralley fed Carrie. After lunch, I went outside and checked on the Eastern Redbud we planted in the front yard. Dyanna Jo called it the "Baby Tree." It had sprouted some branches right below where it broke in the spring. It looked like it was going to rally and make it. I was glad to see that. It made me think of how our miscarriage was like the breaking of the tree. We were broken and felt like we would die. But just like the Redbud was growing new branches, we were getting new branches from being foster parents.

The next day Dyanna Jo came downstairs to the kitchen

terribly upset. "Thyme just called," she announced. "She said one of Carrie's family members from Georgia found out about her and put in a petition to adopt her."

"What? So, what happens now?" I asked.

"Thyme said that this family member must meet the requirements of Tennessee's and Georgia's adoption laws. Additionally, the Interstate Compact on the Placement of Children, ICPC, must be involved any time a child is moved from one state to another for the purpose of adoption. Everything will take time. DCS will have an agency in Georgia make a home visit to see if the home is suitable for a child. Thyme will do a criminal check and start working on the paperwork. Thyme told us in the beginning that family comes first. Right now, we wait."

Just when things were going smoothly, an unknown relative comes out of the woodwork and wants to adopt. Everything was in God's hands, so if He wanted Carrie with us, she would be with us. Period. By this time, she had been with us for four months, and we were all she had known. I'd hate to have her start new with someone else. She was young enough; she wouldn't know any difference in the long run. But Dyanna Jo, Ralley, and I had become extremely attached to her.

Dyanna Jo's **Journal**

I've never been good at patience. It's not in my DNA. I hate to wait, and I will yell it from the mountain tops. Please don't make me wait! Unfortunately, I had no control and was forced to wait.

I decided to keep busy. I had school curriculum to buy; lesson plans to plan, end of summer parties, Church events to help plan and attend, and, most importantly, a preteen and a baby to care for. I had plenty to do, but deep inside, I knew I was only functioning with half a brain. My thoughts were always on the relative in Georgia or the ad in the paper looking for the father. I was acting like a mama bear. I couldn't handle it if I lost this precious little girl. Was I cut out to be a foster parent. It's been five months, and I love Carrie so much. I don't want to lose her. My selfishness was evident. I wanted her; I didn't want anyone else to get her. She wasn't a piece of property; she was a beautiful baby girl I have raised since she was seven days old.

August arrived, and school began. We got back into a groove and continued to wait. Ralley was so good at doing her school work with a baby, swinging, cooing, gurgling, eating, burping, and sleeping. Our school schedule was planned around Carrie. Ralley was so laser-focused. She was a great student and could practically follow the lesson plans all by herself. She was so independent. We were so proud of how she handled the fostering roller coaster.

On September 5, Thyme came for our monthly home visit. We liked to plan them later in the day so Leif could attend. He enjoyed Thyme's visits.

Thyme held Carrie and talked to her as if we weren't even there. With that precious girl in her arms, she completely ignored us. I stayed patient, but I was chomping at the bit. I had a million questions, but I wanted to give Carrie her time. A part of me thought Thyme knew and was messing with me. We had gotten to know each other well enough to where she felt comfortable doing that. Some times, Leif would egg her on.

"Okay," Thyme finally said. "I guess I've kept you waiting long enough."

"You're darn right," I blurted out. I saw a little smile attach itself to Thyme's lips. "You were playing with me, weren't you?" Dyanna Jo snarled when she noticed the slight smile.

"Yes," Thyme said, laughing.

"You're lucky you're still holding Carrie, or I would have thrown this pillow at you."

"I know. That's why I haven't relinquished my hold on her. Now, as for the relative wanting to adopt, her name is Janice Shipley. She's a fourth cousin of Stephanie's. We found out that she was in jail for a few months earlier this year. We have people looking into it further and trying to find out more about her. She hasn't been very cooperative."

"That seems to run in the family," I quipped.

"I know," Thyme laughed. "I don't think you have to worry about anything with her wanting to adopt. I don't think her petition will go anywhere."

"Why do you think that?" Leif asked.

"Because of her jail time and not being cooperative. If you want to adopt, it usually helps to be cooperative and forthcoming."

"Yes, I would imagine so," Leif agreed.

"What about the ad in the paper for the father?" I asked.

"Hasn't been done yet. That's a whole other person, and they are backed up. Nothing goes as fast as we would like. It isn't easy on families, foster parents, or the caseworkers. We can only do what we can. DCS is so understaffed, and we are all overworked. We do the best we can, and at the end of the day, all we can do is pray."

That was the first time I had ever heard Thyme say anything spiritual. I couldn't tell if she was a Christian or not. I am sure that there are strict rules about talking about Christ or faith. Here in the Bible belt, it's common. Coming from California, I wasn't used to that, it wasn't typical. Here in Knoxville, everyone is kind, they talk to each other, even at restaurants out of the blue another table will make a comment or say something across to you at your table. Most people say, "have a blessed day." There's practically a church on every corner. In California, all my friends were Christians, so I was around Christians most of the time, but that wasn't the norm.

Thyme spent a little while longer holding Carrie. We scheduled our next home visit, and before she left, she handed me a list of three attorneys. She said to pick one and let her know who we picked. He would be the attorney who would file our petition.

"I always like it when she comes to visit," Leif said, breaking the silence between us since Thyme left.

"Even though she told us not to worry about this relative, I can't stop worrying about it," I confessed.

"I feel better about it. Janice was in jail earlier this year, and I think she has things she's hiding if she isn't cooperating."

"I know. You know me, I worry about things. I get that from my mother."

"You don't have to remind me. Your mom would worry about whether she'll run out of things to worry about."

Ralley laughed, "You like picking on Nana way too much, Dad."

"So, Ralley, what do you think about this adoption?" Leif asked her. "I know that you know we got into foster parenting to adopt eventually, but now that we have an excellent chance of adopting Carrie, what do you think of that?"

"I think it's great," Ralley answered. "I would like to have a sister even though I am eleven and a half years older than her."

"That's true. You would be venturing out on your own while she's still relatively young."

On September 18, our attorney filed the adoption petition. That was exactly six months to the day that Carrie had been in our home. DCS was paying our court costs and attorney fees since we were foster parents. We picked our attorney from the list that Thyme had given us. We picked Thomas W. Barnett because the Mussina's recommended him. He had handled their adoptions, and they liked him.

We still hadn't heard any word about Janice. We were just concerned that she could cause our adoption to be delayed. We were marching ahead and not letting the unknown hold us back.

December 11, was the day we would appear before the judge, and he would sign the final order of adoption. There was only one more thing to do. The ad in the classifieds would begin on the first Friday of October and run for four consecutive weeks. Until that was over, I wouldn't be able to relax.

I still prayed that God would reveal her name to us. I knew that if this was of God, then He would lay her name on our hearts.

~

RALLEY'S JOURNAL

We kept in touch with Geoff and Melody Mason ever since we had taken Cameron to them. They had adopted him a few days ago and had changed their phone number twice because Cameron's mom kept calling them asking for money. Melody said the mom never asked about Cameron. I thought that was so sad.

The Mason's called my parents and asked if we wanted to meet them for dinner somewhere to celebrate Cameron's adoption. We decided to meet at the Cracker Barrel near the Knoxville Center Mall on Friday, September 19, at 6 p.m. They were already at a table when we got there. I was glad to see cute little Cameron. He had grown some and put on weight. Geoff and Melody looked great, and so did their older kids, Liz and Luke.

"You all are looking good," Dad said to Geoff and Melody as we sat down. He and Geoff did the whole shaking hands with a firm grip macho man thing. Melody had her hair done differently. Of course, it was nine months since I'd seen her so she could have gone through multiple hairstyles since then. Mom changes her hair color like a chameleon changes skin tones.

"Cameron's looking good," Mom said.

"He's doing a lot better," Melody said. "Still in the lower percentiles for his age, but he was below that when we got him. Having a good diet and a consistent home environment has done wonders for him."

"I can see he's a lot bigger," Dad commented. "He was as light as a feather when he was with us."

"So, who's this bundle of joy?" Melody said, pointing to Carrie's carrier. Mom was about to get her out when the waitress came by to take our drink order. After she left, Mom got Carrie out and gave her to Melody. Carrie was awake and looking around curiously. "When will you be able to adopt her?" Melody asked.

"We found out this week the adoption hearing is set for December 11," Dad said.

"It can't come fast enough," Mom said anxiously. "They are starting the ad in the classifieds for the father starting the first Friday of October. It has to run every Friday for four weeks straight."

"She's so cute," Melody gushed.

The waitress came back with our drinks and took our order. We talked and enjoyed our food. During the meal, everyone took turns holding Carrie. She seemed to be okay with it. She just looked at each new face and acted like it was no big deal. I had noticed she never cried much or needed to be held much. She seemed perfectly fine if she wasn't being held. I liked to hold her, though. I enjoyed looking at her and talking to her even though she couldn't understand me. We often put her on a blanket on the floor so she could get exercise. She hasn't rolled over yet. The doctor at the health department encouraged us to see a specialist. The doctor he recommended was extremely busy. It would be a couple of months before we can see her. Mom said there were only two developmental pedestrians in Knoxville, and they both took a majority of the children who come into the foster system.

"We may have to move," Geoff said after we'd been eating for a little bit. "We think Cameron's biological mom has been driving by our house."

"That's not good," Dad said in a typical understatement.

"We aren't sure, but Melody has noticed the same car for several days now going real slow."

"Is she still trying to get money?" I asked Liz.

"Probably," Liz responded as the grownups stared at us as if they just realized that kids have ears and pick up on everything.

"I don't know," Melody said. "maybe. I guess since we changed our phone number, she figures she'll come to our house. It's not as easy to change houses as it is a phone number."

"We'll keep you guys in our prayers," Dad said. "Let us know if we can help with anything."

"Thank you," Geoff said.

We finished eating, and Cameron was getting fidgety. Carrie seemed to be getting a little restless too. She was probably hungry. We said goodbye to them and left. I enjoyed seeing them all. It was good to see Cameron healthy and happy, now if we could fast forward these next three months, so Mom would stop fretting about adopting Carrie.

27

IT'S OFFICIAL

Leif's Journal

Throughout the month of October, the ad ran every Friday. Four weeks of watching Dyanna Jo come out of her skin every time the phone rang. Thyme had told us that she's never had a call come from an ad in the paper; it didn't matter; we were still worried. Week by week, we waited.

November came, and we could finally relax about the ad and the father coming forward. No calls were received. Now they could terminate the father's rights. We also found out that Janice would not be able to get Carrie. After her home visit and a background check, it was a no brainer; she would not be a good option. We could breathe again. We were a month away, and we were looking forward to making it official.

During the last eight months, we had received calls from placement asking if we were able to take children, but we always declined. We felt we needed to put all our focus on Carrie. Because we were so close to adoption, Dyanna Jo, Ralley, and I talked about retaking children. Fostering affected the whole family, and we all had to agree before we continued.

Ralley is so gentle-hearted and incredibly selfless. We're so proud of the young lady she has become. Selflessness is a beautiful character trait; however, Ralley often puts her feelings aside to help others. We didn't want her to get lost in the process. She had to be completely comfortable, or we would put our house on hold for a while. She assured us she was ready. After the adoption was final, we would open our home to more children.

On Thursday, December 11, 2008, we got up early to be at the City/County Building by 9 a.m. It was a cold and rainy day, barely warm enough for it to rain and not snow. We got Carrie fed and dressed, and we headed out the door. The City/County Building was in downtown Knoxville. It housed all the Knoxville and Knox County government offices along with the courtrooms. We parked in a parking garage a few blocks from the building. Fortunately, the rain had slackened to a light drizzle.

We met Dyanna Jo's parents, Pat and Joe, along with my parents outside the parking garage. We all arrived at the same time and walked to the building together. Thyme was waiting for us outside the judge's chambers. Other families were sitting around with specially made signs and t-shirts. There was no doubt; this was definitely an adoption day.

We were called back to Judge Preston. T. Linden's office promptly at 9 a.m. He looked to be in his sixties. His hair was completely white, and his skin looked leathery, like someone who spent a lot of time on the lake on his boat. He was of average height and looked fit and trim. He wasn't wearing his robe over his professional-looking clothing. I guess it's more laid back in the judge's chambers.

After the introductions, he sat at his large wooden desk. Dyanna Jo and I sat in two large leather chairs in front of his desk. Ralley sat on the arm of my chairs. Our parents sat on the sofa against the wall, and Thyme stood off to the side.

"So, we're here to adopt this little girl," the judge said. He picked up some papers and looked them over. "I see here you all want to change her name to Haley Alexis Baskin. Is that correct?" he asked and looked up at us.

"Yes, that's correct," Dyanna Jo and I said together.

He perused the papers some more and said that it looked as if everything was in order. He signed the papers and said, "Congratulations."

The judge stood and came around his desk to shake our hands. With that, we were the official parents of Haley Alexis. Judge Linden posed for a couple of photos. Thyme took our camera and took a couple of family pictures, including Ralley and the proud new grandparents. Finally, we got a photo with Thyme, and then we all filed out to the court clerks desk.

We were Haley's parents, and no one could change that. It was bittersweet saying goodbye to Thyme. We enjoyed having her as Haley's caseworker. She was by far the best one we had dealt with, and we hoped we would get her again with other children we would have in our home.

It was about 9:50 a.m. when we left. We planned to meet our families at 11 a.m. at our usual hang out, Olive Garden. Since we had an hour before we were to meet, we took a fast trip home and changed Haley's diaper. By the time we got to the restaurant, our parents had already gotten a table. What a great celebration. Everyone took turns holding Haley while we sat talking, eating, laughing, and praising God for this precious little nine-month-old girl.

On the drive home, Haley and Ralley napped in the back seat. Taking a nap sounded good, but by the time we got home, Haley had other ideas. She woke up as I was carrying her into the house. She began to fuss and cry. It sounds like she's ready for her afternoon snack. Ralley got a bottle prepared for Haley, but instead of feeding her, she handed me the bottle and headed towards the stairs.

"I see how it is," I said dryly. "You make me do all the work."

"Listen, buster," she retorted, stifling a smile "while you're at work, Mom and I are here feeding and changing diapers. So, bite me."

"You sound just like your mother when you do that."

"Is that a good thing or a bad thing?"

"It's not a good or bad thing. It's just an 'it is' thing. It is what it is is what is... is."

"Oh, bother," Ralley said with an eye roll.

"That's right, my little Pooh Bear."

DYANNA JO'S Journal

Exactly nine months to the day of her birth, we adopted Haley. All I could think about was how good God was. We welcomed this precious baby into our home at just seven days old. I carried and nurtured her for exactly nine months, just like countless other mothers do when carrying their babies in their womb. Was Haley in my womb, no she wasn't, but by the Grace of God, I carried her full term, and she was our baby. The symbolism seems so clear. God gave me my baby. He did that for me.

I prayed for God to name her. We wanted something special that was solely for her. One day in November, I was feeding Haley (Carrie at that time), and I felt this overwhelming feeling of peace. I was looking down at her beautiful ebony face and getting lost in my thoughts. Her eyes were closed as she sucked on her bottle. She looked as if she was at peace as well. Ever so softly I heard, *Haley,* I instantly repeated the name out loud, "Haley?" Again softly, *Haley,* and again I repeated. Our beautiful baby opened her eyes, and again I repeated, "Haley?" She turned her eyes to look into mine, and in that moment, I had no doubt, God named her Haley. She was a beautiful creation, and

God had spoken to me. When I shared her name with Leif, there was no hesitation. He kissed her on the forehead and said, "Welcome to the family, Haley."

Just fourteen months prior, while in church, I couldn't help but notice that all the people sitting around us had babies. Strollers lined the isles. At that time, the loss of our baby was still so raw. I started to ask God, *Why? Why not me?* As I cried, my sweet friend Alexis leaned over and said, "God wants you to know that you will, one day, have a baby." Those words never left me. Four months after she gave me that profound Word from God, she was killed in a car accident driving to Nashville to spend Christmas with her family. God used her, and she was right; one day, I had my baby. Haley's middle name came just as clearly, Alexis. Our beautiful bundle of joy, Haley Alexis Baskin.

HALEY WAS our amazing Christmas gift from God. She was full of personality and doing her best to move around. We created a large playpen for her. Rubber 12" x12" mats covered the floor and connected like puzzle pieces; the total area was 5'x5'. The mats were so colorful and had a number from 1 to 10 right in the middle. The numbers could be removed, played with, and used as teaching tools. We used plastic baby gates that hooked together to create a pen around the mats. She had room to play and stay safe when we needed to homeschool or get dinner ready. She loved it. Her laugh and giggles were infectious. She had a very full-bodied laugh. That seemed to come from deep down in her belly.

It was Christmas Eve, and we were getting everything ready for our traditional finger foods, holiday desserts, and hot apple cider with my parents. Ralley was a tremendous help wrapping presents and making the finger foods. She was also a massive help with Haley. As we worked side by side, preparing the food, I was totally surprised when Ralley told me about how she was feeling about Haley.

"Mom."

"Yes, Ralley."

"Do you ever get tired of changing diapers and feeding Haley?"

"Sometimes. Are you feeling that way?"

"Yes. I'm happy we adopted her, and I'm glad she's my sister, but sometimes I feel more like a babysitter than I do a sister."

"We probably are having you watch her more than you should. You are her sister and not her parent."

"I know that since I'm eleven and a half years older than her, I can help with that stuff, but it does seem like I'm watching her a lot."

"I think so too. Dad and I will be more aware of that. You're so helpful and uncomplaining that we sometimes take advantage of you, and we shouldn't do that."

"Thanks for saying that. I was nervous about saying anything."

"Why?"

"I was afraid you would think I was complaining."

"You're not complaining. You were sharing a concern with me."

"I know, but I was afraid you would take it as complaining."

"You're fine. I'm glad you said something."

Ralley came over and hugged me. I felt bad. She was such a good kid and always willing to help, and we were putting too much on her. We didn't think twice about it. She must have been feeling this way for a while. Immediately, I could tell a significant weight had been lifted off her shoulders. I was relieved she said something because I didn't want her resenting Haley or our decision to be a foster family. It wasn't just about

Leif and me being foster parents. It was about all of us being a foster family.

It was a little under two weeks since Haley's adoption. We hadn't heard anything from placement and wondered when we would be called for another child or sibling group. This Christmas was so different from last year. Last year we were trying to decide if we wanted to continue being foster parents. This year we had adopted a baby and were looking forward to having more kids.

Ralley and I finished all the preparations, and once we were dressed in our Sunday best, we headed to the candle light service at my parent's church. After the service, we all headed back to our house for food, family, presents, and Praise. We had so much to Praise God for; this December was a big one.

After my parents left, Leif, Ralley, and I looked at each other, and in unison, said, "Phew, I'm tired."

It was amazing to look back at the last year and see all the blessings God had given our little family. He has blessed us more than I could have imagined.

I cleaned the kitchen while Leif and Ralley took care of getting Haley ready for bed. After everyone was done and we were dressed for bed, we sat on the couch and played with our new presents. Nana and Papa always spoiled Ralley. This year they had two grandkids to spoil.

28

—————

TAYLOR

Leif's Journal

As we fostered, most of the kids we wound up getting were babies. Most of them were born drug-exposed. I had heard it was a growing epidemic, but never knew how bad it was. A lot of the moms were addicted to prescription pain meds and never set out to be addicts.

The babies we got were birthed by moms addicted to street drugs: cocaine, heroin, barbiturates, and marijuana.

We heard the stories about the biological parents. As time went on, I became convicted about my attitude toward the birth parents. I was critical of them and looked down my spiritual nose at them. Who was I to perch myself atop the proverbial high horse and gaze down upon them in judgment and condemnation? That was reserved for God and God alone. I knew that if not for His grace, that could easily have been me.

So, I began to pray for the birth parents and to be sensitive to any opportunities to minister to them. Dyanna Jo and I had a chance to do that with our next foster child Taylor and his mom Jan.

~

JAN LOWE WAS eighteen years old when her parents, Tony and Christie, found out that she was seriously addicted to drugs. Little did they know that she had started at the age of fifteen. Her parents demanded she go to a rehab facility, but Jan refused. They loved their daughter, but after catching her stealing money from them and losing jobs because of her failed drug tests, they were at their breaking point. They couldn't take her lies any longer; they had no other choice. Tony gave her an ultimatum. Either Jan went to the rehab facility, or she had to move out of their house. They held on to hope that she would make the right choice, but Jan marched upstairs, gathered her belongings, and walked out the door.

Jan was shocked and hurt. How could they give her an ultimatum? She walked slowly to her car, hoping her mom would open the door and beg her to stay. When that didn't happen, Jan got in her car and drove straight to her boyfriend's house. She knew he would let her live with him. It wasn't an ideal situation, but she had the freedom to do whatever she wanted and no one to get on her case. Two months later, she found out she was pregnant.

"I'll make an appointment for you at the abortion clinic," her boyfriend Theo offered.

"I don't want to get an abortion," she snapped. She was horrified that he suggested such a thing.

"You will if you want to keep living here. Cause I don't want no kid."

"Well, I'm not getting one."

"There's the door! Don't be trying to get any money from me. You're on your own. I ain't supporting a kid I don't want!"

Jan packed up her things. *Fine! I don't want a guy like that raising my baby,* she thought as she walked out the door. She didn't even look back. She decided all she could do was look ahead. The only problem was, she didn't know where to go or what to do. Before she reached her car, reality started to set in, and the tears began to flow.

She considered going back to her parents, but it had only been a few months since they told her to leave. She wasn't ready to admit they were right. Being a junkie and pregnant would only make things worse.

She had a beat-up '98 Honda Civic. It didn't look like much, but it ran okay. She threw her stuff in the back, got in the driver's seat, and drove down the road. Where was she going to go? She knew she couldn't keep driving; she would run out of gas. Before she realized it, she was parked in front of her dealer's house. She stared at the house, and then she looked in her purse. She had just enough to score a small bag. She thought to herself; a *small bag was better than no bag.* She made the quick buy and drove away.

Jan couldn't remember the last time she ate. Her stomach began to grumble, and the grumble turned to pain. She drove to the closest KARM, Knox Area Rescue Ministry, to get something to eat. There was no way she could go through a drive-thru; she spent the last of her money on drugs. She knew KARM would have something.

The first few weeks, Jan slept in her car, but there was no way she could keep that going. She had no money, no gas, and nowhere to go. She sold her car for next to nothing. Before she knew it, she was out of money and living on the streets eating out of trash cans. Some times KARM and other ministries would come and bring food, but it wasn't very often. No matter how hard it got, it seemed as if she could always find a little something to keep her fix going. The days turned into weeks and the weeks into months.

The winter cold hit hard on the streets. There was never enough warmth. One night she laid in her wet, soggy cardboard home shaking in horrible pain. Nothing could stop the pain in her stomach. As the pain got worse, she couldn't control the screams that came from her mouth. She had never felt this kind of pain; it wasn't the kind of pain she felt when she hadn't had a fix in a few days. It was worse. Next thing she knew, people were yelling at her to shut up, but she couldn't stop. It seemed like hours she laid there screaming.

Suddenly, she could hear a siren approaching in the distance. Before she knew it, two men were lifting her out of her makeshift home, onto a gurney, and whisking her away.

It didn't take long before the ambulance pulled up to the Emergency Room at the University of Tennessee Medical Center. The baby! Was this it; was she having her baby? Fear set in, and her sobs became uncontrollable. The nurses in the ER told her everything was going to be okay. They would take good care of her. She finally calmed down. Once she was situated, and orderly along with one of the nurses, took up to the maternity ward.

Once they got her in the room, they checked her contractions and found they were far enough apart to have her take a quick shower. She had no idea when she last took a shower. The dirt was so thick, and her hair was so matted she didn't see how she could make it quick. A nurse helped her and instructed her to breathe every time she felt a contraction. Once she was clean, the nurse got her in the bed.

The nurse hooked her up to a couple of machines that beeped and made scary noises. She took a couple of blood samples and left Jan all by herself. Jan had no clue what was happening. She closed her eyes and thought about holding her baby and did everything she could to forget about the scary sounds and painful contractions. She was so tired. When could she sleep?

Hours later, the baby was born and immediately taken to the NICU. Fear came over her, "Where are you going? I want my baby! Please, stop! What are you doing? Please, somebody, answer me!"

Two nurses were at her side, trying to calm her. "Jan, he's been taken to the NICU. He was a little underweight, and we need to be sure he has the proper care," one of the nurses told her.

"It's a boy?" she asked, quieting down.

One of the nurses left the room while a couple of others came in to help clean her up and take care of her. Exhaustion set in, and she slowly fell asleep.

About an hour later, a woman walked in, tapped her on the shoulder, and introduced herself.

"Hello, Miss. Lowe, my name is Mary Wilcox. I am the DCS caseworker assigned to your case."

Jan was confused, "My Case?" She didn't understand why a DCS caseworker was in her room. "Why are you here?" she asked as she started looking around the room. "Where's my baby?"

"Jan," Mary answered, "your baby is in the NICU, and he's doing well under the circumstances."

"What circumstances?"

"When you were admitted, you had blood drawn; the test revealed that you had a considerable amount of drugs in your system. Your son was tested as well, and his results showed the same. When a baby is born drug-exposed, DCS is called, and the baby is placed in our custody."

"You mean I won't get my baby? I've lost him?"

"Losing him depends on you, Jan. If you get your act together, clean yourself up, get a job, provide a stable environment for him, and work your parenting plan. You can get him back, but you have to do the work. What's the baby's name?"

"Taylor Steven Lowe," she said between tears.

"In about a week, there will be a court hearing, and we'll schedule a child and family team meeting. I highly recommend you attend both. I understand you are currently homeless. Is there any family you can stay with, someone to help you get yourself clean?"

"All I have is my parents, and I don't know if they will let me come home again after everything I have done to them."

"Tomorrow, when you are discharged, I will pick you up and drive you to their house. You won't know unless you talk to them."

"Can I see Taylor? I never got to see him."

"They can't bring him to the room, but I can wheel you down for a peek through the window. He is being closely monitored and must stay in the NICU for the time being."

"Oh, yes, please, I want to see him so badly."

~

Dyanna Jo's Journal

We invited the Mussina's to our house for a New Year's Eve party. It was cold and icy, but we didn't mind; it was perfect for an East Tennessee winters night. Dinner was our southern favorite: pork BBQ sandwiches, coleslaw, potato salad, hush puppies, and green beans. You can never go wrong with that meal. A little after dinner, the home phone rang. I excused myself and left everyone fat and happy sitting in the living room.

A few minutes later, I returned to the living room. "That was placement," I began "they have a week old baby boy ready to leave the hospital tomorrow. They wanted to know if we were available to take him."

"Okay, what do you know?" Leif asked.

"Well, I know that I told them, yes, and the DCS caseworker will be bringing him tomorrow afternoon."

"Oh really? So you said yes, just like that, and didn't check with me?"

"That's about the size of it, old man. Whatcha gonna do about it?" I answered, staring him dead in the eyes.

As we bantered, you could see everyone's head going back and forth as if they were watching a ping pong match. I could see Leif starting to crack a smile. I tried to stay straight-faced, but when Ralley started belly laughing, I couldn't hold it in any longer. The whole room broke into laughter. I don't believe Fred and Anna had ever seen us banter like that before. Our banter was usually little fun quips, but this time they weren't so sure we were playing with each other.

When the room quieted down, Leif said, "Give us the scoop."

"His name is Taylor," I said, "he has been in the NICU for five days due to drug-exposure. The mother is an eighteen-year-old who was homeless when she was brought into the ER. Thankfully, she is back with her parents, and they are working on getting her the help she needs. The DCS caseworker is Mary Wilcox, and she will be bringing the little guy here tomorrow afternoon."

"We've worked with Mary," Anna said. "she's good. Early in the process, she is normally able to tell if the parents are truly going to do the work. I don't know how she does it, but she really knows. When she thinks the parents genuinely want to work the plan, she will do everything she can to help them."

That was helpful; it's nice to know a little about the woman who would be working the case. We broke out the dessert. There was something for everyone. Leif got his cheesecake, the little kids got their cookies, and there was a chocolate cake that looked so rich that I knew I better stay far away, or I would regret it the rest of the night. I decided the sugar cookies were good enough for me.

After a couple of games and watching the ball drop, we ended the night. It was the perfect way to ring in 2009.

29

———————

DEVELOPMENT

Leif's Journal

I opened the door to see a petite five-foot-tall woman standing on our front porch. She had a look that immediately made you feel comfortable. If I were to guess her age, I would say she was in her fifties, due to her salt and pepper hair. It wasn't the kind of grey that most women try to hide with color treatments; it sparkled and gave her soft, gentle glow.

"Hello... Is this the Baskin residence?" She asked with a kind and gentle tone.

I suddenly realize that I was staring and didn't even greet her when I opened the door.

"Yes, I am sorry, I was briefly distracted and lost my manners," I said, trying to break the awkwardness.

"I am Mary Wilcox with DCS. I am hoping you can see my ID around my neck, my hands are full and I can't pull it out for you at the moment."

"No, please, come in, let me help you," I said fumbling.

"Thank you; you're so kind."

I took the baby carrier from her hand and led her into the living room. Dyanna Jo and Ralley were patiently waiting for us to come into the room.

"Hello, Mary, I'm Dyanna Jo Baskin. Welcome to our home," Dyanna Jo said.

"Hi, I'm Ralley. Can I help you with anything?" Ralley offered.

"No, no, you're all too kind. I think I have it."

Haley was taking her afternoon nap, so the room seemed a little too quiet. We waited for Mary to finish organizing the papers that she took from her large bag. It looked like a purse, but it was filled with a lot of folders and papers.

Ralley went over to the baby carrier and looked at Taylor. He was a tiny little guy. Ralley didn't dare touch him because he was sleeping so peacefully.

"Please forgive me; I wanted to make sure that I had all the right paperwork," Mary said. "This little man, as you may already be aware, is Taylor Lowe. Today he is six-days-old and has been in the NICU at UT Medical Center since birth. He was born drug-exposed, but he has been doing great. No major symptoms of withdrawal, which is such a blessing."

As Mary spoke, we stayed completely quiet, which for Dyanna Jo, is a miracle. She always asks questions. When someone is speaking, they can generally get about two to three sentences out before her first question comes. They say a couple more sentences, and the second question comes. I asked her once why she asked so many questions. She looked at me as if my question was odd and calmly said, "They pop in my head, and I have to ask. You can't completely learn something unless you ask the questions that your brain doesn't understand. Right?" *Sure, honey, whatever you say,* I thought.

Mary continued, "Taylor's mommy is Jan Lowe. She is only eighteen-years-old and is terribly confused. She wants her son so badly, but she needs to work on some demons that she has so she can be a better mommy to Taylor. At the time she came into the ER, she was homeless, but I am happy to report that she is now with her parents, and they have helped her get into a facility so she can get clean and get her son back.'

"Do you think she will stay clean?" Dyanna Jo asked.

Yep, there it is, let the questions begin.

"Oh, I have no doubt," Mary answered. "I have been doing this a long time, and when I saw that precious young lady in the hospital, I knew the moment she spoke that she would work her plan and fight hard to get her son back."

Dyanna Jo just smiled and nodded her head. I waited for the second question to come but nothing, zero, nada. No question came.

"Is there a child and family team meeting scheduled?" I finally asked when neither woman said another word.

"Good question," Mary replied. "It's on Friday, January 9, at 3 p.m. Because of the holiday, we had to push it out a little. Jan will still be in treatment, but her parents, Tony and Christie Lowe will attend in her absence."

"Are the parents trying to get Taylor to come live with them until Jan has worked her parenting plan?" Dyanna Jo asked.

"Actually, no, they wouldn't qualify because Jan will be returning to their home after leaving the facility. However, they informed me that although they wanted to be one hundred percent involved in the process, they believe Jan will work harder if she knows she has to do the work to get her son back. Her parents can't do it for her."

"They sound like amazing people," I said.

"I believe they are," Mary said, nodding her head in agreement. "They love their daughter, but they will not enable Jan through this process. It's completely up to her."

There was a long silence. I was waiting for Dyanna Jo to say something.

"Now, if you don't mind, I must head out to visit one of my

other cases. Let's see; I will need to get my carrier. I brought a bag of formula, a couple of blankets, burp cloths, wipes, and diapers. I will call you at the beginning of next week to schedule a time to meet somewhere to purchase necessities for Taylor. His medicine is in the bag with the instructions, but I understand you have been down this road before. You're pro's; I'm sure I don't need me to tell you how to give it to him. We will schedule my next home visit when we see each other at the child and family team meeting."

Mary stood, grabbed the bag, and handed it to Ralley. She bent over and took Taylor out of the carrier and handed him to me. She walked over to Dyanna Jo and hugged her then did the same to Ralley.

She shook my free hand, and before she turned to collect her things, she said, "This is going to be an outstanding experience. I am always here if you need me. Here is my card, call me any time day or night and I mean day or night. I am here to help you any way I can. If you don't call, I can't help you. Right?"

We just stared at her. Mary turned, collected her belongings, and walked towards the door. When she opened the door, she said, "Bye now," she didn't turn to look at us; she just walked through the door, and we heard it close behind her.

We all stood there, staring towards the front door. All of a sudden, Dyanna Jo says enthusiastically, "I'm going to like her!"

We all started to laugh. "What just happened?" I asked.

"She was.... she was....um.... what's the word?" Ralley stuttered.

"Mesmerizing!" Dyanna Jo answered.

"Yep, that's the word." I agreed

DYANNA JO'S Journal

Taylor was a perfect baby; he only cried when he was hungry. He slept a lot, which was normal. I found it hard to believe he was a drug baby; he was so calm.

We all liked Mary. She had a glow about her, and she gave you everything you needed to know without even having to ask a million questions. I liked that about her. She made us feel at ease. We talked about her a lot after she left. Each of us coming up with words to describe her.

The following week, we attended the child and family team meeting. Michael Fortner was the Guardian ad Litem. With Mary and Michael on the team, we knew we were in good hands. Mr. and Mrs. Lowe were kind and had high hopes for Jan. They knew how bad she wanted Taylor back, and they had no doubt that she would work hard to do just that.

On Monday, January 12, I made an appointment to see our family doctor because we had concerns about Haley's development. Haley seemed to favor her right side and never rolled over using the left side of her body. Haley just turned ten-months-old. She wasn't crawling or sitting up. When she tried to crawl, she used her arms to pull herself along, but she didn't use her hips and legs. She would drag them behind her. When lying down, Haley kicked and used the lower half of her body so we couldn't understand why she wasn't using her legs to crawl.

We only had to wait fifteen minutes to see Dr. McKay. He has been our family doctor for years. He asked about Ralley and Leif and how foster care was going. After the catch-up, I told him all about our concerns. He was surprised to hear that the Health Department didn't refer us to a developmental pediatrician since she was drug-exposed in utero. He said that most drug-exposed babies have developmental delays, which can be physical, neurological, or emotional. She might need physical therapy, occupational therapy, and possibly speech therapy in the future. A developmental pediatrician could help us determine what Haley may need.

"We can give solid information about what a baby will experience when it is born with fetal alcohol syndrome," Dr. McKay began. "Unfortunately, that isn't the case with drug-exposure. Illegal drug manufacturers cut their product with various chemicals. Some chemicals can be as common as allergy medicine, but others could be rat poison or prescription drugs. No drug is made the same; therefore, it is impossible to tell you exactly how these drugs will affect your child. Let me get you Dr. Rachel Franklin's information. We only have two developmental pediatricians here in Knoxville, and to be honest, most of their patients are children currently in DCS custody or foster children who have been adopted."

He stepped out of the room. I sat there looking at my beautiful baby girl, wondering how the drugs affected her.

He came back into the room, handed me a couple of pamphlets, and said, "here is some literature on drug-exposure in children. Dr. Franklin's contact information is on the bottom of this one right here."

I glanced at the pamphlet, and immediately four to five disorders hit me in the face.

- Attention-Deficit/Hyperactivity Disorder (ADHD)
- Attention Deficit Disorder (ADD)
- Sensory Processing Disorder (SPD)
- Oppositional Defiant Disorder (ODD)
- Obsessive-compulsive Disorder (OCD)

My head was spinning. I looked back up at Dr. McKay, and I could see that he saw the fear in my eyes.

"Now, Dyanna Jo, you listen to me. There is no way to know what Haley's future will look like, but you must remember, God gave you that precious little girl. She is His creation, and He loves her far more than you could imagine. He will guide you and be with you always. Fear not, for the Lord, your God, is with you."

Tears rolled down my face as I got to the parking lot. I prayed all the way home. *God, I know you are with our beautiful Haley and us. Guide us and protect this precious gift. We carried her these ten months, but You, Father, have and will carry her all the days of her life. I Praise You for what You are doing and what You will do in the future.*

RALLEY'S JOURNAL

Mom came home from Dr. McKay's office a little upset. She didn't talk much. I knew when I shouldn't ask questions. Dad looked as if he was concerned too, but he continued to sit in the living room watching Haley play in her playpen. When Mom came home, she laid Haley on the cushion mats and went into the kitchen to get a bottle ready for Taylor.

"Dad"

"Yes, Ralley."

"Is Mom okay? She hasn't talked much since she got home."

"I think she's trying to process the information she received from Dr. McKay. Sometimes doctors give a lot of information that makes our heads spin. They're so smart, and we are so low on the educational pole that they make our heads explode. We're lucky we walk out of their offices alive."

"Oh, Dad, be serious."

"I am, wait till you become an adult, you will see what I mean. They talk to kids more at their level, but we adults, they feel better when they sound smarter."

"Your weird."

"No, I'm not. Your mom loves it when you call her weird. Go into the kitchen and give it a try."

"No way! I don't think now is the time."

"Oh, there's never a bad time to call her weird."

"I heard that!" Dyanna Jo yelled from the kitchen.

"Oh, no! Run! I think we're in trouble," Dad said and jumped out of his chair.

Instead of running away, he ran to the kitchen. I took off after him. We both threw our arms around Mom, and we all started to laugh.

"You guys are weird," she said.

30

UNPLANNED

Leif's Journal

Dyanna Jo waited until Ralley went to bed and was asleep before she talked to me about her visit with Dr. McKay. She was so anxious. The whole afternoon she was on her computer, searching and reading, searching, and reading. She was so focused. She finally told me everything Dr. McKay said.

"I'm not surprised," I said calmly. "I hadn't thought about it, but it makes sense."

"Why does it make sense?" she asked.

"There's no telling how those drugs affected her while she developed in the womb. How they affected her brain."

"The pamphlet he gave me scared me to death. I got on the computer and looked up all those disorders: ADHD, ADD, ODD, OCD, and SPD."

"What did you find out?"

"We've both heard of ADHD, ADD, and OCD, but Sensory Processing Disorder, or SPD, is where I spent the most time researching. It's a condition in which the brain has trouble receiving and responding to information that comes in through the senses. SPD manifests itself in multiple ways. Some examples are children responding adversely to certain fabrics, food textures, or have an extra sensitive sense of smell or hearing. Some children have problems with fine motor skills; they're clumsy or have problems knowing where their body is in space. There is so much to learn. I mentioned SPD first because some of those things remind me of Haley. You know how she gets when she hears sirens? She screams, even at night, when she is sound asleep, they wake her up. She scrunches her nose every time we put her food up to her mouth. It's like she smells it first before she eats it."

"That could explain a few things. Did Dr. McKay recommend someone?" Leif asked.

"Yes, Dr. Rachel Franklin. I called her office and made an appointment. The soonest appointment she has is the middle of February."

"Where's her office?"

"It's at the Children's Hospital Rehab Center on Westland Avenue."

With having only two developmental pediatricians in Knoxville, the wait to see either was about the same. We decided we would wait for Dr. Franklin since she came highly recommended by Dr. McKay.

As we continued to research child development and drug-exposure in children, we had no idea that in just four months, we would be learning about a whole different kind of development—the development of baby John Doe.

KARLEY MANN WAS STILL in shock, even though she's known for two months that she was pregnant. She was forty-years-old. She had a nine-year-old daughter, Mikala, and an eight-year-old son, Jordan. Her husband, Gary, was just as shocked. Having another child was not what they wanted. Gary was forty-two and felt he and Karley were too old to have another child. She was taking birth control, and they thought that would keep her from getting pregnant. But apparently, there's a slight chance you can get pregnant even with birth control.

They went back and forth, wondering how this could happen, what they were going to do, and how they could afford another child.

"Have you ever thought about abortion?" Karley asked.

"Can't say that I have," Gary answered, matter of fact. "I'm not sure what I think. Whether it's right or wrong, I just don't know. Are you thinking that's an option?"

"It's crossed my mind, but I'm not sure. I've never really investigated it, so I'm not sure how I feel. I know this is definitely an unwanted pregnancy, and I can't see us having a kid at our age."

"I know. I'm happy with where our kids are now. Promise me one thing. If you decide you want to get an abortion, you'll talk to me about it before you do."

"Of course, I'll talk to you first. We should both agree, but right now, I'm so mixed up with my feelings."

"I know. I am too."

Mikala and Jordan were straight-A students. Mikala played the piano, and Jordan played basketball and baseball. Mikala's piano teacher thought she had a lot of promise. She was nine but was playing more advanced pieces that would typically take three years of experience. She was a natural. Jordan was decent at basketball, but he excelled at baseball.

Mikala and Jordan were happy about having a baby brother or sister. A few weeks ago, Karley sat them both down and told them she was pregnant. They were surprised; they didn't think she could get pregnant at her age.

Two months passed, and Karley still agonized over what

she was going to do. Gary finally told her to decide one way or the other and get it over with.

She finally decided that she would have an abortion. She told Gary, and he seemed okay with it. Maybe a little relieved. She thought she would feel relieved too but wasn't sure since she'd never done this before. It was two days before Christmas 2008; she decided to do it after the New Year. She would be a little over twenty-two weeks pregnant and kept telling herself that she'd be relieved and that it'd be all over and she could put it behind her. Without "it," they could get on with their lives. She committed to abortion and had no intention of looking back.

CHRISTMAS DAY ARRIVED, and Mikala and Jordan were busy opening presents. Karley was there physically, but not emotionally. She smiled, laughed, and opened gifts, but deep down inside, she wasn't enjoying herself. Gary wasn't either. He just wanted to get the abortion over with. They had to do it the first week of January because Karley would be twenty-three weeks. In the state of Tennessee, you couldn't have the procedure past twenty-four weeks. He had his doubts about whether it was the right thing or not; Karley was feeling the same way. They made their decision and told themselves that they would put it out of their minds and enjoy the holidays. But that was harder than they thought.

After opening and playing with all the presents, they got ready to go to Karley's parent's house. Karley's sister Samantha and her husband Mark were going to be there with their three kids. Samantha and Mark were three years older than Karley and Gary.

Karley's mom, Rita, was sixty-seven, and her dad, Robert, was sixty-eight. They were both retired. Rita had been a nurse, and Robert had been a veterinarian. Both were ecstatic that Karley and Gary were going to have another baby. They thought they wouldn't be getting any more grandkids since it had been nine years since the last one.

Robert greeted them at the front door. When Karley brought her seven-layer salad into the kitchen, her mom rubbed her protruding belly and said, "Merry Christmas in there."

Please don't do that, Karley thought to herself.

"It'll be fun having a little one here next Christmas," Samantha said.

"Mmmubm," was all the response Karley could muster.

"What's wrong, dear?" Rita asked.

"Oh, I'm just feeling it a little today, that's all."

"You go sit down," Rita said as she took the salad and placed it on the counter. "Samantha and I will get everything ready."

Karley went into the living room and sat on the couch beside Gary. He looked as miserable as she did.

"Hey," she whispered to Gary as she leaned close to him. "We need to look and act more cheerful, or they are going to start asking us why we have such long faces."

"I know," he responded with a fake smile.

"That's better," she said with an equally fake smile.

They tiptoed around the rest of the day. Most of the conversation at some point or another was about the new grandchild, niece or nephew, sibling, or cousin that would be joining the family.

Rita asked, "Have you picked out any names?"

"No," Karley answered. "We've been looking but haven't been able to settle on one." That satisfied everyone.

By the time 3 p.m. rolled around, they had enough and were ready to go.

"Mom," Mikala said as they were driving home. "How come we left earlier than we usually do?"

"I'm tired and don't feel good."

"Are you okay? I mean, is the baby giving you problems this time?"

"Well, I am quite a bit older than when I had you and Jordan. So, I think it's affecting me more this time."

"Okay. Can I do anything to help?"

"No honey, I'm fine. I just need to get some rest when we get home."

They were home a few minutes later, and Karley went straight to bed. Gary and the kids brought in the presents Mikala and Jordan got from their grandparents, aunt, and uncle. Mikala and Jordan went downstairs to the recreation room and played with their toys. Gary turned on the TV to see if any basketball games were on.

Karley was relieved when school was back in after the winter break. It was hard to hide her anxiousness and Mikala was picking up on the tension. She had such amazing kids.

On January 6, 2009, after Mikala and Jordan returned home from school, Karley sat both of them down and told them she saw the doctor earlier in the day and found out she had a miscarriage. Telling a lie was difficult, but she couldn't tell them the truth. How could she? She continued the lie by saying that their dad would be taking her to have a D&C tomorrow. She explained that the D&C was necessary to prevent her from getting an infection. Her kids were stunned. Mikala and Jordan saw the shame on her face but mistook it as pain over losing the baby.

"Mom," Mikala said, "I want to go with you tomorrow."

"Oh, Mikala, thank you honey," Karley replied. "This is something I have to do on my own, Daddy will be taking me but for closure, I need to do this alone. I love you, sweetie."

The kids hugged their mom and left the room.

Gary took a vacation day on Wednesday, January 7, 2009, in order to take Karley to the abortion clinic. It was a bright, sunny day, but cold. Her appointment was at 10 a.m. They walked through the clinic doors at 9:45 a.m., signed in, and sat down in the waiting room.

As she sat in the clinic waiting room, she noticed six other women sitting by themselves. She didn't know why they were there, but she couldn't imagine doing this without Gary. Gary looked extremely uncomfortable; heck, she was uncomfortable. She was feeling tiny bits of movement made by the fetus; she just couldn't bring herself to call it a baby.

The women in the waiting room didn't look happy. Some were staring into space, reading magazines, and a couple of them were dabbing their eyes with tissues. Gary just kept staring at the ground. She decided to do the same. Block out everything and hope it all goes away.

At 10:12 a.m., a nurse called her name. Gary kissed her, and she followed the nurse through a door. They got her prepped and had her sign some legal documents. The doctor explained the procedure as an Instillation abortion, which is performed by injecting a chemical solution consisting of saline through the abdomen and into the amniotic sac. The cervix is dilated prior to the injection, and the chemical solution induces uterine contractions, which expel the fetus.

She stared at them empty and numb. The less she paid attention to what they were saying, the less she had to face the truth of what she was doing. She tuned them out and just waited for it to be over.

"Mrs. Mann, my name is Laura, and I am the nurse who will be assisting you today. I am going to take good care of you. I will be giving you something to help you with your anxiousness and for the pain. Do you have any questions?"

"No," was all Karley could say.

After the doctor finalized the procedure, he stood up from his stool and patted Karley on the shoulder. "You did great, Mrs. Mann; Laura will be assisting you now. If you need anything, just let her know. Bye-bye now." He turned and walked out the door.

Laura Kanter worked for the clinic for over a year. She had sat in on countless abortions. After the doctor left the room, Laura checked on Karley. Multiple times a day, she went through the same motions. She would call a patient to follow her down the hall to the changing area, once changed, she would lead the woman to the surgical room, review the legal documents, and explain the procedure the patient would be having. She'd administer her medication and waited for the doctor to come into the room. Once the procedure was completed, the doctor would say the exact same words to every patient and leave the room. An assistant would enter the room and wait patiently for Laura to permit them to escort the patient out of the room. She would begin cleaning by separating the waste from the surgical instruments. Everything was collected and taken to the back of the building to be taken care of later. Once all the surfaces were cleaned, and the room was ready for the next patient, she would start all over.

Karley felt like she was floating on a cloud. She was in a room fully dressed in the clothes she arrived in, and someone with scrubs was moving around the room. She laid there for a long time silent. The next moment she was driving in the car with Gary in the driver's seat. Karley was feeling pains that felt like contractions.

"Gar," Karley slurred, "I don eel good. I f...f...feel like I'mmm hav...ing con...tract..ns."

"The doctor told me that was normal," Gary said. "You might feel like you're having contractions or Braxton Hicks for a day or so, but that is completely normal."

Gary got Karley home and out of the car. She was struggling

to walk upright; he kept hunching over and holding her stomach. He finally got her to their room and laid her down on the bed. He went to get a cold washcloth to put on her forehead. He didn't know if that would help, but he wanted to be sensitive and willing to try anything.

IT HAD BEEN A LONG DAY, and Laura was looking forward to going home. Her feet were barking as they say. She double-checked all the surgery rooms and made sure they were ready for the next day. She still needed to check the backroom where waste and surgical items were taken after each procedure.

There were usually two to three assistants working in the backroom throughout the day, but most of the work got done after hours. Laura always wanted to check in with the team, working after hours, before she left for the night. As she approached the doors, she could hear the music playing. It's too quiet at night; the after hour team loved to play the music to get them through.

"Hey guys, everything okay?" she asked, walking through the double doors to the back.

"Hey Laura, you're so good to us," Cindy said. Cindy had worked there for five years. She was the only employee to have worked there for that long. Turn over was high in abortion clinics. "I think we are good. Can't think of anything. Go home and put your feet up."

"Alright, if you're sure," she replied. "I'm going to sneak out to my car the back way."

Before waiting for an answer, Laura walked through the maze of hazardous waste bins and headed to the back door. All of a sudden, she stopped dead in her tracks. She thought she heard a high pitched squeal. *What is that? Is that the music?* She thought. She followed the sound to one of the hazardous waste bags. The waste looked as if it hadn't been touched yet. She ran to get gloves and ran back as fast as she could. Cindy and the other assistants saw her running back and forth and stopping what they were doing ran to see what was happening.

"Call 9-1-1! Hurry! Now!" Laura yelled over and over again until she saw Cindy running back the way she came.

31

―――――

THE JOURNEY

Dyanna Jo's Journal

In one week, our precious Haley will be one-year-old. It's so hard to believe that we've made it to this point: fifteen months, nine foster children, and one adoption. We have seen pain, destruction, determination, joy, compassion, and love. I am in awe of everything God has given us over these months. The people we have met are amazing: countless DCS workers, lawyers, judges, doctors, hospital staff, WIC staff, Health Department nurses and doctors, physical and occupational therapists, new friends, the families, and, most importantly, the children. We have learned so much about family. It's not always pretty; most of the time, it isn't, but regardless, there is love.

When I get overwhelmed, I try to stop and think of everything that God has given us and to find joy in my circumstances. I'm thankful for these last fifteen months. It's been a challenging but rewarding journey, that's for sure.

When Taylor came into our lives, he was tiny but sweet as could be. When Jan got out of rehab, she made sure to be there for everything, meetings, court dates, visitation, and doctor appointments. At the meetings, we would talk with her and encourage her. She would hug us and thank us for taking care of her baby. We brought Taylor with us every time we knew Jan would be present.

Jan was able to visit with Taylor for two hours every week. Those two hours were special to her, but a couple of weeks ago she asked if we could stay for the visitation. We usually leave, as per DCS request, but this visit Mary approved and said we were welcome any time. Jan wanted to know everything Taylor was doing at our home. She wanted to be a fly on our wall so that she could have a view of everything. The love for her son was evident.

At last week's visitation, I was overwhelmed at seeing Jan playing with baby Taylor. I walked over to Mary, who was at every visitation, and said, "If we felt comfortable having Jan over to our house, to visit Taylor, would that be allowed?"

"I don't see why not," she replied. "She is working hard on her parenting plan, she has passed her drug tests, and she begs to spend more time with Taylor. She has a job, and her boss sees great potential in her ability. He sees a bright future for her. I will have to talk to my supervisor, but if you are willing to supervise the visit and not leave her alone with Taylor, I think I can make it happen."

"Oh, thank you, Mary. Next week is Haley's one year birthday. We are having a party, and I think that Jan would love to see Taylor in our home and see how he is living."

"Your welcome," Mary said. "You and your family are special. You have so much love, not just for these babies but for their families. You have the love of God in your hearts, and you shine brightly. Especially for Jan and her family."

A sound escaped from my mouth, and I replied, "Oh, Mary, you do too. Our family is in awe of how you glow, and your description of our family is exactly how we see you."

"God is Good!" she exclaimed in a whispering way.

THE WHOLE FAMILY made the trip to Dr. Rachel Franklin's office. We arrived at her office in plenty of time to slowly make our way into the building. The long single-story building was welcoming to children of all ages. As we walked down a long hallway to the doctor's office, we saw that the walls were painted with safari animals, plants, and trees. They also had paper mache trees with limbs protruding out into the hall with stuffed animals peaking out as we walked. Ropes were hanging from the ceilings with monkeys hanging from them.

When the nurse came to get us, she took us to a room that had a long, large table positioned against the wall with white paper rolled across the top. There were crayons for the kids to color on the white paper. The table was two feet tall and big enough for our whole family to sit or lay on to color. Ralley enjoyed herself; she colored people and animals and put crayons in Haley's hands to help her color.

The doctor kept us waiting approximately fifteen minutes, but when she was in our room, it was obvious that her attention was only on us. We shared our concerns while she played with Haley. After observing Haley's movements, she highly recommended physical and occupational therapy. We learned that she only saw patients who had experienced trauma in utero. She was passionate and dedicated to helping children of all ages. We liked her immediately. The therapy offices were in the same building, so as we left, we scheduled Haley's appointments.

Every Tuesday, Haley goes to physical therapy for an hour. Her physical therapist, Alicia Haney, worked on rolling her over on her left side and moving her legs and hips so she could crawl properly. Haley loves Alicia. Alicia has a way of making Haley belly laugh, and when she laughs, we all laugh.

On Thursdays, Haley goes to the occupational therapist for her SPD, Sensory Processing Disorder. Kimberly Sparks works with Haley by placing her in a hammock and swinging her gently. The hammock helps with self-regulation and motor skills. Kimberly says that sensory processing is about how our brain and body interact to help us accomplish daily things. She uses things like a weighted blanket, brush, or box of sand to stimulate sensory input.

Our baby girl was getting the help she needed because of services that DCS offered and doctors who guided us every step of the way. We thank God for everything we have learned, and for providing what we need to help foster children and their families. Jan will need this kind of support and information when Taylor goes home. We can be there to help her.

RALLEY'S JOURNAL

It's Haley's birthday, and Taylor's family is coming as well as the Mussina's. I felt strange when Mom told me that Jan and her parents were coming. I thought we were supposed to keep the families away from our house, but when Mom and Dad explained that Jan was working so hard to get Taylor back and that she needed the love of Jesus in her life, I totally understood. Wow, God was using us to guide Taylor's family to Him. It was as if we were missionaries. We were helping people in our own city. You don't have to go far away to lead people to God; you can do it with the people you meet every day.

"Dad"

"Yes, Ralley."

"I've had times when I've resented Haley and Taylor, but I am thankful that God has changed my heart. I didn't understand that God was using us in big ways. At first, I was afraid that Jan was coming to the party, but we are like missionaries, and I really like what He is doing through us. I pray we can lead Jan and her family to Him."

"I pray for that too. God loves them, and He wants them to find their way to Him."

The doorbell rang, and I jumped up, "I got it!" I yelled. Poor Dad, I think I scared him when I jumped. "I hope it's Jan."

Dad laughed, and I took off running. Jan and her parents were here, and I couldn't help but give them all hugs.

The house got loud, really fast. Everyone was laughing and hugging each other. After we welcomed them, Jan went straight over to see Taylor swinging in the baby swing. She loved him, I could tell by the look she got when she looked at him. Jan got him out of the swing and hugged him close. Mom gave Jan and her family a tour of the downstairs; then she took them upstairs to show them where Taylor slept.

The doorbell rang, and once again, I took off running. "That's got to be the Mussina's!" I yelled

Leif's Journal

Jan worked her plan perfectly. She was determined to get Taylor back, and in the middle of April, she did it. Mary didn't have to come to get him and take him to Jan; she came to our house to pick him up. We had a special "baby shower" for her, and gave the baby things she would need at her house. Jan and Taylor became a part of our family, and we knew that by the Grace of God, Jan was on her way to accomplishing great things.

She asked a lot of questions about God, and we told her all we could. She never prayed the sinner's prayer with us, but she is still seeking God and visiting churches near her house so she can learn more. At her baby shower, we made sure that she personally got a special gift from our family. A Bible with her name inscribed on the cover. She was so happy to have her very own Bible to take with her to church when she found the right one.

On May 1, we got a call from Mary Wilcox asking if she could come to our house for a visit. She wanted to talk to us about something. Mary wanted all of us to be home when she visited; we scheduled a time for the following Friday, May 8, 2009.

"I hope everything is okay with Jan," Dyanna Jo said anxiously. "I just talked to her, she sounded fine. Why would Mary want to come for a visit if it wasn't about Jan and Taylor?"

"Don't jump to conclusions," I said, trying to calm her down.

"But, Leif, this can't be good. Are you sure she didn't give you any clues? You should have let me talk to her."

"You would have driven her crazy with a thousand questions. It's a good thing you didn't talk to her."

"That's not nice!" she said indignantly.

"I'm sorry I am just joking. I'm sure that if it were something bad, she wouldn't be waiting a week to come over."

"Well, that's true. I just hate waiting."

"I know, honey. I know."

On Friday, May 8, Mary came promptly at 3 p.m. As always; she had that glow that made you feel relaxed and comfortable.

"Hi Mary, come on in," I said, opening the door wider for her to come through.

"Thank you, Leif. Always so kind."

We walked into the living room, and Dyanna Jo anxiously walked out of the kitchen into the room. She looked like she was about to come out of her skin. I had to laugh, to myself, of course.

"Mary, welcome, is everything okay?" she asked. "Is it Jan or her parents? I talked to her a few days ago, and she sounded good. I....."

Mary cut her off and said, "Sweetie, relax, Jan and the Lowes are just fine. I am sorry I worried you. I just felt it was important to talk to you directly instead of on the phone. Will Ralley be joining us?"

Ralley was walking down the stairs, right as Mary asked.

"I'm right here. Sorry, I didn't hear the doorbell."

"Ralley, sweet as ever," Mary said and hugged her when she came into the room.

"Alright, let's begin, shall we?" Mary began. "I want to talk to you about an extraordinary case. As we worked together on Jan's case, I felt God was laying it on my heart to bring a very precious little boy to your attention. Back in January, a little boy was discovered at an abortion clinic."

We all looked at each other, a little alarmed. "An abortion clinic?" I asked just to clarify.

"Yes. Without going through the gross details," she continued, "the baby survived an instillation abortion, saline injection."

Dyanna Jo and I gasped at the same time. Ralley looked confused.

"I know it's hard to fathom. A nurse, working at the clinic, heard the baby's faint cries and immediately got help. This little fella, fondly called Baby Doe, is in the NICU at Children's Hospital and is doing well. He has been cared for by an amazing team, and he has touched their lives in ways I can't explain. He's been in DCS custody since arriving at the hospital. Because of the sensitivity of this case, we haven't spoken to anyone. As I got to know you, God kept nudging me, and I knew when it was time for him to be discharged, you would be the perfect placement. I was given special privilege to talk to you and see if you would consider taking him into your home."

As if she knew Dyanna Jo was about to start her firestorm of questions, Mary held up her hand. "Before any decisions are made, I want to give you all the specifics; then I want you to pray, discuss it as a family, and then give me your answer next week. He will be leaving the hospital next Friday, and we will need time to find a placement if you are not comfortable."

As we sat listening in silence, she told us the rest of the story. We learned that he had developmental delays and special needs. He would need a lot of care.

When she left, we all walked back into the living room and sat in silence as we individually processed the story we were just told. Before we discussed it, we came together, held hands, and prayed. Prayed for Baby Doe and the choice we had to make.

RALLEY'S JOURNAL

Sitting on the floor, I looked between my sister and my brother. My sister, Haley, was running around the living room. She had the most beautiful dark brown skin, wide dark eyes, and facial expressions that made the whole family laugh. Haley was our hyper, nonstop ball of energy.

My brother is our mellow little man. At least that's what I call him. He has pale pink skin, wispy blonde hair, and bright blue eyes that look exactly like mine and my dad's. Anyone who saw him would look at Mom and say, "when did you have him? I didn't even know you were pregnant." Mom, Dad, and I would laugh every time. He did look a lot like us; he was perfect.

He survived a birth that you only heard about in horror stories, but he was made in the image of God, and we loved him. He will have some challenges overcoming his physical handicaps, but he had a strong determination that we could already see at this young age.

When he came into our home, we knew we would be able to petition for adoption in six months. There was no family to work a plan or come forward. He was ours from day one.

Mom and Dad sat me down one day and asked me if I would like to name him. God named Haley, and I would name my brother. It wasn't hard; he reminded me of a special baby that we lost two and a half years ago; a baby boy with wispy blonde hair and bright blue eyes. He was and is our River.

In December, one year apart, we adopted two perfect children. They were both a gift to our family. December will always be a month of celebration.

EPILOGUE

Leif's Journal

As I look back at the two years we have been foster parents, I see God's hand in our lives. I look at where we were when we had the miscarriage to where we are now. I feel like the Baby Tree. It had a storm break it in half and we thought it died, but now it has several branches sprouting off the top and sides, and it blooms bright with pink flowers.

In December 2008, we adopted our fiery and precocious daughter Haley. We can't imagine life without her. She makes us laugh and always has us hopping.

This month, December 2009, we adopted our calm but joyous son River. He was born a survivor. Just like the baby tree, he made it through the storm.

Learning the back stories of all the children we had in our home, over the past two years, inspired me to begin my own journey. A discovery of my family's back story. My family tree with branches that span deep into history.

I know there is much more to discover about Haley and Rivers family. I look forward to the journey.

Stephanie stumbled wearily up the steps to her apartment. She reached for the door handle, but she tripped over the last step and fell to the hard concrete. She used the wall to brace her self as she stood. Looking straight at her door, she saw the eviction notice still hanging there from yesterday. A letter that said, leave, go away, we don't want you here anymore. *Believe me; I don't want to be here anymore either,* she thought. *I don't want to be anywhere anymore.*

She put her key in the knob and turned. The door opened with a creak, and all she could see was an empty apartment with no one to welcome her. She had no one anymore: no family, no friends, and no babies. Babies, she didn't want to think about that. She walked into the apartment, turned on the light, and fell onto the torn up, bug-infested couch. A spring hit her in the back. She cursed and moved to the other side, hoping to avoid another spring.

She sat there thinking about the eviction notice. Where was she going to go? She had no money and no real job. The only way she ever made money was by selling herself to strangers—men who used her and threw her away. No man ever stuck around. When she got money, she turned around and bought drugs. She needed them to numb the pain and make her stop thinking about her life as a prostitute.

Drugs were all she felt like she knew. She started using when she was seventeen. The cool kids used drugs, right? *Yeah, right, I'm so cool.* Why didn't she listen to her parents? They tried to help her. They loved her then. Why did she have to ruin everything? She never listened to them. When they told her to stop, she did it more. Her sister warned her and told her that drugs weren't cool.

Her sister, she missed her so badly. She would never see her again. She did horrible things to Candace. Things she could never forgive. *I can't blame her; I wouldn't forgive myself either.*

There were so many people she hurt, especially her children. She had children spread out all over the place and a baby she killed. *Who does that?* She had Carrie the first part of last year and left her at the hospital. Took off running right out the front door of the hospital. Six months later, she got pregnant again. If she couldn't keep it, then she didn't want DCS to keep it either. The abortion clinic was happy to help.

She didn't want to think of any of this anymore. She made her final drug buy that afternoon. Enough to feel nothing when she took her last breath. She couldn't do this anymore. This world was lonely and full of people who use and abuse you. Throw you out like garbage. Isn't that what she did; threw her baby away when she killed it?

There is no forgiveness for what she has done. Her parents had taken her to church, and she always felt like she could be forgiven, but now she had done way too much to be forgiven for. *Not even God would forgive me.* Today would be her last.

She had one last trip to make. She pulled herself off the couch, gathered herself, and slogged down the steps to her two-tone white and rust car. The trunk was held shut with a bungee cord, and two hubcaps were missing. They were probably stolen. She fired it up, and it belched smoke, coughed, and finally settled into a hesitant idle. She shifted into gear and drove to her dad's grave. He died in December 2007, two years ago. The two year anniversary had been three days ago. She'd never cared enough to go to his grave, but now that she had been evicted and planned to end it all, she decided to go and say good bye to him. He was a retired Army veteran and was buried in the East Tennessee State Veterans Cemetery on Lyons View Pike in Knoxville.

The brakes squeaked as she parked the car. Her mom had told her where he was buried in case she ever wanted to visit. It took her a while to find, but she finally did. She noticed a few people, but none were close. It had been raining some, and the ground was damp. She didn't care; she sank to her knees. She was going to have her say with her Poppy and then go numb to stop the pain forever. She had called her dad Poppy from when she could first talk.

On the bottom of the headstone, under his rank, name, branch, birth date and date of death, it merely said Poppy. She tentatively reached out and traced each letter.

"Oh, Poppy," she cried, "I know I disappointed you. I know you and Mom loved me. I've done so many horrible things. Things I can never be forgiven for. The things that I did to Candace. Today, I wanted to come and say good-bye. It's time to end the mess I've made of my life. I just wanted you to know how sorry I am for the pain I caused you for not being there when you died. For—" she stopped and took in deep, ragged breaths, "for the mean, hateful things I said to you the last time I ever saw you. The last thing I ever said to you. I'm so, so sorry."

She sobbed for several minutes, deep, gut-wrenching sobs. She noticed the cross centered at the top of the marker. She stretched her hand out, but before she touched it, she drew it back. She didn't feel worthy to touch it. She knew she wasn't worthy to touch it.

She then felt someone kneel beside her in the damp, muddy ground and wrap their arms around her. It was just like she heard about when she was a kid. It felt like God was wrapping His arms around her. The cross was reaching out to her, cutting through all the filth and getting right down there with her in the hell she'd made of her life. Telling her He'd paid her debt, all of it—once and for all. She looked and saw who was kneeling beside her and felt something she hadn't felt in a long time... hope.

WHAT ARE YOUR THOUGHTS ON PLACE OF REFUGE?

If you could take a minute or two to leave an honest review at the store where you bought the book, I would appreciate it. Leaving a review will help other readers who are interested in this type of book to find it. Thank you.

You can sign up for my Reader's List at danielbishop.net. This will allow you to stay up to date on my writings and future books in the series.

DISCUSSION QUESTIONS

Should Christians be involved in foster care and adoption in some capacity? How could they be involved besides fostering and adopting?

The goal of foster parenting is to reunite the children with the birth parents. If it's appropriate, what are ways foster parents can help the birth parents reach that goal?

If you are thinking of becoming a foster family and have biological children, what can you do to acknowledge and listen to their concerns and fears about becoming a foster family?

How does fostering and adopting show God's love for us and how far He's willing to go for us?

ABOUT THE AUTHOR

Daniel Bishop is an Army veteran and the author of Place of Refuge; book one in the Baskin Family Foster Journal Series. Daniel authors faith-based novels of foster care and adoption, guzzles coffee, and occasionally eats ice cream for breakfast. He lives in Knoxville, Tennessee with his wife and daughter.

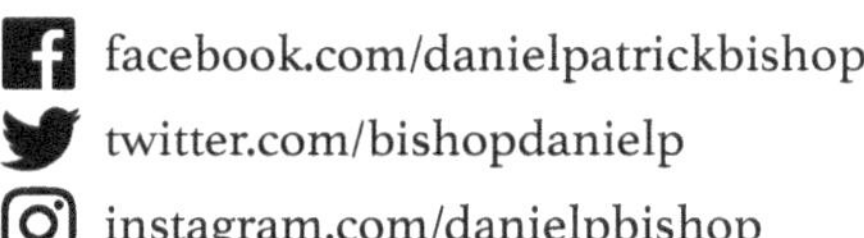

facebook.com/danielpatrickbishop

twitter.com/bishopdanielp

instagram.com/danielpbishop